Strong
Wind

BOOKS BY
MIGUEL ANGEL ASTURIAS
(available in translation)

STRONG WIND

MULATA

EL SEÑOR PRESIDENTE

TRANSLATED FROM THE SPANISH BY
GREGORY RABASSA

Miguel Angel Asturias

Strong Wind

A SEYMOUR LAWRENCE BOOK

DELACORTE PRESS / NEW YORK

Two points in the adventure of the diver?
One, when, a beggar, he prepares to plunge,
One, when, a prince, he rises with his pearl?

Strong
Wind

1

They no longer had to show violent signs of joy. The whole sleepless crowd was inert, relaxed, spread about, after having spent days and nights at work. The terrain where some of them were sitting, others lying down, seemed completely dominated by them. Everything had been dominated except the damp, still, blinding coastal heat. Man's will had been imposed. Hands and mechanical equipment had modified the terrain. The natural course of rivers had been changed, structures had been built for the passage of iron roads, between sliced-out hills, over bridges or fills, through which voracious machines consuming trees that had been reduced to greenish logs carried men and crops, hunger and food. Trees fell while others appeared, planted as a defense against the whipping of the wind for fields prepared for certain crops, and in the gullies, as in the intestines of some poor fabulous beast, tamed, demeaned, but still alive, work was going ahead for the removal of rocks, the drawing off of tons of what little stone there

was, or taking advantage of the topographical irregularities
to open the excited passage of currents of roiled, dirty, needy
water, which grew clean downstream and flowed through val-
leys that were flaming green in color.

Adelaido Lucero's lungs came up to his cheeks to draw in
all the coastal air. He was stripped to the waist and was wearing a pair of pants more like a loincloth, and with his eyes, as
they wandered over the immensity, he could still see the
remnants of that group of weary people who had come from
everywhere, hungry, practically dressed in rags, bony, with
uncut hair, their beards dirtying their rustic faces, Lord,
Lord! . . .

His calloused, sweaty hands, hardened by work, kept on
moving with the grace of a man afire. Squat, rise, squat, rise
. . . all the vertebrae of his spine were jutting out and his
backbone was a copper-colored snake . . . squat, rise, the
hinge of his waist opening and closing, as they filled a platform car with rocks and stones that a locomotive which showed
a thousand years of use would haul away from that remote
siding to the stone-crusher, a huge machine that would vomit
up in showers of pebbles all the larger stones that were poured
down its gullet.

The sea, more violent than on the other coast, was the
backdrop for everything with the echo of its turbulence. A
horizon that was audible and could be seen as a line of blue
fire when someone climbed a hill to take a look at it, from
far away or close by; the newcomers, curious to know what
the Pacific was like, would climb up tall poles and find it there,
with its Creolin color of greenish milk in the morning, and,
in the afternoon, like an open avocado displaying its red seed.

A dangerous neighbor, the coast. The low, tangled vegetation covered everything, and in that green tangle of entwined
threads, the only sign of free animal existence was the presence
of flocks of birds, whose colors, bright as the fragments of a

rainbow, contrasted with the ebony hawks and the jet-black buzzards, all staked out in the depth of the atmosphere which formed a single hot blindness with the vegetation.

"Hot enough for you, Cucho?" Adelaido Lucero asked a humpbacked, stooped companion near him among the thirty-six young men gathering stones for the rosary of railway cars that formed a creaking train; the iron groaned too under the weight of the rocks that had been broken by dynamite and sledgehammers.

"Hot enough for you, Lucero?"

The work gangs passed by one after the other in groups of five, ten, with all kinds of tools, as the foremen led them to the low-lying places where the silence swallowed them up, the silence and the perceptible boiling of minute insect species, invisible but latent, orchestral, frantic, while the sun rose up over bonfires of motionless vegetation and a breath of marshes, the burning coal of noon.

The panting of the workmen alongside Adelaido seemed to envelop the stones that were being moved from the ground to the railway cars with a plush coating of human fatigue that softened the shock.

But it was not that. What was happening, Cucho knew well, was that after hours and hours of that squatting and rising, they were growing deaf; because the panting was closest to their head bones, all they could hear was the opening and closing of their chests, the rising and falling of their arms and hands, as they dug their fingers and nails into the soft earth to grasp the stones and throw them up into the cars, up, down, up, down, opening and closing the hinges of their waists.

Deaf to everything that was not their own panting, blinded by the dust they were raising, sticky with perspiration, the whistle of the boss who was hidden in a hut improvised out of wild cane stalks and with a straw roof marked the lunch break.

The women were cruel tricksters, laughing and laughing,

while they sold them tortillas, new cheese, sausages, blood sausages, cooked chayote, cassava, stuffed bananas, fried beans. The men drank water from a spigot, careful not to get their mouths too close, because the sun had made it like the spit of a grill; they half-washed their faces, let cold water run over their heads, and after drying themselves with nearby leaves, being careful that they were not chichicaste leaves, they turned their eager faces toward the food the lunch women had brought.

The corn tortillas dripped with green chile sauce, beans, fat meat, yellow potatoes, slices of avocado, and cheese, and there was bread covered with hot, greasy sauce. Coffee and milk were poured from earthen jars into pewter receptacles that had once been cups, skim milk, with thousands of black specks, the coffee grounds themselves, like freckles, and into the brim-full cups went everything, fingers, nails, pieces of tortillas or bread, and they would lift them, liquefied, to their mouths, surrounded by buzzing flies and moustaches.

The smell of the women was so pronounced that the men approached them with the urge to lay them right there, just like heaving stones into the cars, with the same will to work in their waists and the same acid smell in their noses; but the women formed a tight knot of food, pigtails, hot breasts in grimy blouses, bundles of buttocks, and they would slip away with promises and vague acceptances for another time, promises which must have been fulfilled, because many of the women were quite pregnant.

The foreman's whistle gave the signal to start work again —they were still savoring their meal; no matter how well they had eaten, they were always still hungry—and to continue what they had been doing.

Someone shouted. A two-hundred-pound rock had caught the tip of his foot. It had almost cut off two toes. The foreman came after they went to get him, with his pipe in his mouth, his glasses riding down the tip of his red nose on his white face, and he ordered them to carry him to the improvised shed nearby, where they kept tools, clothing, and the bamboo tubes of water that the workmen used instead of gourds. And there they laid him on a blanket, while they went to pass the word along farther up the line.

Pain was closing his long eyes for long spells . . . For all of his maleness, as pain asphyxiated him, he was going back to childhood, to infancy. He was moaning like a child. Pantaleón López. They wet his dry lips. He fell asleep, more overcome by suffering than sleepiness. The others were afraid that he had died. But no. He was dazed with the heavy afternoon heat, which never managed to be completely cool.

"Cucho, it's expensive taming the land!"

Adelaido Lucero stuck his face out into the night that was darkened by the night dew of the moonless shadows, no stars, only an occasional light in the camp.

"You see now, today it were Pantaleón, tomorrow it'll be one of us! God save us! . . ."

"If we was to count, Cucho, we'd never get to draw the line so's we could add them up. They're so many that I don't know how come we're still alive and kicking. Just luck. Who can tell. But one thing sure in this kind of work is that when your time comes, it comes, it just comes. All I can say is that I was with León Lucio, the Chinaman, when the rattler killed him. It went over my feet first and didn't do a thing to me. He was the one it was after. Poor fellow. He swelled all up. I noticed that the Mister in charge of the camp had started to get all wrinkled. That poor old man with the sucked-in behind who went crazy. From what I can tell, you know, Cucho, he must have been bit by that spider that brings on a fever that's so strong, so quick that it gets to your brain in a few seconds. Jobaldo nearly died too, after the wrench that all of them that came with him from Jalpatagua got. Three of them were squashed by all that sand that fell on top of them while they were making the cut on the hill from underneath."

"But it all works out, it works out," Cucho said, speaking from where there was the glow of a cigarette, "because they're good men for sticking to something, for knowing what they're doing, and for not hanging around with the girls . . ."

"For having dough, you mean, because without that goldy little fellow even if you want things to come out, they never do. Wanting to . . . You can want an awful lot, but if you ain't got money, it all goes to waste!"

"But they know what they're doing . . ."

"I don't deny that. Besides . . ."

"They do things in a big way, is that what you were going to say? And that's the only way to do it, when you've got to clean out the land to plant what people can live off."

From the distance, along with the wind there were mouthfuls of tar, just the penetrating smell, and along the tracks, far off, the lights of railway cars were passing. They did not rest day or night. The tree-cutting was devouring trees for the fireboxes of the locomotives, the stone-crushers, the other machines that warmed themselves with wood fires; the work was devouring people and more people, tools and more tools; rocks which softened in the even fires of the kilns, changed into raw white lime, and in the construction, the foundations and walls devoured stones and more stones, for fills, bridges, and dikes which held back the water that, as if in a deep sleep, continued moving softly along until it fell into the turbines, giving birth to the electrical energy that began to spread out on all sides along threads of metal in the form of light, of a wasp's sting of fire that amidst sparks and blue halos pierced rails, split steel beams, or joined metal cables in eternal union.

The progress of the work gave the contentment of triumph to all. High and low in the hierarchy of work, they all shared in that pleasure a man has when he conquers the enemy, for they all felt themselves to be equal participants in the victory that had been attained, as in any warlike struggle, at the cost of many casualties, dead and wounded, not counting the mutilated. And as in every army, there were deserters, those who as they arrived on the battlefield turned their backs in cowardice, feeling themselves physically incapable of surviving the epic battle.

Adelaido Lucero, and close by Cucho, both shaking with an attack of malarial chills, were sniffing like suspicious dogs to discover where they were being taken along with so many other sick people, jammed into a boxcar into which some bales of hay had been thrown to serve as mattresses.

They finally reached an improvised wooden building painted with white lead, white outside, wood-colored inside, where some white-smocked men were moving about, putting glass tubes that smelled of cane liquor into their mouths—it was the alcohol they were cleaned with. They tightened the veins of their arms to draw out blood, all of that without even taking a good look at them; they had seen so many sick people, what would they be doing going around noticing them, and they gave them some pills in small, round boxes that they said were good for the fever.

After taking the first pills, Cucho felt the wetness on his back and Lucero also had the feeling that it was raining behind him. A strange illness. It gives hot coldness and icy warmth. Refreshed, without any headache, without any dizziness, animated, with the urge to get up, do something. They faced each other. With no mirror, they had to tell each other about how pale they were, how their cheekbones protruded because they were so thin, their bloodless ears back there, their glassy eyes, their dry, thin lips, and their yellowish gums.

They went separate ways. Cucho began to cough. Not only he, several of them, and all of those several were taken far away, dropped off in the capital, where the climate is milder, they told them, and perhaps they would get better. Adelaido Lucero, with flesh on his bones now, remembered the bony arms of his companion when he embraced him to say good-bye. It was a dead man who was taking leave of him.

"Cucho, I feel awful, because I was the one who brought you here . . ."

"Don't be foolish, I came because I wanted to, I wasn't no kid you had to bring by force, and nothing much happened to me; in a cold climate, without this devil heat, I'll be on my feet again, you'll see, I'll be back . . . don't worry . . . take care of yourself . . ."

The train went off. A train that had stopped at a station that seemed not to be built on the ground, but hanging from the madrecacao trees, from the guarumos, from the vines, from the mass of branches. The whole platform was covered with bark and half-dried eucalyptus leaves. Explosions of celestial electricity thundered down below in the direction of the coast. Two, three skeletons of curs limped off as they ran along the ties on which the rails were resting and which disappeared when they reached the curve where a bridge dressed in red, white, and blue morning glories let the river pass underneath, like a watery railroad that would speed up as it approached the sea, which was its lair.

Adelaido stretched to his limit, tipped his hat back, and, taking his machete out of his belt, carried it in his hand, half-dragging the point along the ground, up to the small village that had sprung up not far from the station.

He made the few purchases he had to, put them in his sack, stopped to roll a cigarette, lit it, and left. Everything was now regular in this new green world where nothing was arbitrary, with roads traced under thousands of leaves which were growing out of fleshy trunks, some with scales and spines like dried fish, others with the color of a genip tree. On the long branches, like oars, they seemed to lose the feeling of fleshiness of the trunk, and the leaves grew thin like butterfly wings. The sensation of an oar coming out of the sea and penetrating the hot air was present in every leaf of the banana grove over Lucero's head. At a crossroads, he ran into a man with swollen feet, very swollen, whose nickname was Chiggerfoot. He had his feet wrapped in rags that were more like scabs, showing the tips of his toes like rotten potatoes. He stood there looking at him with his eyes of a sad old man, and he asked him if he had not seen a girl who had just run away. A daughter of his. Lucero answered him that from the station, no.

"Well, maybe you could do me a favor, just a little one," Chiggerfoot said. "Look for her; and if you see her, tell her I died."

"If I see her around, I'll tell her, and you'd better go back home, because it's no good for you to be wandering around here all alone, because you might get a bad cramp, and you don't need that."

"Better a cramp than what I've got on my feet. For a long time now, years, my feet have felt like they were asleep, like I had two rocks instead of feet. I hope you run into her for me . . ."

From behind a clump of trees, Lucero heard the sound of skirts, and when he turned his head he saw the dark face of a girl who was telling him to keep quiet, putting a finger to her lips.

"Well, if I see her around, I'll give her your message," Lucero repeated, making himself the girl's accomplice.

Chiggerfoot went off, dragging the pillows that were his feet, groan after groan, among the leaves of the shade trees or wet-nurses, as they were called. Adelaido Lucero went over to where the girl was hiding.

"That's being bad," he said to her when he got close, "and being bad like that with your pretty face, that's not right. Because from what he says, he's your pa."

The dark flower lowered her eyes before the reproach, even though her whole face was moving with the funniest grimace to show that Lucero's opinion meant little to her. And she started walking without saying a word, dragging her feet at first to kick up the dust, and then quickly, quickly.

Adelaido looked her up and down from waist to head, a pink blouse, and from waist to feet, a yellow skirt; her black braids over her back underneath her shawl, and he let her go without saying anything. From staring at her, he dropped his machete, and he just had time to move his foot before it was cut.

"Anything else except you can drop when I'm not looking, and that's bad of you," he said to the machete as he picked it up, "you're trying to tell me that a dropped machete means the death of me."

The banana trees growing on that side were waiting for a good cleaning, a cutting of everything dry that was clinging to them, although they looked more like sick plants, like Cucho, who went away nothing but ears, sick like Cucho, because like him, the leaves were coughing with the blowing of the wind.

Lucero remained there thinking all of that as the girl disappeared. And there he would have stayed, if he had not thrown his hat back, spat, and said something as if he were talking to somebody else.

"Oh, you dummy, even if it's late, I'll catch her!"

He went ahead along a fairly wide road, just right for the machines to pass along as they threw sweet and blue-colored acids on the banana trees so they would not get sick. A machine was snoring, dusting them with sleepy rain. Playful butterflies were seen, and from time to time, in the most intimate part of the depths, the song of the cenzontles would please the ear.

"You'd get a whipping from me, if I was your pa . . ."

"If you was," she answered him, "but since you ain't . . ."

"And where are you heading . . ."

"Can't you see, where my face is taking me; now, if you want, I can walk without looking, backwards . . ." and she began to walk backward, while she said to him with the happiest look in the world, "now I'm going where your face is taking me!"

"Don't get snotty!"

The girl was walking backward so fast that she was almost flying away. Lucero was getting close to her without managing to catch up. And they ran for quite a distance like that, she backward, backward, backward, and he following her.

"You can't tell me that a good husband wouldn't do you some good . . ."

"But since there ain't none . . ."

"Course there is, for you there is . . ." Lucero said, quickening his pace.

"But since my pa don't want me to get married . . ."

"What does your pa know about things like that!" He stepped up his pace.

"Why shouldn't he, he married my ma after he'd been married and widowed; married twice, he ought to know!"

"He knows from the man's side, not the woman's, and that's your side . . ." He was going so fast that he could not be understood.

"But my ma don't want me to get married neither. She must have a good reason."

"Because you haven't found the right man."

"And I ain't going to find him, because I want a good man and there ain't none like that."

"Who says there isn't?" They were running now; a moment later Adelaido stopped and she too, at a prudent distance.

"What's your name?"

"Adelaido Lucero, why . . ."

"Just wanted to know; mine's Roselia de León, pleased to meet you."

"That's what I say, I'd like to please you in anything you say or even don't say, because I'd like to please you in what you're thinking too . . ." Adelaido took a few steps forward which she repeated backward.

"I'll bet you say that to all the girls!"

"To lots of them, but I'm saying it to you right now."

"Well, I'd be pleased if you'd be my godfather when I get confirmed, now that the bishop's coming."

"Godfather . . ." He had managed to grasp her by the wrist and he held her so that she could not continue retreating.

"Let me go . . ."

"If you'll stop and talk to me . . ."

"It's best not to talk, it's best you went on your way . . ."

The shouting raised by a woman with the face of a barn owl when she found them, when he had her by the arm and she was struggling to escape, was not the least of it all. And with the owl-faced woman other people came out, most of them women, and children, and barking dogs. All of them as if rising up out of the earth. He let go of her immediately, but it did him no good, because the old woman and the others kept on shouting and dogs barking.

They accused him, both the old owl and Chiggerfoot, who arrived on his mattresses without making any sound as he walked, just like swimming, of everything with their daughter. Underage! Underage! Underage! the old people shouted, drooling something like saliva that was more likely the water of rage.

The machete was the first thing taken away from him by the soldiers who, alarmed by the shouting, had come down from the post. Lucero went along peacefully. In back, the girl's parents were raising a new difficulty, as they were against the patrol's taking her to make a deposition at the jail. It was no use. Behind the girl, Chiggerfoot, limping, and the old owl, giving off a smell of sweat and excrement, climbed up to a

small height where, among some palm trees, the command
post and the jail were located.

The man who acted as justice of the peace, the supreme au-
thority in that place, liquidated the matter immediately.

"Adelaido Lucero, you will take the woman you raped as
your wife, or you'll spend the rest of your life in jail."

"I didn't do anything to her, ask her whether I even tried,"
Lucero defended himself.

"Didn't do anything to her . . ." The old woman was jumping about. "He ruined her."

"Dirty dog! Thief!" Chiggerfoot was reaching the height of
his fury, "he knew I was out looking for her, I asked him to
find her and when he found her he, he, he . . ." From the eyes
hidden among wrinkles, and stubble, and eyebrows, there
poured out the lament of a father who had been wronged.
The old owl was also enjoying herself with good, loud sobbing.

Roselia de León, under the weight of shame, had lost volume,
was a small little animal with human eyes, her mouth was dry,
her tongue as if it had been stung by a scorpion. Without being
able to put two tears together, no matter how much she blinked
and looked all around, she almost tore her shawl with her
hands from twisting it so much, as if she wanted to open holes
in it.

"Well, ruined before or after, you find yourselves in the most
solemn moment of your lives, that in which you celebrate your
marriage." The official made it sound as if he were the one
who was getting married.

". . . Nobody can ever tell. I went out to say good-bye to a
friend who was going to the capital because he was sick, and
the next day I woke up with Roselia," Adelaido Lucero used
to tell years later when the subject was marriage. What he did
know about his friends was that almost all of them got married
through the will of cane liquor. "Me, at least, when they
screwed me, I was in my right mind."

Adelaido Lucero's house came along, brick by brick, row by row, mix by mix and trowel, every Sunday and holiday and times when he was not very sleepy, as at the beginning of the evening, when he would become a bricklayer. A good foundation and the walls lined by a plumb bob. The roof was more difficult. But it was done. One fine day, Roselia's eyes did not come to rest on the empty space above the house, but on the darkness of the tiles supported by the main beams and the cross beams. That darkness was as if the house had braids and they were being seen from the inside. Braids smelling of newly-cut wood, of damp earth, of fresh cabbage.

Lucero mixed the paint in some tin cans, to paint the house. He explained to his wife: the top part of the walls pink and the base yellow. She answered that it would be ugly like that. And he allowed that it would be ugly.

"That's how you were dressed, Roselia de León, the day I first set eyes on you!"

What tenderness he put into the brush strokes that licked the thirsty walls until the colors were smooth and even. It was blessed. For lack of a priest, someone sprinkled it with holy water. It was rare to have a priest around there. It was blessed with a kind of party. Friends. It was decorated with blue and green chains of crepe paper; the pillars were decorated with bunches of wild cane tied together with flowering vines; pine needles were sprinkled on the new brick floors, and Roselia, to top it all off, wore her yellow skirt and pink blouse, except they no longer fit her; she had to let them out, because she was pregnant.

2

From all hoot owls, from all barn owls, from all nocturnal birds, the old woman who was his mother-in-law had drawn her ugliness. That was what Lucero was thinking the day of the party when holy water was sprinkled on the house, and it was an uphill fight for him to realize that the lady there was the mother of his lovely better half, for whom the months of expecting, far from harming her physically, had been a boon to her beauty.

When the guests had left, when they were alone, she went over to her husband, and not because she had taken two glasses of heady wine, almost worth celebrating itself, but because she felt it coming from the child she was carrying in her womb, she put her arm over his shoulders, while Lucero, sitting on a high stool, was swinging his feet like a child who, now that the house was finished, had run out of toys.

The earth, which is life itself along the coast, stuck to the soles of the woman's feet like a burning tongue against the roof of that mouth that feet have on their underside, and licked it slowly until it communicated to her a kind of tingling that ran all through her body, a tingling that only stopped when Adelaido ran his hand across her breasts, her stomach, her legs, as if there were no danger of death in the step awaiting her . . . Ah, yes! . . . As if death were not spread out through the coastal air on the same footing with life, and it would show itself at the slightest carelessness on the part of a defenseless human being, who was so small within that framework of a huge nature, so insignificant, that he was never more than one of a myriad of leaves whose places were taken by others when they died and fell.

Husband and wife were savoring the sleep which had befogged their eyes like a respite in the middle of the heat, as if during sleep they had left the coast and gone walking in the pleasant climate of the mountains; and the air where Lucero had built his house, in Semírames, blew half-cool all night long. Farther down, toward the sea, to sleep meant sinking into all the sufferings of an asthmatic, waiting for dawn, when the heat would be just the same. At dawn her arm hung down from the canvas cot, she was moaning in her sleep, and Lucero's head, with her hair in his face.

The mother-in-law shook them out of their sleep. She was smoothing her clothes, she slept in them, she was running her hands over her hair, which looked as if she had the stuffing from her mattress glued to her head. Semírames was not close for her, but since her husband had left at dawn, she had time to get to the Lucero house before the couple had awakened.

And that old woman! . . . the son-in-law said to himself, becoming aware of the reality that had begun to turn pink with the light of day, the assault of the roosters' crowing, and the distant echoes of motors that were beginning to do their work.

"Oh, Ma!" she complained, annoyed at the imprudence.

"Does she have to start bothering people so early!" he said, aching, rubbing his sweaty back against the warm and sand-like cot.

"I didn't want to tell you anything before, but now I decided that, after all, it was best for you to know. After all. Your pa," she addressed Roselia, who, leaning on one elbow, had raised her head, "your pa took the train, because he says they're going to give him work at the San Juan de Dios Hospital."

"Where's that, Ma?"

"The General Hospital, they call it San Juan de Dios too."

"What kind of work . . ." Lucero asked, as he boldly put his pants on in front of his mother-in-law. With the rage he felt for her, why should he be modest.

"Working as a patient."

"Pa's going to be working as a patient?"

"That's the only kind of work he can do . . ." Lucero said, standing up now, looking for a basin to wash his face in.

"But Ma must mean working with patients, not as a patient," Roselia said as the nipples of her breasts came out from behind a speckled sheet, yawning.

"As a patient . . ." the mother-in-law repeated, glad that they were awake.

Lucero gave his face a good washing, he threw lots of water on his hair, even his shoulders got wet, then he took a towel and rubbed his forehead, his cheeks, the back of his neck, his ears, his chest, and underneath his arms.

"Leave him be, he'll be on his way back soon, some notion of his, you can't blame him for getting desperate, the shape his feet are in."

"Well, the shape his feet are in, who'd have thought it, is what they're going to pay him for. That's what he told me before he left. There's a doctor who wants to show that what your pa's got isn't big leprosy, it's little leprosy, brought on by all those chiggers that have got into him. Since he was always drunk, he wouldn't dig them out or let me dig them out, and his feet got the way they are. A regular breeding place for chiggers."

"So his leprosy came from chiggers and liquor then, so what, will he get cured or will he still limp around, walking like he was going around on his heels, *tuco-tuco-tuco*, like instead of feet he had a pair of bananas."

"Well, I don't know whether he'll get any help in the end. I tell you, Adelaido, it's funny what he's got, because he don't stink much and it don't make him cry; it's made him peel, you could say, fish scales, dirty ashes."

"But if it's for sure that they're going to pay him for showing that it isn't real leprosy, he should take advantage of it, what the devil, people pay in circuses to look at the freaks, and with him it's something worse."

"That pa of mine gets some ideas, I don't know, I really don't know . . ." Roselia had fastened her hair with a comb and was running back and forth getting breakfast ready; she stopped and said to her mother: "Stay and have breakfast with us."

"I took a physic and I have to leave, because if I don't I might lose something back there, with all the stealing that's been going on since the word got around that people make good money here, and they only come to get sick and see what somebody's left laying around so they can get their paws on it."

The trains were bringing in coachloads of men on their way to work on the plantations, their tanned faces under yellow straw hats, silent. Some smoking, others motionless, eyeless before the endless passage of thousands of trunks of banana trees, which were holding up the blades of their green machetes like a host armed with swords to cut off passage to the sea.

With them, after them, at the same pace, there came liquor, beer, prostitution, trumpet-shaped phonographs, expensive victrolas, drugstores, a garrison of sad soldiers, the lovestruck telegrapher, until the village took shape on a piece of land donated by Tropical Banana, Inc., where the freshly-cut stumps of trees that had been felled to clear a space for the buildings alternated with ditches and bramble patches.

And all those men, awakened by the heat after daybreak and blinded by the darkness of the burning night, were moving about the rudimentary village, having trouble seeing where they were stumbling, using their hands to help them wander about. All those men would most often fall into a stupor at night, worn out, smelling of fatigue, because fatigue stinks when it becomes too great, it stinks of that, fatigue, of torn flesh, of suffering, of a back that pains from being stuck to the ground with no blanket underneath, a hat over the face and a jacket opened at the chest and raised up to the shoulders, as if someone face-down on top of them were hugging them without arms, just empty sleeves, as they slept.

Far off, in the darkness everything seems so distant, a light shows where the Chinese store is, a pitch torch, a food counter, coffee and bread, sausages, stale cracklings; and there they would crowd in one behind the other, or in groups, saying hello to the woman behind the counter and ordering something to eat. She would serve them and they would squat down with their plates and mugs of coffee, setting their table on the dark floor, all squatting. The ones who had already put time in on the coast with glassy eyes until night came on. The first fevers confused with the heat. The newcomers, in better health, stronger, joking, reminiscing, anxious to go pay a good woman out there. There, in the tight darkness, in the frames of doorways like gold-toothed phantoms, women waved at those who passed, calling them, insisting that they come in: Honey! . . . Sweetie! . . . Dreamboat! . . .

Everything was quiet but not in an absolute silence, because one could actually hear the sprouting of the leaves on the branches, of the branches on the young trunks, of the trunks on the roots as they appeared at the surface, growing with the sound of a jet of water which rises up and up until they attained the height of a bush or a tree; and one could also hear the footsteps of the animals as they took advantage of the darkness to come and go secretively in search of food or a place to hide.

Adelaido Lucero, overseer of the plantation called La Maroma, ate breakfast as soon as his mother-in-law had left; she mentioned leaving and she left, afraid that thieves would break into her house, taking advantage of her husband's absence; Chiggerfoot was good for something, for staying there so that nothing would be stolen, and Lucero left with his usual trick, joke, or caress, putting his hat on his wife's head for a moment so that she would remember him while he was gone.

Riding breeches, leggings, a fringed shirt, and a wide-brimmed hat to protect himself from the sun. He was soon at his first duty of the day. The foremen formed a circle around him. Man to man, bare fists. One of them was saying: I knocked him down. He wasn't man enough for me. Muggsy Zaldívar went off with Lucero to tell him something very important. The cutting season was almost there and his crews were undermanned. The ones they were sending from El Jute had not all arrived. Three, that was all. If they didn't give him people, they shouldn't put the blame on him. Nigger Sologaistoa, another one of his foremen, talked to him about the same thing. They were shorthanded. And since the cutting season was getting "frantic." Nigger Sologaistoa used words, as he said himself, like a "stampede." And, as a matter of fact, the cutting of the fruit did have something like the frenzy of small animals about it as they detached the bunches from a gigantic green mass with the cutting edge of their hooks. The movements of the cutting crew at the foot of a banana tree which looked like a green cross resembled those of Jews with ladders and spears as they tried to lift down a green Christ who had been changed

into a bunch of bananas which descended among arms and
ropes and was received with great care, as if it were a case of
an overdelicate being, and carried off in small carts to receive
its sacramental bath and be placed in a bag with special
cushions inside.

The water gurgled hesitantly as it flowed along a new irriga-
tion outlet opened up between piles of dirt to keep the ground
moist. Under the banana trees the earth was exhaling the hot
coastal dampness, and it was that water-breathing which fed
the vegetable world as it went from seed to flower in a matter
of an instant. A lakelike vegetation of trees that formed large,
broad green expanses and continued on toward the infinity of
the sea. Rows and rows of banana trees. On all sides. Everywhere, until they became lost on the horizon. Thousands of
plants that seemed to multiply in successive mirrors. So much
alike and so symmetrically planted that they looked like the
same plant, equally spaced, the same height, almost the same
color, the same eternal growth and flowering. The polished
trunks, a metallic gloss, and branches that formed arches made
of fans, ringed the vista with a vegetable light, the cells of
future emeralds.

"A land that swallows people up . . ." Lucero observed; and
he had really seen it, he was one of those who had arrived there
when everything was yet to be done; and it would go on swallowing them, he thought, as he discussed the way to get hands
with the foremen, because if they didn't, the whole thing would
be worse than fouled up. They were in bad shape the year
before because of that. If the fruit ripens too fast it just gets
ruined when there aren't enough hands for the cutting, because it has to be cut when it's nice and green. And some
thousand or two thousand or three thousand or five thousand
or ten thousand bunches are lost . . . That was how accounts
were kept, in losses as well as profits, at Tropbanana, as they
called Tropical Banana, Inc. Lips Torres was the last foreman.

And he came with the same story. People. No matter where they got them from. Because if they didn't, the results. With the ones they had, impossible to get it done.

The demands of the foremen to the overseer and his to the head men and of the head men to the central office mobilized a set of secret springs in the telegraph office. Those tiny machines in the midst of that tropical jungle, that disconcerting concert of creation, which in its effort to outdo itself touches death almost at birth, it lives so rapidly, received from the operator's finger the signals of alarm that went to other plantations, communicating the request for "more men," "more men," and "more men."

The trains passed by, loaded with people. To work on the coast. To work on the coast. Others came on foot, to work on the coast. Others came in trucks, to work on the coast. Without families. Why did they need to haul them along. With nothing but their ponchos and a few reals for the road. For just in case, a machete. For just in case, a relic of the Christ of Esquípulas, brand-new on a boy's hairless chest or the gnarled chest of an adult. Soon that holy adornment would be a little string worm that would get sweated up until it fell apart.

The train dumped them, bored already and with their bodies asleep, at the station nearest to the plantings. From there they would set out in military formation. There was no lack of eager ones who always wanted to get there first. Others, the conformists, wherever they were put. And others, the laziest, behind, in the rear. They would all get there at the same time, just as with a levy of troops. Except that in a levy they were sad when they reached the barracks, while here they were lively and merry, because the pay was twice what they could hope for. With a few months of work, they would lift up their heads. Go back with something they could use. The heat was softening them. The cold jerked-beef flesh of the mountain people was giving way under the heavy drowsiness. They began by taking off their clothes, unsticking them from their honey-colored hides, as if something were burning them, distressed, thinking about leaving after they had earned the first few pesos. All of them, in the end, all of them would bear it and stay on. Some were overcome by sleepiness and others by insomnia. And a feeling of nausea. Always thirst and nausea. There were people. There were people in greater and greater numbers. But they were always asking for more people because they needed them for the planting. Worse yet if, as they say, work has begun over there in Río Hondo. They had already begun. Theodolites. Men in pith helmets. The clearing operation, attacking the underbrush with fire or machetes. The plowing. The planting of the shoots. The plants growing after putting roots into the ground. The plants, as they grow taller. The plants, now full-grown, with offspring at their feet. Irrigated banana trees. The magnificent sword-leaf banana trees. And being able to see that everything that glitters is gold, because water, sun, moon, stars all join to produce the bunch of bananas that will be sold for its weight in gold.

Workmen, foremen, overseers, administrators, even administrators, the human organization was arriving, it could be said, because from that time on, with a different type of man, the blind, implacable machinery was beginning to work, one which converted everything into figures in its books, unalterable, chronometric, precise.

One of those different men, Mr. John Pyle, conscious of his role as a small cog in a heartless machine, was showing it all to his wife, Leland Foster, down from the Dakotas on vacation, showing her Lucero's house, he was the oldest overseer on the plantation. Flowerpots, vines, a macaw. That was enough to give the house some flavor. Moved to the different men's section, where the higher-ups lived, the macaw and the flowers would become artificial.

"That artificiality of our life here, set apart from this magical world of flowers and birds," Mr. Pyle was saying, "makes us feel out of place, the same as in boarding school or in military service. We don't know what to do after working-hours, which are the same as classes, meals in mess halls where we're always together at the table with the same people, just like army recruits. But these people, on the other hand, Leland, they live," and he repeated, "they live, and what's good is good and what's cruel is cruel. We're neither good nor bad, just machines."

John Pyle's blue eyes were dancing behind his glasses which were sparkling because they were so thick and clean, happy to have his wife look out over the terrain and see the inferiority of men like him who worked for powerful companies.

"We're robots," Pyle said, "denied life as an adventure, because if we're lower down the scale, the slightest change in the routine of the job makes us lose our reputation and our position, and if we're big bosses, money does away with any possibility of risk, and without risk, there can't be any vital adventure."

Pyle was rubbing his hands, waiting to see the effect his words were having on his wife. She was contradicting him. Great enterprises, for her, would always be an adventure for many lives.

"Agreed! Agreed!" he said twice, jumping like a little boy; "but the men of adventure in this enterprise are not the ones running it now, those others perished in the adventure itself, devoured by the climate or by life itself and replaced, replaced by us, the ones who aren't good or bad, happy or sad, just machines."

3

The atmosphere was suffocating and they had to walk, wear out the soles of their shoes. The walk helped them get through the night. Get tired, digest, speak, as they calculated among the expanses of grass to find the steps lost among the brightly-lighted houses and those that full-volume radios had turned into music boxes.

The Pyles were silent: he with his white shirt, impeccable, his pants made of a special weave which allowed the air to circulate around his legs, and she with her white shoes, a white tailored suit, her hair fixed like that of one of her grandmothers, the one she looked like, the one who had been painted by a famous Dutch artist of the last century. A beautiful woman.

And those were the precise words said by Carl Rose, an old-time employee of Tropical Banana, Inc., as he joined them in the nightly stroll they were taking on a ship anchored in the depths of a Tropic of Cancer night. His arms, with their golden fuzz showing in the lamplight, became active, so that he was speaking mostly with gestures.

Leland, bumping into the shadows that fell from the branches of the ornamental trees up above, bathed in the light, thought that there were steps where everything was one long strip of concrete, and she was maintaining that the gigantic exploitation there was still an adventure.

Carl Rose knocked his pipe in the palm of his hand, tall, built only of bone, and he ventured:

"It did have, it did have its epic hour; but what else can you expect now, it's nothing but cheap exploitation, the dreary exploitation of natural resources, of those invaluable lands we're looking down at!"

Mr. Pyle agreed with Carl Rose that there had been a moment of adventure, when the plantations were set up, when the machinery went into the jungle; but he could not accept it as a stupid exploitation now.

Leland, modulating her voice, with that clear intonation of a person being consumed as she speaks, was impassioned and beautiful; she accepted Carl Rose's feelings: exploitation was something more than dull, it was stupid, completely stupid. Her feelings about that were so violently feminine that she repeated the word twice before stating:

"An enterprise with so much money behind it, operating right in its own backyard, in virgin territory, with a labor force that's practically free might be something else again."

"The days of adventure were something else, weren't they, really, old John!" Carl Rose exclaimed; "there's a difference between the man who goes into the unknown to bring out beneficial natural resources and the one who follows him in the absurd routine of never getting beyond going along with what's been set up."

"And the worst part, the worst part," Leland rested her arm on her husband's, "is that when time is lost, everything is lost, because business, just like people, has a right time for every age. If adventure is a sign of youth, then this business burned its youth up very fast and passed into old age, senility . . ."

"An opera of the tropics!" old John shouted.

"Let me finish; I was saying that this business burned its youth up very fast and passed into old age, and right now it has the body of an old man who wants to be sure that in the last years of his life he won't be upset or bothered by anything."

"I'm not following you too well," Rose said, turning around to look as if someone were following him; a feeling that often came over him ever since years ago when he had been in a railroad station and had seen someone shoot another man in the back; he always felt the threat behind him. "I'm not following you too well, but I do insist, Leland, that this banana business has got itself into an impasse that it can't get out of . . ."

"Because a full-fledged adventure would have been building up a kind of human cooperation around this whole world of vegetable emeralds; not being satisfied with just an artificial domination where we've come to deprive ourselves of life so that we can escape death, living like so many corpses preserved behind glass, in wire cages."

"And in alcohol!" Pyle exclaimed.

"You're right. Men only seem to be alive here when they're drunk."

Leland felt so far away from her usual calmness when she said that, as far away as any of the stars shining in the pale dome of the sky and which seemed to be dying of the heat, breathing with difficulty, twinkling to give themselves air, just like them. Except that they were going to have something to drink and do some bowling.

Old John bowled and made a strike. He wanted to make up for losing the night before.

Leland put her beautiful bare shoulder into play as she bowled and there was another strike.

"Underneath it all, you're a pair of adventurers!" Carl Rose shouted to them as his ball left the alley, climbed, jumped, and was returned to him. "The second ball is already routine. Old John should tell us when, where, and how routine starts!"

"This is where it ends; when the ball leaves your hand, you stop being a routine bowler, and the adventure of a solid round mass impelled toward its goal begins, and its collision there will produce another chapter in your personal adventure."

Sleep was always necessary and it was a bore. Behind the screen walls, in the half-darkness, people there like naked ghosts, desirous, alternating digestive salts with sleeping pills.

Leland, while the men were working in the office, ventured off by herself—it is easy to lose one's way in the banana groves —to the house of Adelaido Lucero, the overseer. Her dress of raw silk, pale lemon in color, made her look younger. Although it was not an original, it was a beautiful dress with kimono sleeves. A Japanese parasol drew a flowery hemisphere above her greenish-golden hair which was held in a turban the same color as her dress.

It was easy to get lost in a place where there were no points of reference, where the land, covered by a growth of pretty, damp flowers, does not vary and always seems the same under that fish net of noisy insects. A team of crop sprayers appears in the distance, looking more like soldiers of a war among divers at the bottom of the sea. To shield themselves somewhat from the calcifying force of the sun, they have covered themselves with intertwined branches until, closer now, they look like moving plants. Some quickly connect the hoses to the spray pipes, while others direct the liquid onto the emerald showcases, some loaded down with bunches weighing over two hundred pounds. The banana grove is becoming covered with a light, sky-blue layer of perspiration under the rain of the "Bordeaux broth."

Leland quickened her step. A kind of desire to let herself go came over her, to give her body over to the feeling that her senses were giving her of what was around her. Yes, stay there, under the white rainbows of the artificial rain which was dampening the hot-coal atmosphere as it threw water from the sleeping canals in pulverized clouds of millions of cool droplets over the plantings that are now green rows standing at military attention.

The pruning gangs watch her pass. So many dangers that threaten the plant which produces the "fruit of wise men," that in two long shifts every day they are examined from top to bottom, while the sun sends rivers of gold dust over the crumpled leaves.

Small and large parrots and other slow-flying birds, foamlike clouds, and other men, moving like moles as they pour crude oil on the pools of water to prevent the mosquitoes from breeding.

Doña Roselia de Lucero was quick to offer her a chair. The best in the house. For such a fine lady, so fresh in spite of the heat, and to whom, if she did not show her those attentions, she would have no way of expressing her pleasure at having her in her house, for she could not speak a syllable of English and Leland could not speak a word of Spanish.

Their looks softened as they sat. Leland sat down opposite Doña Roselia, who had brought out a small bench for her visitor. What else could they do but look at each other? They laughed. Now they were not looking at each other in a scrutinizing way as at first, but pleasantly, like two people who knew each other. Leland tried a Spanish word that would be the equivalent of "purty" to her, speaking of one of the little Luceros, the runt, because the other two were men already, as he came crawling out. The mother, in a burst of tenderness, picked the child up from the floor, up to the level of her dark face; she almost lifted him up over her head, raising him higher, then she hugged him to her breast.

Leland saw how high the language barrier can be between two people who cannot communicate. Each in her own world, in the world of her own language. The mystery of languages. The confusion of the Tower of Babel. She crossed her pretty legs that ended in slim ankles, took out her alligator cigarette case, and offered a cigarette to her silent companion, who thanked her with a gesture but did not take it.

Leland was startled by the laughter of someone guffawing like a clown. A feigned laughter, but one which had an insulting pugnacity about it. And she was even more startled to find between them a man, who was still laughing boisterously: Ya-ha, ha, ha, ha! . . .

He had on a shiny jacket, frayed at the cuffs and the collar, the color of ipecac; pants of a lighter color, half-gray, striped, with knees almost worn through and very short legs. His green eyes were the color of young banana leaves, a thin nose, thin lips, and blue shadow on the ruddy skin of his clean-shaven cheeks, as perspiration rolled down over the cleanliness of soap and water. Some called him Cosi, others Stoner, others Lester Mead.

Cosi, Stoner, or Lester Mead did not give his possible customers time to flee. With the outburst of his strident laugh, there he was in person with his merchandise. "Everything a seamstress needs." That was what he said when he stopped laughing, falling then into a deep silence in which he would dilate his green eyes, bugging them out until it looked as if they would leap out of their sockets. "Everything a seamstress needs," he repeated, gazing at his merchandise, following it with another endless laugh: Ya-ha, ha, ha, ha! . . .

Leland congratulated him on his methods of salesmanship, combining his announcement with the laughter that bubbled up out of his mouth like gargled water that had burned him as he swallowed it and which he then spat out. "Everything a seamstress needs." Ya-ha, ha, ha, ha! . . .

Cosi did not answer Leland's congratulations, contenting himself with looking at her silently, piercing her with his green, round eyes, a will turned into glass. Suddenly he half-tilted his head, showing the back of his neck, where his long hair had the shape of a kind of wig, and after a moment of looking as if he had no neck, he raised his head and released his laugh, which wounded the ears of those who heard it as if a barbed wire had been pulled through: Ya-ha, ha, ha, ha! . . .

Leland asked him who he was. His Adam's apple moved as if he would let the answer out after he swallowed some saliva. He replied in a measured voice, like a professor, a Protestant minister, or a diplomat. He spoke Oxford English, and Leland could not have made a better find that morning. Señora Lucero could not understand a word of what Leland and Cosi were talking about. As he was leaving, he took the hand of the beautiful Mrs. Pyle and, with the voice of a man who has found a word that he has not spoken for a long time, he called her: friend.

"Hissing . . . the way snakes would laugh if they were able!"

Those were the last words that Leland heard from the strange person of "everything a seamstress needs." Hissing . . . the way snakes would laugh if they were able! He was leaning his hand on one of the posts. Beside his feet, the bag with his precious colored thread, needles, thimbles, pins, knitting needles . . . One of his shoes had holes in it. The other had a flapping sole.

Leland tried to smile at Doña Roselia. She could not. She fixed her mouth as if she were going to, but there was more affliction than smile on her lips. Her eyes, the color of bread crust, slightly golden, watched the man attentively before he left. He was not the poor-in-spirit that he seemed to be. Who was he? She had just taken leave of Doña Roselia, who was carrying her youngest in her arms, raising up her parasol to say good-bye. Cosi let her pass, talking to her with his eyes, which, like two hopes with eyelash feet, penetrated her through the cold white of her corneas. Then she heard him go away with his feigned clown's laugh. Ya-ha, ha, ha, ha! . . .

For the sake of doing something, Leland Foster, the beautiful Mrs. Pyle, spun her flowered parasol nervously on her shoulder and headed toward her residence. Old John Pyle celebrated his wife's decision not to stay penned up at home while he was working in his office. Had she begun to like the place? Would she stay for long in the tropics where she had come for a vacation? What showed on her pleased face as she came close on her return from Lucero's, closing her parasol and asking for a Scotch and soda with ice? She greeted her husband with a kiss, then she shook hands with Carl Rose and Ernie Walker, a poker player with a lock of hair hanging over his forehead.

Before they could speak, Leland told them about her chance meeting with that apparent poor-in-spirit who spoke impeccable English. The argument started right away. What did she mean, what did they mean, what did the world mean by impeccable English? There was the smell of must in those cases of impeccability. People like to use fossil words and they speak a language impeccably. But the English they spoke was much more alive, even though Leland thought that it was shamefully poor and the barbarisms of giants who had reverted to childhood and no longer really spoke, but babbled, speaking half-words in order to save time, or mixing them all together to invent words for a damnable commercial jargon.

Little was done in the afternoon. Rather, nothing was done. Siesta time, lying naked on their beds. The silent employees who had left work pending in the office went back to work for a short time. Amidst the smoke of locomotives doing yard work in a station teary with willows, with no buildings, beside tall water towers that had been silvered with aluminum paint, the first stars in their great office, in their nocturnal work of sending and receiving messages to and from the Supreme Being and the drowsy croaking of the frogs.

Adelaido Lucero returned home for a deserved rest. There are days when there is no time for anything. Lucero organized the work according to a timetable, but not even in that way was he able to get everything done that should have been done during the day. His children surrounded him. When he got home at night, he would sit down like a tree with several coconuts on it, as he touched the three heads that formed the bunch. The last was his favorite. When his father sat down, he would crawl over to him. He looked like a newt. That was what they lovingly called him.

"Look, there comes the Newt . . ."

And the cinnamon-colored child, as if he understood what his father had said, would beat the floor with his hands to get there faster, and when he reached his feet, he would grasp his knees, struggling to climb his legs. The paternal hand would come to his aid.

"God-dammy! That's my boy, that's why I put up with you! You toothless little bugger, your teeth won't never grow out, you're going to be the first toothless individual in all creation!"

"Don John's wife was here," his wife told him, "but it would have been better if she hadn't come, because I wasn't able to entertain her very well. Because I couldn't understand her and she couldn't understand me."

"Did you have her sit down?"

"Naturally, I've got my manners . . . She was here for quite a while, until Cosi came; she spoke that gabble they talk with him, and only the devil could have understood."

Lucero made a gesture that he understood, and they fell silent. The Newt was trying to stick his finger, along with the moustache there, into his father's nose.

"Give him a whack," she told him.

"What an idea, eh, boy! Me whacking my boy! And what did Cosi do?"

"Well, like you know, he came up from out of nowhere. That man, he's nowhere to be seen, and when he lets out that laugh, he's already right on top of you. And he disappears just like that, and a body never knows where or when. Nutty as a fruitcake!"

"Nutty or not, he's the son or stepson or adopted son of one of the people who licked the jungle by fighting against swamps, mosquitoes, fever, alligators, poisonous snakes, and the devil himself to get all this nice land ready for planting. If it hadn't been for them, none of this would be here now. The ones who opened it up . . . and now that I think of it—cut it out, Newt —I forgot some papers, Mr. Pyle must have them, I'll have to go over and see him, I'll be right back!"

The Newt wept hard when he was separated from his father. Lucero reached Mr. Pyle's house just as he was saying good-bye to his friends.

"Come in, Lucero," Mr. Pyle invited.

Adelaido took off his hat, listening without understanding what they were saying as they left. The one who was doing most of the talking was Doña Leland, who accompanied Carl Rose and Ernie Walker to the door. When Leland came back to go up the steps that led to the entrance to the house, she had the impression that her husband and Lucero were talking in a wire cage, just like two birds dressed like people and peck-ing in the air. Lucero folded some papers, took leave of Pyle, and passed her on the stairs.

"I just heard," he said, without knowing whether to put his hat on or not, "that you met that wheedler who laughs like a howler monkey; have Mr. Pyle tell you who he is, because someone like you ought to give him some advice. My wife tells me that when you spoke to him he paid attention, he listened to what you said to him. Your husband can tell you.

All of us, myself included, hate to see him like that, half-barefoot, with hand-me-down clothes, no hat, crazy . . ."

Leland did not understand a word of what Lucero was telling her with the aplomb of a person who thinks that by speaking slowly he can make himself understood; but her husband translated it for her. When Lucero left, she fixed her mouth, trying to remember how she had done it to smile at Doña Roselia, but she only managed a sign of affliction.

Rainy days followed, days and nights of rain, which obliged her to stay at home. Her husband came and went like a ghost, with a hooded raincoat, an umbrella, and galoshes. Friends were absent. Everybody in his own house. Cigarettes, books, whiskey. They spoke on the telephone, and on the telephone one day at dusk Cosi arrived, he dropped by on the telephone, through the receiver of the telephone, laughing with his horrifying locust laugh, moving his green eyes like a statue that had suddenly begun to move its eyes from side to side.

Leland saw him, soaked, dripping water, and laughing like that, she brought out a towel, slippers, some of her husband's clothes so that he could change. He changed, he took a cigarette from a lacquered box that he had been looking at for a long time, and he scratched the match to light it as if he were going to set fire to his face. Now, Leland thought, what will I do if he doesn't leave, even though I don't want him to.

Tury Duzin, youthful and slim tennis champion, neutral, so much like an adding machine, her breasts the size of two tennis balls, welcomed in her quarters of an important employee, Mr. Dimas's secretary, one beautiful Sunday morning, horsewomen whose close and daily contact did not prevent them from coming by on Sunday as if they had not seen each other all week.

Nelly Alcántara dismounted after the ride and Tury Duzin helped her. They spent every Sunday afternoon together. A

friendly frugal lunch, and then the tyranny of the tennis champion as she demanded amorous declarations from her friend.

Tury Duzin, the lady colonel of the office, had the color of
dry sand, which, along with her short, black hair, parted in
the middle, gave her a masculine look. Her exaggerated refine-
ment hid her instincts of a desert marauder so deeply that no
woman near her would suspect the danger she was in except
at the moment when the claw struck, too late already for any
salvation. The shifting quicksands of a sticky sexual tenderness
would then replace her unexpressive way, until she would
weep, drop by drop, as if she were filtering her tears. "Oh,
desolate virgin," she would say to herself in her husky voice,
"you've eaten up the woman there was in you and all that's
left is the man who can't be satisfied with you anymore and
looks for the flesh he wants in other women!"

Tury Duzin's love for her favorites was born of that need
for females, and outside the office, therefore, she could not
bear men and was surrounded by girl friends, who were
pleased by her exquisite treatment of them, her delicate
coquettishness as she courted them. Enthusiastic, giving, she
worked like a machine all morning long; except for her masculine looks, she was a beautiful man-woman who at six in
the morning would do her exercises, eat fruit for breakfast,
work like a machine all morning and part of the afternoon
after a salad for lunch, and when she returned home and felt
lazy, she would lie down on a divan like a small animal to
await the arrival of her girl friends, among whom Nelly Alcántara was now the favorite.

Tury Duzin clasped her friend's body, putting her arm
around her back, her right arm, and she kissed her on the
mouth, while her left hand sank its fingers into the division
of her buttocks, between skin and panties.

From the growing village, to wake up the happy lovers, the

breeze brought the sound of the clapper of a bell located high up on the half-built church, where people were entering to pray, although there were also the curious, who went in to see what was going on. Nothing was going on. But someday something had to be going on, and one had to be present. Something had to be going on there where God was present.

Adelaido Lucero, his wife, and his children, the two older boys, Lino and Juan, as well as the Newt, how could they not be there as everybody walked through the square, looking, listening, showing off their new clothes? Some on horseback at the corners. Officers on leave, no doubt. Others around a wheel of fortune. Spending their dough. What's dough for if not to be spent. Samuel, the bootblack, with his future wife taking subversive looks at the showcase of the Chinese store and the perfumes there. A Negro, with two other Negroes, waiting for the public dance to start.

Lucero, his wife, and their brood go into a barbershop called The Equinoxes. The barber made a bad face because he thought it meant work for him. But when he found out it was a visit, he embraced Lucero's children and picked the smallest one up in his arms. Then he offered them the barber chairs. Doña Roselia did not want to sit down where only men sat. She would rather have a regular chair. Lucero had gone into The Equinoxes to close a deal for some land that he had been wanting to buy for some time.

"You see, now, Roselia, something had to happen. That's why God's around on Sunday afternoons. Now we have the land for the boys. Lino and Juan Lucero here are going to be landowning farmers."

"You know," Doña Roselia said back home, as beside the plates of whole beans with wild chile sauce pouring off them she was serving the father and the children black coffee full of sediment, sweetened with brown sugar, "you know what I was thinking on the way home: these two, with the land you just bought them, are going to be better off than we ever were, because we never had nothing we could call our own!"

"That's right, there's nothing like having something of your own; somebody who works for somebody else is always a buzzard and never gets to be a hawk; if I don't look out for myself after working all these years, I'll be just the same and maybe worse, because it's not the way it used to be, when everybody worked with their mouths shut, happy to get what they were paid . . ."

"That's right . . ."

"Now they've woke up and we're the simple ones, like me when I have to stand there and tell them to be patient, that everything's going to work out all right . . ."

"Yes, because they've been making threats, maybe Lino told you."

Lino lifted his eyes from his plate of beans, swallowed a mouthful, and with his voice a little blurred because he was still eating, explained:

"But that business, Ma, that was about something else, it didn't have so much to do with pay . . ."

"Yes . . . " the father said, "about the tricks they play on the women; don't you see, because a woman can't walk around alone without them following her to see where they can get her on her back!"

"And the worst of it is that the ones in charge, they trick them into coming into their houses and they get them there," exclaimed Juan, Lucero's other son, who seemed to be very upset by that infamous procedure.

"You seem to be all upset by that, boy! Tell me about it, that's why I'm your pa!"

"It doesn't just upset me, it upsets all of us!"

4

"An extremely volatile liquid . . ." Mr. Pyle said, leaning over a cupboard as he took some benzine for his lighter from a small bottle. Then he turned around and showed his smiling face to his friend Carl Rose, who was deeply upset.

Losing a friend of so many years like John Pyle was as painful as having an arm amputated, a leg, some part of the body. His face was mournful when he left. The least he could ask of old John was not to force him to drive him to the station in his little car. He looked for pretexts. The motor got so hot that you'd think it ran on steam; and when the steam came out of the radiator cap, it fogged up the windshield, and since there weren't any windshield-wipers, there was no way to clean it off. And if it wasn't easy to see where you were going and talk, what was the use of going to the station?

Because of Carl Rose's arguments, John Pyle used the office car for the last time, driven by the Negro Soledad, who knew that the boss was leaving for good and was more solicitous than usual, helping him load his baggage, his hats, his coats, other items.

The divorce had left John Pyle free to marry again. It was the only disadvantage that he saw in divorce: the danger of a second marriage. Tury Duzin, accompanied by Nelly Alcántara, came to say good-bye. Nelly imposed on him with a letter for a friend in Chicago. When the car stopped by the Lucero place, Doña Roselia could not hide her grief. They were the tears of an old Latin woman, coming forth each time she told him: good luck, Mr. Pyle. Ernie Walker, the poker player, with the lock of hair on his forehead and the ever-present Virginia cigarette between his lips, was at the station. Someone had to give him a good handshake before he left.

John Pyle had never seen the countryside so green, Soledad so black, the cool morning so drowsy with its opals of mist, the bunches of bananas so much like bunches, the Bordeaux poison that the sprayers were hurling into the air so softly blue, and the banana trees that had Panama disease so close to nothingness.

In the train, he took the last empty seat, next to a fat lady, whose flesh, as if it had a will distinct from that of its owner, began to fill that minimum space which he had tried in vain to keep for his bones between the hemispheric lady and the edge of the seat. He even began to feel that he was fat. With her flesh clinging to one's bones, anybody would be fat.

The burning heat of noon. The tightness. The discomfort. So many people in a single coach. He rolled up his shirtsleeves. The fat lady had already smiled twice with the sweet laugh of a chubby schoolgirl as she practiced piano pieces on the windowpane with her bejeweled fingers. The window was kept closed to keep out the dust from the slopes that trembled and crumbled as the train passed and the smoke from the engine with its sparks and soot. The heat was not for talking, but

when it grew cooler they spoke. When the train began to climb
up into the highlands. After all, destiny had joined them together body to body in a narrow space for that trip. What else
is every union between man and woman? They opened some
bottles of beer that Mr. Pyle had bought, she unwrapped several sandwiches of ham, cheese, chicken, and some hard-boiled
eggs. As they were friends now, Mr. Pyle was able to settle
himself better, attempting to see to it that some of his bones
did not have to support so much flesh, and letting others carry
the lady's adipose stuffing, on loan for the rest of the trip.

"I make this trip sixty times a year," she said, "and I'm sick
of asking them to put on more coaches when people are traveling from Mexico, because then it fills up and a person comes
along and doesn't know whether she'll make it or not; you
must be high up in the company, maybe you could say something; it's for everybody's good, you people too; it's bad for
your reputation, you don't want people . . ."

Mr. Pyle did not answer.

"You can't give me any answer, but I can tell you that we
do like you, we like you because you get so much out of us."

"Thank you for the part that I've gotten out . . ."

"No, we don't separate you; we like you altogether, the ones
of you who've come to fight this climate so that other country-
men of yours can live like kings back there; it's true that the
ones in charge here are most likely not what they are among
us back there; but that's the way things are . . ."

The vegetation was changing on the plateau, trees with
metal-colored leaves on the surfaces of which green, oily paint
had been spread. A deep feeling of freedom and coolness coming from the soft breeze that was blowing among the leaves.
The trees were bodies that could be breathed, they came in
through the nose, passed through the lungs, and came out
again to remain where they were. On both coasts, on the other

hand, every tree was a compact mass, a green mattress, pressing against people just like the comforters that gypsies throw over themselves when they sleep.

The passengers were taking out jackets, sweaters, and coats.

"You should put something on, don't forget that we're leaving the coast," said Mr. Pyle's companion, who, as she was getting ready to say good-bye now, told him that her name was Clara, "but because of my coloring they call me Clariona. At the Hotel Buena Vista in Ayutla, ask for Clariona and they'll treat you like a king . . ."

A passenger who was dozing in the beat behind, woke up halfway and, without raising his head, said:

"They'll give you your Last Supper . . ."

She turned around and said:

"Boor, meddler, who asked you to butt in!"

"Speaking of butts . . ." the one dozing on the seat behind mumbled, his head resting on the back, his hat over his face, breathing with difficulty.

Clariona paid no attention to him. Pyle rolled down the sleeves of his shirt over his thin and hairy forearms and put on his jacket after checking to see that all of his hand luggage was there. He mechanically brushed off his shoulders. Always that dandruff.

At the hotel (he did not seek out the hospitality of his friends the Thorntons) he sat down in a chair beside a round table covered with a cloth where it could be seen from the marks that men's clothing had once been ironed, and he began to open the letters they had given him to deliver to various people. In the past he never would have done it; but on a certain occasion the idea came to him to open one of those letters he was to deliver, and perhaps it would start like this: "The idiot bearing this letter . . ." Since then, any letter sent with him was a letter opened; if it did not interest him, he would skim it, merely glancing at it, and if it did interest him, he would read every word of it.

He adjusted his glasses as he began to read the letter which the gentle Miss Havisham was writing to her mother. Miss Havisham was a woman close to fifty who made an effort to please everybody with her manners and good breeding, but she was unsuccessful because she had an innate haughty way about her, pedagogical, that of a person who is always in front of a class, and because she was implacable in matters of schedules and duty. She would twist her depilated mouth, frown, and all of her would nervously change as she spoke of uprightness, character, punctuality, and other virtues that were holy to her.

She was writing her mother a letter about John Pyle and Leland Foster's divorce, in which she said:

"You can use the map you have as a guide . . . that map I sent you two years ago is still good for locating things around here. The heights you see to the north, where birds with beautiful plumage abound, had a good deal to do with Leland Foster's decision, I think. The hills where the mineral world lies under thick layers of vegetation attack the very innermost part of the soul with a dampness that turns into a feeling of vague melancholy, of dissatisfaction with what one has. Mrs. Pyle laughed when I told her that she shouldn't go horseback riding in that place very much. Her personality, which had seemed so well adjusted to our most rigorous traditions, became unhinged. You know all the rest from my previous letters. An adventurer got her, and her poor husband . . ."

Mr. Pyle could only scratch his head when he saw that part about her poor husband and continue on . . .

". . . her poor husband is one of those people who thinks that we women are different from men because we're women; he was always enthusiastic and he got everybody enthusiastic about what he called the epic of the people who founded this great enterprise; the builders, the ones who rescued these fertile and workable lands from the jungle, and when Leland found herself face to face with one of those great adventurers, she did not see what he was like, she adopted him, because that is what we women of a certain age will do, we adopt the men we love . . . Lost youth, dear Mama, means that the life of the days when we had love without adoption has sunk into nothingness . . ."

Pyle laughed heartily. The letter was a very close account of something that had happened to him. The only thing new to him was that part about the heights to the north, where birds with beautiful plumage abounded and the mineral world lay under thick layers of vegetation . . .

He put the incomparable Miss Havisham's letter on the table and opened the envelope of the letter from Nelly Alcántara, Tury Duzin's girl friend. Mr. Pyle thought those little ladies were adorable because they made up a world apart, comfortable for the male sex because man was really a creature of no importance for them as far as the normal importance man has for woman was concerned. When he talked to them, old John would have the pleasant feeling of not having to defend anything, his sex first off, which is what a man is always defending in the presence of women. Old John felt that he could let himself go, like a person swimming on his back when there is no danger of any kind.

"Leland Foster," Nelly Alcántara's letter said, "broke up with her husband, an adorable person in the opinion of Tury Duzin because he was so inoffensive, and now she's making me feel that she adores me; the world will have to go back to what it was before, when love was between people of the same sex, the only formula for happiness. The worst part is that Leland has gone after another man, who will soon be her husband and she talks such nonsense about rehumanizing the

world, implanting social justice . . . I can't stand her . . . I
only like seeing her when she plays the piano; Mozart becomes
adorable for me under her fingers, and Tury Duzin isn't jealous
of Mozart, she's jealous of Leland's fingers. And speaking of
my love for music, something very amusing happened. Coming back from a ride we stopped at the house of some natives,
well established and good people called Lucero. We were
talking about the harpsichord, which I think is an adorable
instrument. In the midst of all the lofty talk going on there,
the natives sat wide-eyed without understanding a word; I
was being teased for being a melomaniac, a supermelomaniac,
a hypersupermelomaniac . . . and what do you think, after
siesta time, the owner of that house appeared at the door with
a basket of golden fruit, some exquisite melons . . . And the
funniest part, they'd thought that I'd had an urge to eat some
melons because I was pregnant; and these people think that
the baby will turn out to be an idiot if the mother doesn't
satisfy her whims. Me pregnant? . . . Pregnant by Tury
Duzin, maybe, when the gods come back to earth."

The other letters that he read, five in all, were from his
fellow-workers in the office, those entrusted with the preserva-
tion of the immortality of cretinism on this earth. One, the
leaden Mr. Kobler, was criticizing him for his inclination to
fantasy, his lack of solidarity with the Company, and from that
he drew the conclusion that since Leland, his wife, was part
of the Company because she was an American, by opening a
crack in the faith that she should have in its methods, he had
left her free to pluck other fruit, and a woman who plucks
fruit, well, we all know what she plucks . . .

Mr. Pyle crumpled the letter and spat out a curse. The
leaden Mr. Kobler's nastiness had reached such a low point
that the last word was written in such a way that the *pl* could
have been read as an *f*.

After all, what else could one expect from that honorable

pig, who never lifted his behind from his comfortable office chair except to break wind, who never took his nose out of his ledgers, who had a hysterical wife . . .

Pyle relit his cigarette which had gone out in his mouth, hanging from his lower lip as he read the letters. He could not censure his fellow-workers for that sort of thing. He had written to his friends in New York too the time that the healer, witch-doctor, or Shaman, Rito Perraj, had tried to cure Mrs. Kobler of her hysterics.

He had them hoist her up a coconut tree with her legs open as she rose, giving the impression that she was not being raised by the ropes around her shoulders, but that she was climbing by herself using her hands and feet, as she rubbed up against it, massaging herself, feeling herself. It worked. The good lady went for a year without any more attacks.

Called back when the attacks reappeared, Rito Perraj, the great Shaman, smelled Mrs. Kobler and said: "She wants to go back and screw the tree again."

The look on the face of the leaden Mr. Kobler . . .

He tore the letters up into small pieces. He would not keep them and he would not take them. There was some truth in all of them. Even in the other two, where they called him a "magnificent cuckold," an "Othello with the spectacles of a Protestant minister," in which the writer also said that all his wife had done was to change madmen. The only thing that bothered him when he took the pile of paper in his hands to flush it down the toilet, just as if someone had defecated, was having torn up the letter with the heights to the north, where birds with beautiful plumage abounded and the mineral world lay under thick layers of vegetation . . .

Grounds for divorce, he stood there thinking as the water in the toilet bowl carried off the paper, poetical and unknown. He went back to the room, undressed mechanically, and lay down. There was a bottle of whiskey in his suitcase. People like him who respect themselves for what they are worth and who have been on the coast for many years do not go to bed without at least a quarter of a bottle safely inside their torsos. He savored the liquor. He had to drink it from an ordinary tumbler that smelled of toothpaste.

A new day, a new life. In the morning he took care of some pending matters that had to do with the company agency. On the rugs, among the walls festooned with beams and windows with California Spanish grillwork, rugs of a uniform brownish color, his shoes sank in and gave him the feeling that he was going to an audience with the archbishop. As he saw him enter, a man much taller than Mr. Pyle stood up simply, greeted him with a strong voice at the same time as he cast on him a pair of eyes that hung from the cornice of a narrow forehead, out of which there arose upward and toward the sides, a tuft of hair shaped like a rooster's tail. The man seemed thinner from behind than from the front. A gray-haired secretary was typing on a noiseless machine.

Surrounded by walls decorated with maps and panoramic photographs of the Company's fields and buildings, the tall agent continued speaking in his strong voice, keeping his eyes on Pyle, and half-wrinkling the small forehead that was left by the tuft of hair.

As the telephone rang faintly, he took a bundle of papers from the desk and handed them to his visitor. Then, almost without moving his body from the waist down, he turned half around, just as if he were on hinges, and he picked up the telephone with a hand that had long, fleshy-tipped fingers.

Mr. Pyle, who was quite familiar with the sheaf of papers, did not even look at them. He held them in his hand, and when the agent hung up the receiver, he said slowly:

"It's not worth going ahead; my opinion is this: if instead of making new plantings, we buy fruit from the individual growers, it'll be much better for the future. Working conditions in the world are changing every day, and unfortunately we can't count on any poisonous substance to do away with socialism the way the Bordeaux broth holds back sigatoka."

"All right. The report is being typed up to be sent to the big-shots up there."

The vague term with which the agent designated the head-quarters of Tropical Banana, Inc., in Chicago, always bothered old John, but now he rose in rebellion.

"Those big-shots up there had better find out pretty soon what's going on down here, or it'll be too late for threats to pull up stakes and go somewhere else, and gunboats and diplomacy won't be worth much either!"

"Maybe they all feel that way, but since there's always some-thing to be done up there, the people have to get that done first, and when they've done that they can get to what else has to be done: the reading of your report, Mr. Pyle."

Old John took leave of the agent, who stood in front of his desk with his arms hanging uselessly in his sleeves. One cannot lose time speaking in a vacuum with people who are on the outside of a reality that is taking shape, the reality which is replacing today's reality.

He took refuge in the American Club. The same people. The cordial greetings from the bartender and the waiters, from the Negro doorman, from Chilo, the man in charge inside. He did not have to order his drink. As he was leaving his hat and his briefcase at the end of the long bar, they brought him his usual glass of whiskey and a bottle of mineral water that seemed to be smiling at him with its effervescence.

"Some hot hors d'oeuvres, Mr. Pyle . . ." Jacinto Montes, the bartender, said.

The daily customers were coming over to have a drink and celebrate old John's appearance with a few rounds. Each tried to think of how long it had been since he had seen him last; some had been at the plantations and had met him there, and in those calculations they found a pretext to have some more drinks. In the middle of the afternoon, the only ones left in the main room were Jacinto Montes, Mr. Pyle, and an occasional waiter, waiting for the last customer to leave so they could close.

"This is my business now, Jacintón," he said, holding his glass up to the bartender as an excuse for his being there when everybody had gone back to work; the poor scruples of a man who felt guilty when he was not at the office, as if he were robbing someone.

Jacinto Montes, trying to make conversation, told him that a woman he knew had been murdered near the seminary. Old John did not pay any attention; he was caressing his glass of whiskey and some of the precious liquid spilled on the bar.

"Poor woman! Look at the way she ended up, finished off in a dirty way like that!"

They turned on the lights at the American Club. Pyle, dead drunk over his eternally full glass, could barely blink his eyes anymore. His greatest displeasure was to see his glass empty and therefore they kept filling it for him; and when it was full, he would empty it.

"I'm not drinking because I like to or because I have to, or for any other reason except this: I hate the sight of a full glass . . ."

When he emptied it, he would bang it down on the bar, shouting in a thick voice:

"The thing I hate most is an empty glass. Fill it up for me . . ."

And when it was full, without losing any time, having trouble pronouncing the words, he would repeat that a full glass was the worst thing that could happen in the world, and he would toss it down, spilling some of it out of the corners of his mouth now.

The Negro doorman came in with the newspaper. There was

the picture of Jacinto Montes's friend, the murdered woman.
Mr. Pyle noticed the picture of the dead woman as he handed
the paper to the bartender. It was Clariona.

"I knew that woman and I know who killed her . . ." Pyle
said with his chin over the bar, his hat down over his eyebrows.

Jacinto Montes made a signal to the waiters who had come
back on the job again which meant what can you expect from
this poor gringo; but old John, guessing what he meant, perhaps, straightened up the best he could and asked them to call
him a taxi to go to the police station. He was sure he knew
the murderer.

Jacinto Montes, whose shift was ending, offered to go along
with him. He took him by the arm. Luckily he was not very
big. Short men are easier to lead when they are drunk. At
the police station, Pyle told about the scene he had witnessed
on the train. The person who was traveling behind Clariona,
pretending to be asleep, and that she had provoked him, just
before they reached the central station, when the train was
in the yards.

Suddenly old John was overcome by a great love for
Clariona. Shaking his head from side to side, he demanded
that they get a cab, he would pay for it, and go to the morgue.
He had to see her for the last time. He seemed to be sobbing
at times, but it was more of a drunken hiccup.

"Well, we'd better go if he wants to," Montes said to a
companion who had joined them on the street and who also
knew Clariona.

They hailed a cab by the telegraph building, put their
precious American cargo in the back seat; Montes got in beside him, and the friend alongside the driver.

Pyle's drunkenness left him when he came close to the slab
where Clariona was lying naked. Her thick hair, black as coal,
was a kind of mortuary cushion. Her twisted face, out of shape,
her eyes half-open, her pupils staring into space, her double

chin falling to one side, the side toward which she had her face half-turned. Under one of her dark, black-nippled breasts the knife wound began, and as it went down to her stomach it opened up into bloody and viscous rims.

They left without saying anything. The morgue attendant, a gargoyle of a man, an octopus, a spider, with spoon ears, lame and palsied, took the coin which Montes handed him, showing his white teeth as a sign of thanks.

At closing time at the American Club, where Montes and his friend had left Mr. Pyle, the latter was downing his last drinks for the night so that he could forget that cut made by a razor or a sharp knife which had torn the life out of Clariona. One of the waiters had told him that it had not happened near the seminary, but by the statue of Columbus.

Two sub-chanters dressed in their long robes, six Moors dressed as horned devils, a donkey the size of an elephant, and he behind, naked, with a basin in his hand. He was dreaming. His feet like fringed trowels, his knees like growths on a tree trunk. The secretary to the Trophanana agent was following him with a violin bow between her legs. Two suitcases, twenty suitcases, thirty suitcases. It was horrible having to travel not like a simple passenger, but as the representative of a theatrical company. He managed to dive off a board into an empty pool where he never landed. Those "big-shots up there" were nowhere and, yet, before leaping from the diving board, he had been their incarnation on the plantations. It was probably one ten-millionth part of those big-shots which he, John Pyle, had made incarnate for thirty-six years, three months, twenty-three days. And he made them incarnate for "the poor people down here." It wasn't bad, that tactic of having one thing oppose another. The simplicity of the system made the masses enthusiastic. Put white against black, clean against dirty, beautiful against ugly. A simple speech beginning like this: Your houses are twelve feet wide, their houses are twelve hundred feet wide counting just the garden. In yours there's nothing, in theirs there's too much. Your women wear cheap under-clothes, theirs wear silken things as thin as a butterfly wing. Not just you, the silkworms work for them too! S. O. S. ten cruisers, six destroyers, nine torpedo boats, all at full speed to undo the evil thought that not just you, but the silkworms too work for them. He must go to the judge and make him have the statue of Columbus tell who had killed Clariona. What good was it for him to have discovered America if he can't tell who killed Clariona? She was killed by a man who had a hand on one side and on the other just an empty sleeve. He sank the knife into her with the arm where there was just an empty sleeve. She fell like a sack of black sand . . .

. . . He was awake for a long time without knowing where he was. The light from a window was bathing the unfamiliar room. He knew that he was in a bed, under some blankets, beside a night table, but he did not know where he was; he knew that it was not the place he had been dreaming about, building, house, or whatever it was. A hotel, no doubt, judging by the furniture. His hat was on the rack. He decided to press a button and a bellboy came. It was the Hotel Metrópoli.

"Metropole?" he asked to be more certain.

"No, sir," the bellboy answered, "Metrópoli."

It seemed better than the hotel where he was staying. He would go get his luggage. He would have to pay his bill there. Better yet, you go. That was what he said to the bellboy, and when he was alone he muttered: Fate brought me here, and here I shall remain, except that my briefcase is missing, I must have left it at the Club . . .

The bellboy told him that he had been brought there around three in the morning by some gentlemen who spoke English and who had paid for the room. Pyle pulled up the bedclothes and went back to sleep.

He talked about all that with his friend Thornton that afternoon. The Thorntons would not forgive him for not having come straight from the station to their house, where there was always a room for friends, and the meal could have been taken care of by watering the soup. Pyle half-excused himself. He finally decided to say it right out.

"I didn't want to; discreet as you are, you would have asked me about Leland with your eyes, and I didn't feel like talking about her, even if it was only with your looks, because even then I would have had to answer you: she's not with me, I am and now I shall always be a single man until the day I die."

When Pyle left them, much as they asked him to leave the Hotel Metrópoli, he refused; the Thorntons came back from the garden gate to where they had accompanied him as if from a burial.

Old Thornton finally said:

"I can't believe what John says: Leland Foster in love with that nut with bats in his belfry. Such a well-balanced and beautiful woman. Losing her head . . ."

The last news they had from John Pyle was a Christmas card from New York.

5

Chiggerfoot was changed when he came back. There he was for all to see, people who had predicted in their disbelief that he had gone off to the hospital to die. The illness had been reduced in such a way that he could put shoes on, shoes that were half-canvas and half-sole, but shoes nonetheless. Previously he had only been able to use those wrappings gradually becoming veritable pillows as the disease progressed.

Sara Jobalda, Lino Lucero's godmother, had burned her foot in a bonfire on St. John's Eve some fifty years ago, and she could still remember the fat foot she had got and all that her parents had done so that she would not lose the use of it. That was why she, always keeping in mind that this serious illness had not struck just one but both of Chiggerfoot's burlapped feet, never ceased slapping him on the back and congratulating him on his miraculous cure.

Sarajobalda, running her names together like that, was getting the reputation of being one of the most dangerous women in the region. No one knew why, but everyone was afraid of Sarajobalda.

Chiggerfoot dug into an agave bag in which he had brought back some small items to give as gifts and he gave his old friend some vanilla beans. Sarajobalda's dark eyes were the color of vanilla. She put them in front of her nose and as she exhibited her impeccable teeth, she expressed her pleasure with that gift from Señor Blas.

"Blas, Chiggerfoot, has come back healed!" they shouted into the ears of deaf Ambrosio Díaz, a gentleman who had arrived wearing shoes and who had to go barefoot there because he had become so poor.

Señor Ambrosio Díaz went over to Lucero's house in Semírames to see him, to touch that miracle with his own fingers. And after seeing and touching, laughing his thin laugh between his parched-grass teeth, he asked if perhaps there wasn't some kind of medicine which could grow shoes on his feet without his having to pay for them.

"You go shit!" Chiggerfoot answered; but since he did not shout, the other one was at a loss as to where he should go.

The lady of the house, Roselia de Lucero, and Chiggerfoot's wife, Roselia's mother, were preparing a punch for the people who had come to see the man who had been cured of leprosy.

"Because what he had was leprosy . . ." his wife affirmed, forgetting the shouts and insults that she had been wont to give when someone during the time before Don Blas's trip would insinuate, if he did not say so outright, that the old man was a leper.

"Chiggers and liquor brought that on, m'boy . . ." she would go around repeating through the streets so that everybody would know that the man was sick from chiggers and liquor.

Now that he was cured, no talk about chiggers and liquor, it was leprosy, pure and simple. She was proud of it. Ha! Leprosy

isn't any ordinary sickness; in the first place, it isn't for com-
moners, because they say that Philip II had it. In the second
place, it's not catching, even though they say it is. I lived with
this one as man and wife and I didn't catch it. And in the third
place, not everybody can be cured: my husband's the first
one.

Sarajobalda drank the tasty punch. They'd thought the foreman was killed by the kicking he got from his horse last night,
somebody said. It was melon-seed punch and Sarajobalda bit
into some of the seeds when she heard the news.

An anguished look, a girl's eyes unable to hide what she
feels pass over the gathering; but only Sarajobalda noticed,
and she watched the girl looking at her with her cold ebony
eyes as she trembled, as if telling her: You got what you
wanted, now you should go to the hospital as often as they'll
let you in, be kind to him, bring him what he wants; the man
is yours, it took a lot, but he's yours now! . . .

Adelaido Lucero said something about one of his foremen
who had got a bad kicking from his animal, and that was why
he was late for the party. Behind him were his two big sons,
although only recently accepted into adult society.

"Go on in, don't be a-hanging back there . . ." he said to
the two boys, almost shoving Juan, "say hello to your grand-
mother, to Señora Sara Jobalda, to Señor Ambrosio, and to
Pablita . . . Say, is Pablita leaving so soon? . . ."

"What do you think? Three big men can frighten a girl . . ."

"Especially the old one, right, Roselia?"

Sarajobalda knew what her client was up to. The love of a
man is hard work. You have to chase him a lot. And sometimes
not even by chasing him. That boob of a foreman had to be
made to fall off his horse to bring him around. The poor girl
was in love with him and he wouldn't tumble. There's nothing
that can't be moved. The suffering will do him good.

"There's no sugar in this punch . . ." Lucero protested.

"You like it just like honey . . ." his wife said, going for the sugar bowl to sweeten it some more.

"When I die, the worms will say this guy was made out of honey."

"They won't find much honey, right everybody?"

"I'm still sore at my father-in-law. Look what he's done to me: he forced me to marry his daughter . . ." Roselia looked at him with tender annoyance, "and even though I'm his son-in-law, he won't tell me what the secret is of getting his toes full of chiggers and feeding them on cane liquor so he can pass himself off as a leper and get everybody's sympathy first and then meet that doctor who paid him to get cured."

"It looks now that if the cure is final, he's thinking of taking me to Paris in France, because without me, what good does all he's studied about this kind of leprosy do him; he wants to take the proof along with him . . ."

"I'll be whipped . . ." his wife said, "I was the one who got stuck with your daughter, then I got stuck for the rest of my life with your two big feet, and now himself is cured, traveling all alone with his doctor . . ."

"Around here," Lucero said, "the general manager is the only one who travels with his doctor along."

"Now we got two, m'boy! Except that the manager pays his doctor and my doctor pays me."

"You should have let me have all them secrets, not that I haven't spent my life trying to get them, and I can't even get my body to town to have a little fun."

"Dirty old man . . ." Sarajobalda interrupted, giving the proper stress to her words.

Lucero's sons, Lino and Juan, drank punch until they were ready to burst; then they left the gathering to unsaddle their horses, who were nodding their heads under some paradise trees as the hot flies punished them.

Whenever their mother looked at them she would feel her

eyes get large with tears. The older one, Lino, could already
read quite well. The younger one, Juancito, was more easy-
going. Having brought them through all the troubles of life.
With that town there that had not existed before and which
now was just like her father's festering feet before they had
been cured. Swollen, foul-smelling, where no more vices were
possible because there were no more vices left. It may have
been God's will. And Adelaido, who makes no attempt to stop
them from going down there when something is going on.
Parties. Bitter and poisonous flypaper.

Sarajobalda said good-bye, thanking them for the punch
and the pastries and the vanilla beans that Señor Blas de León
had remembered to bring; his kindness was that of an old
young swain.

"And you know, Sarajobalda, one of these nights they're
going to see us in town having a good time kicking up our
heels."

"Whenever you say; I'm going to order a dress, because you
probably won't want to take me the way I am; what would
people say, and your friend the manager who travels with his
doctor."

They all laughed. Sarajobalda was such a good person. They
all thought about that. But how did she make her living? A
mystery. From something rotten like what happened to my
old father-in-law, Adelaido Lucero said to himself.

The boys came back to the house with their spurs ringing
on their heels. They drank some more water and then they
both went to bed. The hammock was empty outside. Lucero
and his wife counted out some reals to make a payment on the
land they were buying in installments.

"Just look," Lucero said to his better half, "that plot, like
I've always said and I'll say again; I want to buy it so the boys
can plant their own banana trees. That's all I want to leave
them: their own independence. I'm a father who doesn't want

his sons to have any bosses over them. Like I was telling Muggsy Zaldívar . . ."

"That dark-looking fellow is no friend of ours . . ."

"Because as far as I'm concerned, Roselia, the main thing a father should leave his son is independence; I can't understand how fathers who've always been dependent on someone like me don't try to see that their sons are free, because you can't tell me that this business of working for someone isn't the worst kind of slavery there is. Oh, yes, I'm dreaming of the day when the boys will have their own land and they'll live off their land, without depending on no one. Poor but free!"

"And from the message you got from Cucho, there are a lot of them who want to come and try some banana-planting."

"The best would be if he could come, but he says he's sending a godson of his who, what did you say his name was? . . ."

"I don't know, they gave you the message."

"Well, I can't remember what name they told me. He's going to look us up."

"Cucho was a good friend . . ."

"He sure was, especially if you compare him with Muggsy Zaldívar. That guy really is no good. But, God forgive me, I have the feeling that Cucho's lungs are all messed up."

"I never met him, but I heard you say he was in bad shape. You said he coughed a lot, and a cough isn't any recommendation, especially around here, where anybody with a cough has one foot in the grave."

"The day I put Cucho on the train I met you for the first time; I was on my way back from the station when I ran into your old man, and right there and then, boom, I fell into the trap . . ."

"You're teasing . . ."

"Wasn't I forced into marrying you?"

"Because you were aiming to do me harm."

"That's real pretty, that is, everybody has the same aim with women, but they don't all get married just because of it . . ."

"Well, you've still got time to go your own way whenever you want to . . ."

Adelaido, smiling, was holding the money for the payment on the plot of land. His sons were snoring. A short time later his wife was also snoring. He was the only one awake, adding and multiplying to see how much they would plant, how many bunches of bananas they would get, and what they would get paid for each bunch . . .

6

Cucho found Bastiancito, his godson, and between coughs he spoke to him with words that came from the voice of a damaged person, and even though they broke apart in the air the way that clods of soft earth turn into dust when tossed up high, they became engraved in his ears to such a degree that all he had to do to hear them was to wish to.

"Don't be an animal, Bastiancito, staying here where the land doesn't grow anything anymore! Stuck here like your folks, not even earning enough to live on; cutting down live-oak trees to make firewood . . . What kind of a future is that! The old folks, you can understand, they haven't got the strength, let them cut up their wood and sell it by the cord; but you, Bastián . . ."

Bastián was walking through the woods alone, but his eyes were even more alone, walking in space as if searching in the gulleys and small rises that hemmed him in for some weighty reason to use against his godfather's words. Even if he had

to move a mountain, he would move it just to tell his godfather
I'm staying here because . . . He could not tell him he was
staying because that was where he was from, because according to the according-to's of his godfather, a person came from
where the land was good to one, and that land there between
precipices was terrible to everybody; and if he came out with
the reason that his parents owned land there, he would be disarmed with the fact that it was land that wasn't worth anything
anymore: burned-off land, scraped away down to bedrock, the
fine hand of erosion . . .

Bastián beat his hands against his head and stamped his
feet on the ground as he felt himself split in two by his godfather's sparkling eyes: somebody without money, a pitiful
beggar almost, and a coward who invited disdain.

The appearance of a horse far off in the fields with a rider
who could not be identified because of the distance brought
Bastiancito Cojubul out of his thoughts. Horse and rider drew
near quickly and then he saw who it was. One of his uncles.
Uncle Pedrito. He brought his horse over close and clapped
the boy on the back a couple of times and asked him what he
was up to.

"After a calf that got lost, Uncle Pedrito, that's what I'm up
to, and you, where are you off to?"

"I'm going over to your house, Bastiancito. I left home early,
I was supposed to see your father before noon; he must be
waiting for me, because I sent him a message yesterday; so
I'll be on my way, I'll see you back home there, and, God willing, I hope that calf hasn't fallen off a cliff."

The horseman lunged forward, spurring the animal, and
soon he was just a cloud of dust in the midst of some earthen-
colored and lifeless groves that were like the insides of an old
mattress.

Uncle Pedrito Bastián thought when the horseman had disappeared. Uncle Pedrito, the prototype of the person who has

spent his whole life here, never doing anything better, growing old and filling my aunt up with children, and not just my aunt.

He could not hold back. He forgot about the calf and ran, crossing a field of dry hay. What else would he be except a calf, Bastiancito Cojubul, if he stayed there.

Bastián in front. His wife behind. Bastiancito Cojubul in front and following the trail of his open pace, that of a long-legged man in a hurry, the tiny steps of his wife who was following him. They stopped at a bend in the road, far from the house they had left unoccupied. They had to put a fire together to make some coffee. Dawn was coming up.

Bastián slid down a path to the bottom of a gulley to get some water from the river. His wife, meanwhile, was searching for some dry twigs and a match. They had everything in the basket: coffee, brown sugar, matches. The glow of the fire made them happy with its warmth and light. They did not show it. They felt it. Soon the water was boiling in the small pot. Then she released a handful of coffee into the bubbling liquid and shortly after, before it boiled too much, a little cold water to stop it and settle it. That was how Bastiancito liked it. He took some pieces of tortilla and some new cheese from a cord pouch. They put out the fire with the water that was left over, and forward.

Whom did they leave behind? Whom else, their parents. Whom were they going to look for? A friend of his godfather. What were they bringing along? A bit of money with which to buy some land on the coast, and they were bringing themselves, he, himself: sturdy, he could easily toss two hundred pounds up on his shoulder. And she, herself and something more. The way things are, women can carry something more than themselves and not know it. And men too. Ah, but it isn't the same! Men always carry it, but women only carry it when they walk along the way Gaudelia Ayuc Gaitán, Bastiancito's wife, was walking along.

They were going to find work growing banana trees, buying some land as his godfather had advised him. The banana groves, Cucho told them with his voice of a damaged man, his laughless laugh, have green leaves like gold-backed banknotes. When you see a lot, but many, many gold-backed banknotes clinging to a clothes rack, that's what just one leaf of a banana tree is like. And the bunches are like many leaves, a lot of green banknotes all pressed together, turned into green-gold bricks.

It was hard for them to say good-bye to their parents. They went over one Saturday and by Tuesday they were back at the place, their place, which now, of course, they had left abandoned. They spent about two days at the house of the old Cojubuls. Señor Bastianón was talking about necessities, sickness, calamities. A glass of cane liquor was given them as they were leaving. They stayed less time with her people, the Ayuc Gaitáns. There they gave them beer. To everybody's health and to the trip.

Bastián Cojubul, Bastiancito, answered the questions they asked him at the Ayuc Gaitáns' with the assurance of a person who knows what he wants. I'm going to look for a Señor Lucero, a good friend of my godfather's, to see about buying some land and growing bananas. Everything I had here, some cattle, what was left in the bins, tools, six mules, a few calves, we took to market, Gaudelia and I, and we have it all in cash, but not to spend, to spend it only for the land. Gaudelia's brothers accused Bastiancito of being brainless. A dreamer, they repeated to him as they smoked with their hats on and spat.

What they had to spend was just enough to buy the railroad tickets. The coffee they drank on the road was all that went into their stomachs that day. He in front, breaking trail, and she behind, they passed through the city to the railroad station, practically without looking to either side so as to avoid the sight of food; and when they reached the station, they purchased their tickets.

From a new wallet, the color of jerked beef, Bastián took out what he had kept aside for the tickets. Two small pieces of cardboard, quite stiff, the tickets, both the same size, the famous tickets, two small pieces of cardboard the same size with letters and numbers that were alike. And they had cost so much. At once they looked for a place to sit down. Right there. Without talking. Without seeing each other. They no longer saw each other because they had been together so much. Maybe they had seen each other only the day they were married. They were occupying some wooden benches. Through the windows that opened onto the outside part of the station, passenger coaches and freight cars could be seen.

They left at night, hungry, cold, sleepy, but neither he nor she said a word. The second-class coach in which they found two seats, one seat for both of them, rather, was half-dark. The faces of the passengers could not be seen. Over the hazy bodies, felt hats, and more straw hats than felt. For every pair of bare feet a straw hat. For every pair of shoes a felt hat. The train left, passing between men swinging lanterns with white, green, and red lights.

Gaudelia yawned and adjusted her shawl, getting comfortable in the discomfort, buttock to buttock with an old man who stank of turpentine. Bastián sat there looking at her, but he did not see her; he yawned because he had caught it from her, while a man in military uniform opposite them got up to stretch and his revolver almost dropped. He pushed it back with his hand, just like a hernia.

After leaving the yards, the train slid away smoothly, as if all of its parts had come to the agreement that they would roll along interminably in one single direction, hour after hour, all night long.

Gaudelia fell asleep on Bastián's shoulder. Bastián did not

close his eyes because he was watching the money. He sank them into the dim light that the lights of the train were giving off, or he cast them onto the floor, as if he could see passing by under the coach the rails, the ties on which they were laid, and the earth. His ear meanwhile was following the iron cud-chewing that as it went rolling along up front was swallowing distance, something to eat, something to eat, it was leaving something that was like the dark manure of space far behind . . .

People around were scratching themselves, *racky, racky, racky;* others were snoring; others cushioned the hard wooden seats with noxious breezes that the fortunate wind from the countryside, as it came in each time the doors between coaches were opened, would blow away. It must have been . . . what time . . . who could tell . . .

The train stopped, whistled, coupled or uncoupled some cars, and forward. A slight breeze which chilled one's bones announced the dawn. Bastián, his head thrown back and his mouth open, was snoring. A whistle woke them both up, and the bell which said that it was time for the train to put on its brakes. Bastián stuck his head out of the window and his eyes were drenched in a purple color, purple dew, then lilac, blue, pink, golden. Dew and light. Dew and light were the same thing at that hour. And dew, light, and leaves were also the same thing. Some leaves in the shape of fringed hearts. Others with jaguar spots, and others with a great red splotch, as if they were animal hearts. From the train his eyes sought out the banana groves in vain, those leaves that were green like gold-backed banknotes, the ones that on the advice of his god-father Cucho he was coming to seek with Gaudelia.

They got off the train and they remained standing on a patch of road as the locomotive approached a tall water tower; and from one gigantic funnel another funnel fell to quench its thirst. It gave off white steam from both sides, the spray from a sneeze, which, when it passed them, bathed them in steam, which immediately turned to dampness on their clothing.

They asked how to get to the plantations, and Bastián in front and Gaudelia behind, they started walking through some woods. That was the way to the plantations they were told. Birds the color of fire and blood arose from the trees, and Bastiancito explained to Gaudelia that they were cardinals. And some that were like sky-blue doves with black trim and eyes like the sparkle of the sun. And turbulent lorry parrots and armies of smaller parrots that crossed between tall ceiba trees like flying leaves.

Woods and hills on both sides of the road, where some work-men were beginning to appear; ox carts, carts drawn by mules, and riders on fine-stepping horses. They asked the first person they met after walking quite a while, a man with red hair, where the place called Semírames was. He told them how to get there. Bastiancito in front, Gaudelia behind.

Lucero was the name of his godfather's friend. "Señor Don Adelaido Lucero, Semírames, courtesy of Señor Sebastián Cojubul," the envelope said all of that. Cucho had given them a letter of recommendation which was in the envelope and in which he said that they intended to buy land and plant bananas.

"Semíra—"

Bastiancito could not finish the word because he had opened his mouth and become one with his wife, both of them unable to take a step, wounded by a sort of rain of machete blows given by some leaves of a most beautiful green in color, not the green of mountain vegetation, not the green of parrots, not the green of a forest, but a green made from the mixture of the green of the sea and the green which was carried down by the golden light above the leaves and the deep and fleshy, light emerald green of the blue water flowing under the leaves. The sunlight, as if it were passing through torn canopies, was like a clustering of diamonds in the dark shadows. Rows of banana trees on both sides, in movement and motionless, as they continued on their way toward Semírames.

They looked at each other to show agreement. His god-father had not deceived them. It was exactly what he had pictured to them with his voice of a damaged man, when he had told them that when they reached the banana groves they would feel as if they were going into a sea without fish, without water, but a sea, a sea in which the trunks of the banana trees looked like columns in the shape of swords, swords that after wounding the atmosphere of fire would let loose up above small arrows of leaves, soft as a dream in the eyes, cool as gauze placed on a wound. They were made of green gauze.

Lucero . . . Semírames . . . They met the man himself on the way, riding a fine mount. He pushed his hat back from his forehead to read Cucho's writing in the light.

"Ah, fine . . . so you've come . . . ah, fine . . . so you've come . . . ah, fine . . ."

But it was better to talk at home. He told them how to get there.

"Go along here by all this movement of leaves you see," and it was so, for a distance of more than a mile the leaves could be seen moving, and moving, and moving, "and when you get to where there's a crossroad, bear right, and pretty soon you'll see a kind of rise: that's the way up to Semírames. Semírames is on top. That's where I live. Tell my wife that I met you, that we saw each other, and that Cucho sent you. I'll be back there at lunchtime to arrange things with you."

Bastián watched him as he read the letter. His wife too was examining his appearance as he told them where Semírames was. He made a good impression on both of them. His god-father had not deceived them about Lucero either. He had told them that he was a good man, and he probably was.

Sebastián Jerónimo Cojubul, or as they called him since his son had grown up, Don Bastianón, appeared at the house of the parents of his daughter-in-law, Gaudelia Ayuc Gaitán, to talk to his in-laws about how suddenly the children, his son and their daughter, had been taken with the idea of going to try their luck on the coast. Gaudelia's brothers were not there, only the old people, his friends, when Don Bastianón appeared and said in a hoarse voice:

"They said they were going to go on the train, they've got so much nerve I wouldn't be surprised . . . I tried to make them see that someone who plants in land that's not his, when he can plant in his own, is taking a risk, and it's no good taking risks off somewhere else when a person has something that's his own."

Bastiancito's mother-in-law, Gaudelia's mother, putting her eyebrows together to see better, muttered something that her husband repeated without moving his lips, as if he were speaking through a funnel. In their marriage this was always the way of speaking in the family. In speaking they were a kind of team: she would mumble in a low voice something that he would repeat aloud in a stiff sort of way.

"Well, they didn't pay any attention to us either; but we said that we would have done the same thing at their age, because in places like that a person can earn something, better than around here, where what a person can get is nothing but trash. From what I heard Bastiancito say, on the coast you can get land for a song, and all you have to do is take out your machete and cut down the brush, chop down the trees for lumber, burn, plow, and plant banana shoots."

"Bastiancito, m'boy, he said all that, but who can say whether it's the truth or not. With talk, everything's easy; but going up against what's real, and the climate's not healthy, lots of poisonous animals—God help the pair of them—that are all hot with burning poison and they make people puff up like toads. I wish I could have said it's a good climate, you'll have plenty to eat, you won't miss the nice, cool water we have here when you get desperate because the ocean sun makes you thirsty."

They were silent. The mother-in-law was tapping her fragile, reedy hands on her thin legs. Then, accompanying herself with the movement of her hands, she spoke, as Don Bastianón took out a bundle of cigarettes rolled in corn husking to start himself and them smoking.

"As far as I'm concerned, and God forgive me, the one who put all that nonsense in their heads was Cucho; he came around saying how as soon as the banana crop was cut, it was sold to some foreigners who paid for it at the price of gold; that hunchback made it sound like a king's ransom."

"Cucho is my old friend, Bastiancito's godfather, but . . ." Don Bastianón said, bringing up the end of his cigarette which he had lighted from the lamp to his in-law's cigarette, while the latter interrupted him to say before taking a puff:

"The exaggerations of a man with TB; everybody with a touched lung dreams like that, they get delirious, they see things."

"The only thing sure is that they did leave . . ." the woman said with a voice of wet ash as she smoked, sucking on the cigarette with the few teeth that remained in her gums, as the sun began to hold its hot coals of noon against the dry trees, which would have caught fire if they had been tobacco.

And the visitor was getting ready to leave after the cigarette had been smoked slowly and with long drags, when Gaudelia's brothers appeared: Juan Sóstenes, Macario, and Lisandro. They arrived on horseback, and without dismounting, they greeted Don Bastianón, telling him that someone was coming up the road on foot looking for him with a letter from Bastiancito.

The noonday sun was bringing sadness and loneliness to

those lands that had been worked for centuries and where, after the trees had been cut, the good soil had been washed away, leaving the mountains all limestone, the gullies bare, and like some tragic signposts, a few kilns for burning lime-stone.

The Ayuc Gaitáns started dismounting after they gave Don Bastianón the message about the letter. On foot, they tied up their animals and, one after the other, with arms folded and hat in hand, they greeted their good father and their good mother, while old Bastianón, without speeding up the pace he had already set, went off in search of the person bringing the letter from Bastiancito.

Juan Sóstenes, followed immediately by Macario and Lisandro, reached Cojubul's house and asked him what else the letter had to say, which slyly meant that they already knew something of its contents and was a suggestion that the old man show it to them; but Don Bastianón, the devil is wise because he is old, stopped them then and there:

"Oh . . . it doesn't say very much . . ."

"My good father," said Juan Sóstenes, a short man, with bowlegs and a large head resting on his shoulders, "told us to bring him news if Gaudelia is all right, if everything's fine with Bastiancito, if they found work . . ."

"Hmm . . . yes, they're all right, they're not sick, they've got a place to live; but I better go show the letter to your father myself; or look, I'll be over there by the bridge, because I've got to go to town right away; tell him to meet me there; I'll be along shortly . . ."

"Poor sister! . . ." Lisandro exclaimed, his black eyes fastened on Gaudelia's father-in-law, the wrathful hammer blows of the beating of his heart nailing him to an imaginary cross, where he would have liked to have left him for the rest of his days. And he added insolently:

"Even though you weren't to blame, my poor sister . . ."

They left, Juan Sóstenes, loud-voiced, short, big-headed; Lisandro, after he had spoken, and Macario, dark, greenish, the color of a bottle. When the Ayuc Gaitán brothers had gone, Don Bastianón went out the door, and shaking his white, white head with hair combed over its forehead, he sighed:

"What else did the letter say? . . . They won't ever set eyes on it . . ."

When he left for town, Don Bastianón could make out a small shape on the bridge which stretched across the river that had channeled through a gorge, and as he approached on his nag, it became his good in-law. He was already there waiting for him. Sometimes he would forget what his first name was. Now, for example, he could not remember. What was Ayuc Gaitán's first name? Until he was next to him and shaking hands from up on his horse, then it came to him like magic: Teo.

"You must have been waiting for a spell, Don Teo, but . . ." Cojubul essayed politely, "I really hadn't thought as you'd get here so fast, and I was busy looking for some deeds of mine . . ."

"I come just as soon as the boys give me your message, because that way, I said to myself, I can get over being worried about m'girl; this letter coming was so funny that it's hard for me to imagine but that everything isn't all right and you just didn't want to tell the boys . . ."

"I've got it right here, Don Teo, I've got it right here . . ."

"It's to get real things out of words that's so hard, Don Bastianón. Sometimes a body would like to put a bridge like this one across what he hears or reads so he can get across the river of words and reach the other side . . . But hold on, stay up on your horse, don't get down for me, I've got to buy some things for the house, a few things we need . . . candles, flour, salt . . ."

The small village of straw-colored houses hidden among the

trees descended as if it were washing its feet of laid-out clothing in the river. The main street, paved and steep and called
Calle del Calvario, was where most of the business went on,
the sale of cane liquor more than anything else, in rundown
houses that looked like adobe eggshells.

"I was thinking of inviting you to have a drink and that way
we can read the letter; you read it, because I already know it
by heart; I couldn't help it, I must have read it over sixty
times . . ."

In a room decorated with colored paper that hung from the
ceiling and bamboo stalks (there must have been some party
in the offing) the old men sat down at a table to read the letter
over two glasses of cane liquor that the waitress served along
with a plate that had some salt on one side and three slices of
green mango on the other.

Out of the tin can in which he had his rolled up deeds, Don
Bastianón took out Bastiancito's letter and gave it to Don Teo
Ayuc Gaitán. Old Ayuc Gaitán, with his head on his hand now,
crossed his legs, his thin and workworn legs, and put his hand
on the table to pick up his glass and toss down the liquor before
reading the letter. He hoped that it wasn't bad news. Don
Bastianón was spying on him out of the corner of his eye,
watching his wrinkles flow with pleasure.

"Señor Don, Don, Don . . ." Señor Teo was reading, ". . .
Los Macabeos . . . Say, how could he remember that this
place was called Los Macabeos? A sad kind of name. The kind
that ought to be forgotten, but young people never forget anything."

"And even less when they're far away, Don Teo, then they
remember the fleas that have bit them and where they did it."

"Dear Father and Mother: after saying hello," Don Teo was
reading half-aloud, "and hoping everything is all right, the
same as it is here, because thanks be to God we've been well,
I want you to show this letter to my godfather and to my wife's

folks so they'll have some news of us and our hello; and it would be a good idea too for the boys, Gaudelia's brothers, to come to the coast. There's so much land to be planted that a person feels guilty not planting it. On the plot we bought we've already got a house half-built; for what I got for the firewood I cleared off, I was able to pay for half of the land, and maybe I shouldn't say anything more because I want the boys to be impressed by this beauty of a land when they come. Gaudelia is fixing up a chicken house. She sends you her best. If you see my godfather, tell him that Señor Lucero, the one he recommended us to, has helped us so much that we'll never be able to pay him back, the same as his wife, Señora Roselia, and his sons, Lino and Juan, who are grown men. My godfather never knew them. Near the property of these Luceros we bought our land and we're all working together. On the other side and behind us is the property belonging to some foreigners we've made friends with, Doña Leland is her name and he's called Don Lester, because they're setting up their banana farm too . . ."

"Don Teo . . ." Bastianón interrupted, he had already seen his pleased face, "I've got to go and attend to these deeds; I'll leave the letter with you on the condition that you don't show it to your boys, because they'll want to go off too . . ."

"As far as I'm concerned, they could have gone already; when a person's young, it's best to try his luck where there's some chance and not stay behind like us. We never changed from buzzards to hawks; a buzzard eats dung and a hawk eats meat . . . What do I need with sons who call themselves farmers when the only thing they know how to do is chop firewood . . ."

"Oh, Don Teo, listen to what you're saying!"

"Amen, friend, because this business of a person's staying where he was born, like a blind chicken nestling in its mother's

belly, is brainless, thinking that there isn't anything better
away from here . . . bah . . ."

Night was coming on. Lights were seen here and there in
the village, but they too, like the houses, were hidden. The
river that was boxed in between the banks made noise at night,
just like a drunkard.

"Uncle Pedrito, you still ain't left?" Don Bastianón said when
he got back to his house from the village.

"No, I ain't, you'll see 'cause of what . . ."

" 'Cause of what, Uncle Pedrito?"

" 'Cause of . . ."

"Speak up, Uncle Pedrito, that's what relatives are for."

" 'Cause of that girl of mine married to Guberio."

"María Luisa's the one married to Guberio . . ."

"And she's going to be all right, but up till now Guberio
hasn't collected the few cents they owe him where he sells
his wood; he's bringing in cordwood . . ."

"Well, yes, I better tell you no before you go any further,
Uncle Pedrito, because I just offered to put my deeds up as
security for some cash I need and they wouldn't even look at
them. They don't give anything anymore on this burned-out
land, this stripped land . . ."

"But firewood's worth something . . ."

"Charcoal's worth more, Uncle Pedrito, but only the Indians
make charcoal because it means work, and we cut wood, because it's easier, and that's why we're farmers, to cut wood
. . ."

"Bastianón, I could let you keep . . ."

"Your horse and saddle, because you don't take the saddle off
all day long, that's how we do it in the family, Uncle Pedrito,
we keep our horses saddled and all ready to go out and work
while we lay around on our backs talking or playing cards."

"Well, at least you can offer me a glass of water . . ."

"Don't get upset, Uncle Pedrito, but it got me so mad that they wouldn't give me nothing on my deeds, and you caught it because of those girls of yours who breed like rabbits."

Bastiancito's mother, Doña Nicomedes San Juan de Cojubul, appeared, her head covered, a good wool shawl over her shoulders of a woman who always has a cold; ample skirts, and two copperish gold rings buried in her enormously fat fingers, which looked more like toes.

"Praise be to the Most Holy Sacrament!" She was carrying a candle and was looking for a holder to put it in.

The men took off their hats, lowered their heads, and answered the prayer. Meanwhile, she set up the candle and wished them good evening.

"Water, Uncle Pedrito . . ." Don Bastianón said and went toward the kitchen.

"Watch out, Pedro," Doña Nicomedes intervened, "this husband of mine is a sly one. He's just as apt to bring you water in a bowl . . ."

"Just what you say . . ." Bastianón came back, "but it's no ordinary bowl, it's a gourd; I can only get rid of my thirst when I drink water from a gourd or from a jug."

"What's this all about, here's a glass, don't pay him any heed, Pedro."

Doña Nicomedes took the gourd full of crystalline water and poured it into the glass she had in her hand and gave it to her brother.

"God bless you . . . I've got to go, I've got my troubles, that's the only thing a person gets from children; you were lucky to get Bastiancito off your hands so soon . . ."

"What? Didn't my husband tell you how good things have been for them on the coast? Have him show you the letter so you can read it."

"I left it with Don Teo, Gaudelia's father, my daughter-in-law's father, because Bastiancito says in it that Lisandro,

Macario, and Juan Sóstenes ought to go out there with them."

"Now that's an idea, brother; your daughters' husbands ought to go work on the coast too."

"They don't want to, Nicomedes; I think they married the girls for the land and they're happy stripping it; as soon as a new live-oak starts to grow, they cut it down; they're regular savages."

"Then, they married the firewood, Pedro . . ."

"Well, that's the way it looks, because there hasn't been any lack of offers, and good ones, to go work on the coast, and there they be, just the way you see them, they won't take any risks . . ."

"And what kind of risk would they be taking?" Don Bastianón joined in.

"They're loafers," Doña Nicomedes contended; "they're the kind of men who don't like to do anything, find something wrong with everything. They like to warm their nests like hens, and to have a lot of children so they can leave them just as stupid as they are, to get old before their time, because it's laziness that makes a person grow old the fastest."

The wild face and the suppressed sobs that Guberio brought in made the old people fall silent. Finally he was able to speak. He spoke by pulling words out by their roots from among the hairs that were sprouting out of his shirt. It was like hair standing on end in mourning. His voice was sad now, and there was a heavy weight on it, a tragic weight.

Doña Nicomedes brought another glass of water, she put in a few drops of essence of orange blossom, and after Guberio drank, they all took small sips.

People appeared on all the roads. Relatives in endless numbers, friends, acquaintances, even neighbors who, if they had time, stopped work to put in an appearance at the house of death.

Uncle Pedrito, buried in the silence of a poor, worn-out

beast, soaked in his paternal tears, looked out the window to let his eyes see into the night as a leaden moon began to climb up over the distant peaks. Everything seemed so dead. People came over to him as soon as they arrived, they embraced him, and they gave him their sympathy. Slow and heavy feet came up every road leading to his house, where a fresh rose had succumbed, the victim of frustrated motherhood. He was not listening, but he heard . . .

"That son-in-law of yours, Uncle Pedrito, he's an idiot; why didn't he leave some time between one child and another, the dirty animal! And look at the results; he was the one who killed her, with that love of his like a beast in rut; no, when a woman gets married, she should take a look at who she's marrying; she could marry a Christian, not an animal who doesn't know anything except being always after a woman so the poor thing can only obey the law of God and keep on having children like they were some kind of gift . . ."

Guberio, the widower, was going among them all, silent, with a sorrow like cotton soaked in cane liquor. His small children, orphaned by their mother a few hours ago, were following him everywhere. Sometimes a small one would grasp his leg, asking him to carry her, saying that her bare feet were cold because there was nobody to put her shoes on for her. Guberio carried her. And while he was carrying her, she urinated on him. But they would not even give him time to shake out the child's wetness, which had penetrated his sleeve, reaching his arm, because an older boy called him to light a lamp in the kitchen, and another little one tugged on his jacket to have him put him to bed.

In the room where the dead woman was laid out, her coldness spread to the atmosphere, the air, the candlelight, the furniture, and to some frames with pictures of saints and family portraits among the fronds from Palm Sunday which protected against storms, and other relics. Her working-woman's hands, the weak arms of a woman who had been a mother many times, her oval face between the jet-black hair that had been parted in the middle, the closed eyes under her broad forehead, and her thick-lipped mouth. Later on they brought a handkerchief and tied her face up as if she had a toothache. So that her jaw would not drop. What difference did it make, Uncle Pedrito thought, now that nothing made any difference to his daughter, whether it dropped or didn't drop . . .

Meanwhile, up on a hill where the cemetery was, two men were digging the grave, pausing from time to time to breathe in that mixture of newly-turned earth and the strong smell of the suquinay plants; a smell that would intoxicate a person and make him sigh. It was night, and they were working by the light of a large bonfire. Until they finished the grave and went to the wake without any sorrow. Like pounding in the hollow of a dull bell, that was how they were pounding. One was opening, splitting, swinging his pick to dig, and the other one, when the first one stopped his pounding, would lean deeper and deeper into the hole and bring out the earth, first with a shovel, then with a bucket, which he filled and slowly raised. They were sweating. The stars were like the eyes of people who can see underwater. Golden-eyed people. Heavenly people. Angels perhaps.

"The oven's hot now and it's going to get cold!" a woman's voice shouted several times in the courtyard behind the house. Not much could be seen, for although the moon had come out early, dark clouds had hidden it almost immediately. A jocote tree with a ladder full of birds, pure horrors, as if they knew someone had died in the house. A hollow log with water in it as a watering trough. Some stones laid out to dry clothes on; it seemed, yes, there were some pants stretched out, and two barrels of water with scum on top into which the night sent down the reflection of a crocodile's eye.

"You've hurt my eye!" someone exclaimed as he went toward the oven, two figures. A man from his voice.

"I should have put it out for what you tried to do, what on earth are you thinking about, that just because . . . show some respect, that . . . can't you see that someone's dead . . ."

"Don't be like that . . ."

"You watch out or I'll scream . . ."

"The oven's getting cold, hurry up, I don't know what they're doing, they're taking so long!"

"You devil, but I'll make you pay . . . Listen, they're calling us . . . I'm going to get rid of this . . ."

All of the back courtyard, in pitch-darkness, was filled with amorous whispering, as if the hens and roosters were dreaming that they were people, and the people had turned into roosters and hens behind the house as they took advantage of the wake.

From time to time some old woman would come out with a lantern. She would raise her arm to light things up better, but she could not see anything.

In the hall, in the front of the house, where the entrance was, chairs and couches had been placed, everything that could be sat on that was in the house and around it. People who came in, hat in hand, passed through rows of people already sitting down, men, women, who said hello to them in low voices, out of good breeding, answering their greetings, or with more affection when they were friends or acquaintances. In that case, also in a low voice, they would offer them a place, call them over to sit down.

In the rooms, from one to another, the members of the family were circulating, wandering like people who had been struck but did not know where. Some would sit on the beds and cots after walking back and forth, or they would remain standing, chatting, smoking. Solicitous people were serving glasses of cane liquor or making bread and preparing dishes for something to eat after midnight.

Bastiancito Cojubul's letter passed from hand to hand, and if a person did not comment positively or negatively, in favor or against it, it was because he did not wish to.

"They're lies," one of Uncle Pedrito's sons-in-law, not Guberio, said, "and even if it was true, who wants to leave his folks and go grow fruit somewhere else!"

Uncle Pedrito was not listening, but he heard . . .

"The fruit that you, my sons-in-law, have grown here is bitter fruit, the fruit of death; laziness, sitting with your hands folded, it breeds a wanting to be snuggled up with your wives all the time. God bless the sons who leave their parents, who get detached from them and grow leafy trees where God wills it! God bless the sons who do not turn into scabs on their families; scabs that can only increase the dryness of the old people; sons who go far away and flourish in branches and bunches of fruit, to return later, they or their messages, to rejuvenate the old trunk, so that their parents can feel themselves living again from the ones who knew how to squeeze the juice out of life and not perpetuate death's placid ashes!"

"There's nothing new in the letter," another member of the wake was arguing; "who doesn't know that planting bananas brings a good profit? But there's so much sickness in those places, so much danger, and if you don't believe me, there's Cucho, with lungs like the drums on Corpus Christi Day every time he coughs . . ."

"You make me laugh. You've got to take some risks. It'd be nice to have someone peel your potatoes for you, for the land to be good for sowing a good crop and no dangers. If that's what you want, you'd best die and go to heaven. One thing's sure, that if a person doesn't need anything, he's fine that way, the way he is; he needs a lot of things, but he gets along, well, he's better off that way . . ."

Uncle Pedrito was not listening, but he heard.

"Plant a tree, have a son . . . We've had many sons here,

but none of them can be called a son in the sense of what a person ought to mean by son, a continuation of a person, progress . . . and as for planting a tree, shit, we've cut them all down for firewood, and we make our living chopping down the woods!"

A cadence of leaves that the night breeze dragged along would invade the house at times. It was as if it were carrying off the dead woman, more yellow now as she got farther away from life, turning into a bag of dry skin, skin that was beginning to wrinkle, with a slightly purple tinge at dawn.

Dominica, Uncle Pedrito's other daughter, came in with an enormous bundle in her belly. Her husband, a farmhand with bristly hair, was talking about Bastiancito's letter.

"That's pretty good talk, coming from you, Bushy . . ." Don Bastianón said to him when they passed in one of the rooms where the older one was smoking a store-bought cigar.

"It's not talk, it's just that I can take anything except their telling me to go to the coast, where they've got so many mosquitoes; and a person doesn't have to go if he can get by here, I know you can't make very much, I know the land is overworked, I know how it hurts to see the way the corn and beans turn out, but maybe if we used some fertilizer . . ."

"Fertilizer costs money," Don Teo said, "the only way would be if instead of eating up the last of our live-oak groves to sell as firewood, we all sat down to shit."

"Uncle Teo, why do you always have to be so crude!"

"And you've got the same thick head you were born with; all the responsibility of that big family you saddled yourself with, because with this one now it'll be Dominica's seventh . . ."

"It'd be worse if I took off and went to the coast and died of malaria or one of those fevers they've got there, or came back like Cucho, who ain't good for nothing."

"You're going to die poor here, little by little, and not just you but your whole family, because there's nothing to feed them with, there's nothing for medicine, there's nothing so your children can be the way they ought to be, and there they are, growing up with skinny little legs that look like wire, with their dirty faces, looking like fetuses, and with their big wormy bellies, and their mothers can't give them enough from their breasts."

The cough told the group where Cucho was, more hunch-backed every day, with his eyes like thick glass sunken into the bones of his face, his wrinkled eyelids hanging from his brows, and his nose that had an edge of death.

"Who am I?" Cucho was saying to a small blind man who had come over to say hello and was feeling the thick, hairy, woolen clothes, while the other friends in the group were tell-ing the blind man that he ought to be able to guess who he was from the hump.

"By your voice I say you be . . . Who be you?"

"Make a little guess . . . I'm a sick person who preaches life to good healthy men, men who God hasn't taken health away from, or understanding, or hands to work with, or young years they can make use of . . ."

"A professional corpse!"

Even Cucho laughed at the blind man's sally.

"That's exactly what I am, a corpse who works for a funeral parlor, a corpse who's been losing what voice he has left in his chest advising a whole army of young people to get out of here, to go work on the coast, where there's a battle starting for men, men, a battle against the sea for the land."

"Cucho, you've got a good tongue, but you won't convince them . . ." a member of the group said.

"Hell, if I can't convince them, they could listen to me at least!"

"Men, men . . . what do you mean by that?"

"Laziness turns men into women; drivelers who do the kind of work where they should wear skirts!"

Cucho coughed, coughed, coughed . . . After the attack of his cavernous cough, he took out a silk handkerchief to blow his nose and remove from its tip, very sharp now, the shudder that had run up his backbone, which had shaken his ankles, his wrists, the transparent lobes of his ears.

"A battle against the sea, Cucho, you make me laugh!" The one who said that, one of the group, came over and gave him a loving pat.

"If I had my eyes, by God, I'd go have it out with the sea, which to my way of figuring is more fake than anything else. Bums with eyes and scared to leave this godforsaken place and take off to see how much they could make out yonder!"

"Looky here, Cucho, tell us about this business of fighting the sea; because I don't think you even know about it yourself and you're just shooting off your mouth."

"That's what happens when you talk to people who haven't let go of their ma's petticoats, or if they've left their ma's petticoats they've run over to the ones that belong to the woman they've married up with. Fighting against the sea, as I see it, is being like the trees on the coast that go right down to where the breakers are. Foam and rocks all around, you should see it, the green branches of the mangroves and other tough trees that face up to the sea. That's why with those thousands of trunks, branches, leaves that are always fighting off the waves—and it's worse when there's a storm—that the sea hasn't carried off the land on that side. But who is there behind those trees, who's there? . . . Not a single one of us . . ."

"There it goes, here it comes, the sea . . . I've seen it too, Cucho . . ."

"And that's why I never get tired of telling them over and over again that people who are healthy have got a place there,

in those lowlands where the green is parrot-green and eve,
thing grows like wild . . . Just take the corn, the way tl
ears grow, the bean fields look like liver spots on a pregnan
woman's face. Look, when I see the fields around here, I get
the feeling that the things coming out of the ground aren't
leaves anymore, they're dead chicken feathers . . ."

"When I was young," the blind man said, "a man came
through here looking for rare woods, and he wanted to take
me along with him to explore the land along the Pacific; I was
all ready to go with him, but I didn't, what got in the way were
the comforts of my parents' little house, the ebb tide of a child's
love; it would have been terrible leaving the old folks, the
rounds of relatives and visitors, my sprees, my girl friend, and
it all ended with my being blind ever since that Conception
Eve when the rocket blew up in my face . . . If I'd have gone
with the lumberman, I might have still had my eyes now, and
if it was God's will for me to be this way, I might have still
been blind just the same, but I wouldn't have been poor . . ."
The blind man sighed deeply, shook his head, which was like
the mane of a dappled horse, and added. "Not even the devil
. . . I'm going to touch the dead woman, I want to make sure
it's her, the woman with the biggest heart in the world, who
never should have died, the one who died . . . I want to get
an idea of how big and cold it's going to be for me, all alone
without her, because she was the one who gave me shelter
here in her hallway, and something to eat in the kitchen . . .
When there are so many sons of a pig who are too many already, why do people who are needed have to die! . . . And
all because of that damned Guberio . . . isn't he the one to
blame? . . . I can tell them, because since I'm blind I can see
lots of things with my ears. The big lout would get drunk and
stumble in and start pestering her, waking her up, be pulling
her, feeling her, as if he'd never had a woman before . . . Son
of a bitch! . . . What a pig! . . . A grown-up man acting

with the mother of his children like a boy of twenty, knowing that one of these times it was going to leave them without a mother . . . just the way it finally happened, but it shouldn't have happened like that . . . the world's unfair, God's unfair, men are unfair! . . ."

The tears ran down the blind man's cheeks like hot mud. When he was beside the body laid out there, he leaned over: she smelled of flowers and myrtle sprays, and he touched her to make sure it was she, the good one, the sweet one, the delicate one, almost bruising her . . .

A little boy came out from a door and hit him with his fists to make him stop. The poor thing thought the man was hitting his mama. They carried him off to calm down his rage against the blind man.

The weeping of the child, grief-stricken, the penetrating shriek of a sad little animal, mingled with the quiet sobbing of the blind man, bearded and with the straight, gray, long hair of a dappled horse.

In other parts of the house, active now with people serving coffee, glasses of cane liquor, rolls, and passing out cigarettes rolled in corn husks or yellow paper, there were women wrapped in blankets and mourning shawls; men were squatting down in the corners around gas lanterns, people shooting dice or playing cards.

With the hand of his heart, as it followed the ridge of a vein, a sleepy lover could feel his loved one's blood flowing under the tip of his finger. That night of death was the first one that the lovers had spent together and by letting themselves be seen they showed the sure signs of adolescent anguish.

"Love, but far from this land of ashes, of ash piles used to make lye, where there are nothing but bushes that bear thorns, thistle patches, the green cutlasses of maguey and prickly-pear cacti. Love, but far from these limestone peaks where there is no hope for anything that blooms . . . And death, death far from here too, where a person can soon change into something else besides a poor exhausted stump, a dry forest decorated with spider webs that have old flies and drops of pitch, on which the dewdrops look like tears . . . If it were left in my hands, I would take my dead daughter and bury her far away, far from these rock patches, far from this dismal bed of clay, so that in the future, tomorrow even, she would be a flower, a fruit, a leaf, and not adobe, because the dead who are buried here have no future except someday to be part of an adobe wall, of some sickly plant, of some tree that has no springtime."

Before dawn, the women knelt to pray in the room where the corpse was. The candles were barely showing in their holders after burning all night long. On the chairs and benches some of those who had kept the vigil had their hats over their faces and were dozing; others, chilly and stepping carefully, wrapped in ponchos and blankets over their thick frieze clothes, set out for the kitchen in search of steaming coffee and corn cakes with beans, some of the ones that had come out a little burned but were still edible. The dice shooters and the card players were still squatting by the lighted lamps, and now, in the daylight, their suicidal faces were intent on their last bets. A hiccupping drunkard was not missing. Cucho's cough sounded even more cavernous in the light of dawn. With the hand of his heart, the fingertip in love was following the path of the blood in his loved one's vein.

7

The friends of Leland Foster, the wife of old John Pyle, were still the friends of Leland married to Lester Mead, among other reasons because it was always something new for them to visit a place where the coastal table had a frothy fringe like a Sunday tablecloth, and the countryside was always bright with sun, tall palms, seabirds, unfailing sunsets, and in the small and comfortable living room there was a piano, whiskey, cigarettes, books, magazines. The only new friend was Tom Baker. He measured several feet in height. His head seemed small because he was so tall. Quite blond. His hair was the color of white honey. The peculiarity of his face, one which gave him the look of a friendly dog, were the teeth that jutted out over his lower lip.

Leland, leaning her arm on the edge of the piano behind her, reached out her other arm to touch a page of the piece of music open on the stand; but she did not get to touch it because Tom Baker said something that she would have challenged at once if Lester, her husband, had not beaten her to it:

> She lov'd me for the dangers I had pass'd,
> And I lov'd her that she did pity them.
> This only is the witchcraft I have us'd.
> Here comes the lady; let her witness it.

"*That I did love the Moor to live with him,*" Leland said, shaking her green-gold hair as tall Tom showed the tips of his teeth in a cold smile of disbelief, "*my downright violence and storm of fortunes may trumpet to the world.*"

Carl Rose had come in from the back, he could barely hold his pipe after an attack of dysentery that left him all skin and bones, and he added aloud, almost shouting as he interrupted:

> Look to her, Moor, if thou hast eyes to see:
> She has deceived her father, and may thee.

They all began to laugh, even more so when Tom Baker, hiding his teeth as he rang the curtain down, said:

> I will incontinently drown myself.

The sea could be heard resounding close by like a setting as the friends, bathed in perspiration, each holding a glass, received the whiskey that Leland was pouring for them. Then they helped themselves to ice and soda.

Lester Mead was emptying a can of anchovies onto a green saucer, tapping the can so that they would come out to go with the olives, salted almonds, and pieces of cheese, as an appetizing odor was already flowing through the small living room.

Ernie Walker always arrived late; but this time he overdid a little his "never let your feet catch up to the hands of your watch," as he explained his lack of punctuality. He brushed back his lock of hair and went over to serve himself a good shot of whiskey. What he liked best was an old Scotch with a heavy aroma.

"The scandal of the day! Tury Duzin and Nelly Alcántara are getting a divorce, they've already separated! The pair of them look as if they'd been run over by a gravel train; they had a fight that went on for six hours."

"I propose a moment of silence as a token of mourning," Carl Rose said, asking with his dysenteric face for the support of toothy Tom, who even with his mouth closed showed the edges of his comb of teeth.

"Not a bad idea," Tom Baker exclaimed, "especially for Lester, who never laughs or says anything."

"You used to be a wholesale laugher, right love?" Leland intervened in defense of her silent husband.

For a moment there appeared among the group of old friends the figure of Lester Mead when he was Cosi and went about dressed in clothes that were too small for him, with long hair and scuffed shoes, offering "everything a seamstress needs," and they could almost hear his insulting loud laugh: Ya-ha . . . ha, ha, ha, ha!

"You all know very well that I'd rather listen," the one referred to said, taking Leland's hand as she suggested they all sit down and be more comfortable.

"If we don't these chairs are going to be just so many useless objects; you've all turned into real businessmen, people who leave their jobs to drink cocktails standing up; who talk standing up all the time . . . People who don't sit down are the despair of me . . . The good old days of sofas, easy chairs, benches have gone out of style, nobody sits down now, as if they didn't have the time, and they spend hours on end talking like that, moving their legs as if they were tied up in a stable . . . Nothing bothered me more about New York than drinking cocktails after work, standing up."

In order to get a breath of fresh air in that coastal atmosphere, Leland rolled a small cart with the whiskey, bottles of soda, ice, and the saucers with olives and other hors d'oeuvres into the den; but they did not move as they talked about a new drug that was more effective against malaria than quinine.

"I'd just as soon catch malaria if I could lose my insomnia; why don't they invent something to make a person sleep . . . The desperation, a person sucking on the night like an endless piece of candy that must be swallowed, because as soon as it starts to get dark, a person who can't sleep begins to feel the night in his mouth, like something that burns him, dries up his saliva, makes him tremble . . ."

"I had a spell of not being able to sleep, not being able to close my eyes," Tom said for the sake of saying something after the funereal silence that came after Ernie Walker's words.

"There's no cure for that . . ." Rose added.

"That's why it's so annoying to have them discover this and that against malaria, syphilis, scurvy, and God knows what, and not to invent or find anything so that when a person lays his head down on his pillow his eyelids will seal themselves up."

"It's not an illness . . ."

"What is it, then?"

"A bad habit . . ."

"A bad habit? I used to sleep for nine hours back home; I came here and I go through the whole night without shutting my eyes, and I can't live on a combination of soporifics and whiskey, whiskey and soporifics . . ."

A soft melody. The piano. Leland now had an étude by Mozart under her fingers. They grew silent to listen to her, bathed in perspiration from head to toe, then they went over to the piano, sat down in the chairs one by one, without making any noise. Only Tom Baker remained standing.

They started playing late that night. Lester shuffled the deck, his eyes heavy with fatigue. The heat was intense. The fans were humming after having been on for one, two, three hours, and like fans, the hands were dealing the cards in hand after

hand after hand after hand. The last hand. No. One more hand.
Yes, one more hand. And the last hand never came. The "word
of honor" that this was the last one. But it was already four in
the morning.

When he left the house, Lester Mead would change into
Cosi, his popular name, his nom de guerre, the one he used
when he laughed and sold his wares, "everything a seamstress
needs," ya-ha . . . ha, ha, ha, ha!, and that was why he did
not like night to fall and dawn to come as he played cards like
a condemned man who sees the beautiful and cruel day come
up.

He rode off on a jet-black horse to Semírames in search of
Adelaido Lucero or one of his sons, and on the way he ran into
the cutters, all excited, waving their machetes like silver
tongues of flame in their copper-colored hands, showing their
threatening white teeth, as if peace had become war in their
mouths too. When he met them, Lester found out what it was
all about; there were no secrets from the popular Cosi, and
Lester Mead, or Stoner, as they also called him, was still that
man with the Ya-ha, ha, ha, ha, ha, ha, ha! for the cutters,
harmless as a child or a bird.

"This time," they shouted to him, "we're not asking for
better pay, but guarantees for our women . . . Either they
respect them or we'll kill them all!"

The cutters were raising their voices like their machetes,
with the smell of women turning around in their insides; that
smell of women's clothing, the more intimate it was, the more
desperate the need it aroused in the surging blood of the male;
that smell of women's hair; that smell of the coastal air, which
is the sex of sun and vegetation.

The great savage had taken off her clothes and let her run
naked through the banana grove; another one who was more
of a man had cut her off and put her down; but another one
even more a man came along and took her away from him, and

she took advantage of that moment to run away, and she would have made it, she would have escaped from all of those savages if the twins hadn't cut her off . . .

The ground, old and familiar earth to Cosi, ran rapidly under the hooves of his horse until the distance between the group in arms and Lucero's house was reached. Adelaido was not at home, nor were his sons. That was what Doña Roselia told him. They were probably out calming down the people who refused to work until justice was done. The lead-heavy sun would probably serve to smother the flashes of honor as the men would become asphyxiated, without the coolness of perspiration, in that atmosphere of white fire, and malarial fevers would break down all of that rebellious drive with a mask that was yellower than the hateful lycopodium powders they were sold to put on their children's navels. All of those up in arms, beaten down by sun and malaria, would end up by accepting the insult, the dishonor, the whole monument of shit, as Adelaido Lucero used to say to avoid saying something else when he lost his temper.

But this time he was in a good mood and in the struggle of his duties when Lester Mead found him. Their horses were their thrones. Each on his own. That is the way business should be done. Lester Mead asked Lucero what price they were buying bananas at.

"They're paying twenty-five gold cents for a nine-hand bunch."

"That's robbery," Lester said.

"What isn't robbery around here?"

"I'm going over to complain . . ."

"You'll be wasting your time. It's better just to sell. The fruit'll go by and everything'll be lost. Sell, all right? And the next crop will give you time enough to complain before it ripens, just as long as you don't have to go all the way to Chicago."

"I'll go wherever I have to . . ."

Lester turned his horse. When he got to his house he could figure out who they were from the muddy footprints on the porch. The young Luceros, Lino and Juan, Bastiancito Cojubul, the Ayuc Gaitáns. They were all talking animatedly with Leland. She in half-words and they repeating to her word by word so that she could understand them.

"Lovies . . ." That greeting from the time in which he offered everything a seamstress needs was very much like Lester.

They all spoke at once. Lester cut them off, announcing to them that he was ready to go and talk to the people so that the prices would be better.

"But while you go and talk, the fruit'll go to the devil," Bastiancito said, consulting his companions with his eyes.

"It doesn't matter, we'll lose this crop, but we'll set the price. They'll pay us a fair price."

"That might be all right on the one hand, that might be all right; but . . ." Macario Ayuc Gaitán was speaking very slowly and repeating himself; "but the fruit's starting to ripen and why in hell should we work . . ."

"I always thought it was a trap," Juan Sóstenes let fly at Ayuc Gaitán, moving on his bowlegs; "a trap with a double bottle that we've fallen into, where we don't make anything if we sell and we lose it all if we don't."

"Well, you do what you want, I'm not selling, my soul can ripen, but not my bananas," they all let out a laugh, including Lester, who unconsciously turned red, "and I won't sell a single bunch, not because I've got anything to hope for; I'm in it up to my neck, but a man in this place has got to defend himself against people who want to lay down laws that are unfair."

"The unfair thing here is the price, and the trap is in the contract, because it is a trap . . ."

"Of course it is," Lino Lucero said, backing up what the

pumpkin-headed Juan Sóstenes had trumpeted; "because if they're getting more for the fruit, why shouldn't they be able to raise us a few cents?"

"Agreed, agreed . . ." Leland said in her half-Spanish as she came in with a bundle of letters she had gone out to pick up at the door.

Lester explained to Leland the reason for the discussion, but it was only a change of languages, because he kept on arguing with her about the same thing, because his wife too thought that the fruit ought to be sold at whatever price they wanted to pay for it.

When he finished his heated and brief dialogue with Leland, speaking Spanish again, Mead exclaimed that he was for what they had said: to go and make them pay what was fair, insist that they don't make a mockery of the good faith of the people who grew fruit on their own lands.

"The hell of it all is the trap. They give us all sorts of help. You can't deny that. They even give us things to fight crop diseases with. And when the fruit is ready they refuse to buy it."

"That's where I see the trap!" Juan Sóstenes stated as he kept on moving his head like a huge pendulum, backing up Juancho Lucero's words.

"I'll bet they haven't lowered the price on them when they sell it up there. And they don't keep their word. What would they lose by paying us a little more? A screwing. They're bad people and the worst of it is that they pass themselves off as good people. They've turned good into bad, just like themselves. That's what stinks, laughing so we'll think they're nice and generous."

"Hey! Now you're getting sentimental too, like a bunch of poor devils going around with your chests puffed up with gratitude," one of the Ayuc Gaitáns shouted.

"No, Dad, I'm one of the ones who's always said more than

anyone else around here that all the good the Tropbanana people do is far from being charity and we'll have to pay it back!"

"It's no use talking about the fruit here," Bastiancito said, "I saw one of the superintendents yesterday, that one who's always chewing tobacco, Mister . . . Mister . . . I can't remember the names of all of them . . ."

"Exactly," Lester said, "because that's just what they all are, Mister It-doesn't-matter-who, because they're all . . ."

"They're all a . . ." Macario Ayuc Gaitán exclaimed; "I almost said something dirty, and Don Lester is and at the same time isn't from their country."

"What I was going to say," Mead continued, "is that whoever they are, when they get down here they're all the same, and what's worse, especially with good people, is that in their jobs they turn into . . . what Macario was going to say." Then, cutting himself off, he added: "Friends, if you want to sell, you can go ahead, I'm not going to."

They left. Their footsteps could be heard on the floor of the house as if they were bearing out a corpse. Bastiancito was slapping his broad-brimmed hat against his thigh above his leggings; Lino Lucero was biting his lips; Juan Sóstenes was shaking his head, which was hanging down from the back of his neck by its own weight and the weight of his painful thoughts about the injustice, as if it had been half cut off.

"I'm going to sell the fruit after you've gone," Leland said with a tired voice in the midst of the terrible heat as she sought relief from one of the fans.

"You won't sell it, it's cost more than what they're giving us for it and that should never be; making deals with injustice is the beginning of the whole moral defeat of our so-called Christian civilization."

"But they're the ones with power, child."

"Powerful today, damn it!, because they're robbing us; but

a white sheep can change his teeth; you used to write stories before for those magazines where we show ourselves to the world with all the infantility of superannuated children, you ought to write a story not about the wolf in sheep's clothing, that's an old one, much too old, but about the sheep a dentist fitted with a good set of wolf's teeth so that he could live among the wolves."

A hat on a man, a suitcase beside a man, and pipe in the mouth of a man. A firm, resounding step that accompanied him to the stone entranceway suddenly disappeared as if it had been lost on the surface of a dream. He did not look down because he could feel very well under the soles of his heavy shoes that it was the cushiony carpet of the Tropical Banana, Inc. agency in the small city.

"Mr. Mead," the general manager said, "I have no intention of prejudicing your interests, but we can't buy fruit at that price."

"I can wait while you send a cable to the home office; come on, you could call Chicago on the telephone; it's a matter of hours before the fruit spoils on us."

"Mr. Mead, I can't spare the time, my time, which is worth more than your fruit. We've just thrown two loads of fruit overboard . . ."

"But . . ."

"Two shiploads of fruit totaling a million bunches thrown overboard."

Lester Mead frowned, took out his pipe to refill it with tobacco while the manager spoke to a clerk who reminded him that he was due on the golf course; when the clerk left, Mead stood up, shook hands with the manager, and went out step by step until he found the sound of his person walking on the paved floor of the entranceway.

His bags went with him on the Atlantic. Nothing sadder than one of those ships like whited sepulchers, one of those that bring poison to fight sigatoka and carry back huge bunches of bananas to the great markets.

"The great fleet of white corpses," Mead said to the Negro cabin boy who, whenever he came or went, gave the impression that he was going to hit his head against the top of the door, which did not happen because he would stoop just at the right moment.

Some employees of the great banana enterprise were traveling on their vacations, without losing their habits of office fowl, their clothes smelling of patent medicine.

Lester Mead, for some of those employees, the older ones, was still Cosi, the one with the laugh (ya-ha, ha, ha, ha, ha . . .), except that he had a new madness: explaining to them that none of them knew what it meant to plant that miserable little thing that smelled of dampness, was the color of dirty coffee, was almost like a small piece of a tumor, and to see it immobilized for many days, and suddenly and all at once, to see it begin to move, and move, and move until it was a prodigious plant.

A Protestant minister noticed that the passengers were hiding from Lester. They had established among themselves a kind of espionage system so they would not run into the madman. Hand signals, low whistles, rapid sounds of *psst, psst* gave the signal of his presence, and a person coming along a passageway would retreat and someone on deck looking at the sea would go over to the side opposite Mead, and someone sitting in the saloon would seek refuge in his cabin.

The minister was interested in that harmless madman. The ship was dancing like an eggshell in the Gulf of Mexico, but that did not stop the minister, holding onto the walls, the railings, from reaching one of the deck chairs and sitting down beside Lester Mead.

Mountains and abysses of water; that was how the world must have been when it was being formed, except that instead of water it was boiling matter, solid, treacherous, and muddy. What interested Lester Mead most as he talked with the minister of what he had read about the formation of the terrestrial sphere was the moment in which man found an ally in the plant that produces the banana.

"And do you think, Reverend," he sat up in his chair with his green, green eyes, his aquiline nose, and his sunburned face, "that the earth, igneous matter, life put forth extra effort to produce this plant so that those miserable people could enrich themselves without end until they became the most powerful financial group in the Caribbean?"

The minister made some reference to the Gospels. Lester, sitting up straighter and straighter, although he had to hold himself in the chair as the ship bucked like a young horse being broken, exclaimed:

"Ah, but Reverend, no matter how much you try to stretch the language of the Gospels, it's still inflexible, there are no half-tones, it doesn't allow for compromise, it doesn't accept any arrangements: 'If thy right hand offend thee, cut it off . . .' Perhaps the role of men of religion is to conciliate those inflexible mandates with man's convenience, especially the convenience of those who get their millions by exploiting the land and the men who work that land, acting like highwaymen without having to be swine," and after a brief silence that the sea filled with the hammering of the waves against the shell and the machine room with its incessant vibrations, Lester Mead went on: "Because that's why a person is a millionaire, so he can stop being a rich swine, a millionaire is that, a rich man who can afford the luxury of ceasing to be a swine . . ."

The hat, the suitcase, the pipe. Alone among millions of people, waiting for the traffic light to allow his taxi to pass, the one he had taken at the station in Chicago where he had arrived by train from New York.

He slept through the night and woke up very early. From

his bed he followed the sounds of the immense city as it awoke under an impenetrable blanket of dark fog. He moved his body under the sheets of pleasant English linen to stretch, and he sank his head into the pillow, closing his eyes tightly, opening them then little by little, and with his eyelids half-open he felt himself overwhelmed by a sort of thankful feeling toward life for having taken him far away from those cities and to the vegetable world of his banana groves.

He shaved, bathed, dressed in a hurry. His hat, his brief-case, his pipe. The time. The clock. Running to catch the elevator and go down. The door. The street. The struggle to get through the thousands of people who were passing by until he found the first empty taxi.

The Green Pope was waiting for him. A bad joke in this case. The Green Pope was waiting for him, but it was he who had to waste almost three hours before being admitted to his presence.

The top man in the hierarchy of Tropical Banana, Inc., stuffed into a gray suit of very fine material, a salmon-colored shirt of Italian silk, a yellow tie, was waiting for him behind his desk. When he saw him come in, he stood up, shook his hand, and offered him a seat.

They were face to face at last. The Green Pope in his swivel chair, looking at him, two small, insignificant eyes behind two thick lenses that were set in very dark black tortoiseshell frames, and Mead was looking back at him. It was that quick instant in which two people see each other for the first time and in detail. A cigarette. The Green Pope leaned back in his chair to answer Lester Mead.

"We agree, Mr. Mead, everything you say is true; but not only can we not pay any more for the fruit, but I've already given instructions to stop buying it."

"That's ungrateful . . ."

"We're a commercial enterprise, and a commercial enterprise, Mr. Mead, is not a mutual aid society. It's just that the utopian ideals of some altruistic millionaires have made people think that Tropical Banana, Inc., is an enterprise set up for the benefit of humanity when actually it's a financial organization."

"But don't you think that there are probably some stockholders of Tropical Banana, Inc., who wouldn't want to see their money grow that way, who would be ashamed if they could only imagine the procedures that are followed?"

"The stockholders are only worried about their dividends . . ."

"Do you know them . . . do you know all of them?"

"That's of no interest. It's not a matter of people, it's a matter of shares."

"That's unfortunate, because some stockholders would be upset. Most of them don't know that their dividends come from illegal deals. If the stockholders only knew that in exchange for their enormous, fantastic profits a tremendous fifth column against us was being created, the kind that springs up out of a hopeless life . . ."

Mead, underneath his peaceful appearance, could feel the blood boiling in his veins, as if it were irrigating him under his skin.

The Green Pope was looking at him with his caterpillar eyes behind lenses that were so thick that they formed concentric circles under the office lights, just as if at the bottom of two luminous cartridges, in the depth of two spirals, there were powerful, unexpressive, firm little eyes made out of the lead used for bullets.

"If the stockholders only knew what it is like to cultivate a piece of land, plant banana trees on it, and when the first fruit appears like the sweetest hope in life, to take it off to be sold, carrying it with great difficulty and care in ox carts or on muleback and laying it out where it can be bought, and to wait under the sun for hours on end, filling themselves up with illusions about the benefits gained from the fruit of honest work, and suddenly to receive a negative answer from the inspector, who refuses to buy the bunches, giving the thousand reasons they come out with in cases like that, and everything a person owns becomes so much battered fruit discarded alongside the railroad tracks like something dead, like something worthless, something that was cultivated in vain because it has no price, because it doesn't represent anything for anybody, not for the person who produced it, not for the company, not even to be given away . . . and a person is left with the corpse of a living thing that cost him so much and which is not dead, because it is alive, it is a green reality, a definite, obvious presence, but since it was not purchased it's lost its value in relation to the market that you people manipulate at your whim."

The Green Pope's silence did not disarm him, it aggravated him. Mead felt that his effort was useless. Human life was alien to the Green Pope, a creature of numbers, of figures written in chalk on the blackboards of the New York exchange.

"And since the growing of this product is the hope of a man, of a family, of a village, which has not only seen hard work but also the sacrifice of what is most valuable in life, a person's health, one must calculate the meaning of the disdain received in payment for so much effort as the inspector does not even turn around to look at the product because he knows beforehand that he is not to buy it. Malaria, tuberculosis, blindness, dropsy, bits of physical misery, blood, pus, sweat, and cane liquor . . ."

The Green Pope, spinning in his chair, rapped the knuckles of his right hand twice on the desk before saying:

"That's why we have hospitals, clinics . . ."

"Ya-ha . . . ha, ha, ha, ha!"

Lester Mead let out that loud strident laugh which, when

he was Cosi on the plantations could be heard for many miles, and which made the windows shake here.

"We sell meat and everything cheap in the commissaries . . ."

"Ya-ha . . . ha, ha, ha, ha!"

"And we've invested millions of dollars to make unhealthy countries worth something, and what we spend in salaries and wages is more than the governments themselves spend . . ."

"Ya-ha . . . ha, ha, ha ha!"

A man with a round face and a red nose dressed in a dark military tunic appeared from behind the curtains of one of the windows and stood next to the Green Pope cradling a submachine gun, tiny, like a pet. Mead no longer saw him, he was walking out with long strides, and when the elevator stopped at the fifty-third floor, he occupied a small space among the forty people going down, changed into a sardine, his eyes moist from having laughed like that, violently, freely.

8

Leland was at the station. She had failed in her efforts to open a vial of perfume. Between the honking of Carl Rose, who was driving her to the station and the voices of old Roselia and Bastiancito's wife telling her to hurry, there was no way to open the bottle, not even by heating it in the flame of her lighter.

The men, all lined up and hugging the wall, were waiting for Mead's return. There had been worse news. They were no longer buying any more fruit at all. The work of two years. Their jaws were tight with the pain of it. The Ayuc Gaitáns were cursing Cucho. It was a bad day when they had listened to his advice. If he were alive, they would spit in his face, because you don't come here to fight against the sea but against a gang of sons of bitches.

"He hoodwinked us, he hoodwinked us," Macario said as his brother Juan Sóstenes repeated:

"I was right when I said it was a trap, and a trap with a double bottom."

"What do you mean, Juan Sóstenes, a trap with a double bottom?"

"It's that now they'll take our land away because we'll abandon it because it hasn't given us anything, and even if we sell it then they'll get the good of what we've done here and that's all there is to it."

"But didn't you hear that they're not even picking all of their own bananas?"

"That's a trick, the bastards . . ."

The passenger train came to a stop noisily. Mead got off with his hat, his pipe, and his suitcases, one in each hand. His figure stood out among the handful of greasy and copper-faced passengers.

"Let's hurry up," Carl Rose said after the embraces, greetings, and handshakes, "because it's clouding up and it's going to rain hard."

Bastiancito, the two Luceros, old Lucero could not make it because of an attack of rheumatism in his leg that had hit him a few days back, the Ayuc Gaitáns, all jumped on their horses after the welcome, while into Carl Rose's car climbed Leland, Lester, and Walker, who had barely got to the station on time.

"Did you hear the news?" Walker asked Lester while Carl Rose was starting the car.

"I heard it from the mouth of the Green Pope himself . . . They're not buying any more fruit. We're ruined."

"Not at any price?" Leland asked, showing great affliction in the last part of her question.

"Not at any price."

The cloudburst was not long in coming. It fell on all sides and, it must be said quite frankly, Carl Rose's automobile was an old jalopy.

"Why haven't you got yourself a new car?" Mead asked him as they all made jokes about that great gasoline-propelled coffeepot in which they were all getting soaked.

"Because I'm a sentimentalist and it has sentimental memories for me and I get a funny feeling whenever I think that memories and all, they're going to toss it into one of those gulleys that the company fills up with worn-out cars. I've had to put up a fight so they won't shove it off a cliff to lie on its back among hundreds of other cars, nothing but old iron. It still runs."

"In your place," Leland said, "I'd put it in the living room of my house like royal coaches in museums, and I'd write a description for tourists of what it meant, pointing out that Carl Rose had an adventure in it which began this way . . ."

"Cut out the jokes, once and for all!"

"No, I'm just starting, and it's not a joke."

"Let's hear how it starts," Walker said in the best of moods.

"I'd better keep quiet, because he's liable to wreck the car."

"No, because it's something sacred for him. Right, Carl Rose, you wouldn't be capable of wrecking the car because you know that if you did, it would go to rot at the bottom of the old-car gulley all the quicker."

"Well, this sentimental chapter begins the way all adventures in a car begin . . ." Leland's repressed laugh could be heard as she went on to say, "with the horn demanding that the date be fulfilled; beep, beep, beep . . . until the instant in which the sleeping beauty appears, because it's at night, she wasn't sleeping during the day. The door opens to her nervous touch and slams shut, and the lady is now inside the vehicle. She can't escape because the door is locked on the outside. The motor. The vibration of the motor coming up through her feet to her legs, through her legs . . . Then a little speed to make her scalp tingle and bring on a loss of senses as she leans her carefree head against the shoulder of the one intent upon the curves in the road behind the wheel . . . The gears must be shifted, and there is an unexpected relationship of continuity between the speeds and the loved one's lower extremities . . . First, second, and her thigh, with a certain softness, third . . ."

Carl Rose, faced with the impossibility of quieting Leland down, pushed the accelerator down to the floor. Gossip versus motor. Suddenly he stopped in front of Mead's house. He was safe. He stopped the car and Leland's gossip.

Mead opened one of the suitcases in his room and came out with gifts for the friends who were arriving on horseback later. The most expensive of the gifts, they all could see, was a beautiful pistol, a request from old Lucero. Some regal handkerchiefs for putting on airs, some electric lamps and other showy things that his partners' wives were receiving amidst much bustle and thanks.

In spite of the gifts, the important part was missing. Had he fixed things up or not?

"We'll talk about it tomorrow, boys," Lester said, pressed by the eyes of all those good people, which were asking him anxiously without daring to put the question.

Carl Rose's automobile, taking Ernie Walker along, and the horses were lost in the hot darkness of the evening. The men were not riding. They were going on foot with the women, leading their horses by the reins.

That night Leland felt wrapped in a deep and mysterious nullification of her faculties when she went to bed alongside her husband. Her existence previous to the moment she was living was somewhat hazy. She had the sensation of being suspended, without memory, without will. She was in her senses, but not in her senses as they had been before, when seeing was seeing, hearing hearing, feeling feeling. Now, lying beside her husband, she saw, she heard, she felt without seeing, without hearing, without feeling. Where do clouds

come from? Where does the rain come from? Where does the
loving integration of one's being as it thirsts for sweetness and
is ready to drink in a look come from?

"Leland," he said, a sob? . . . whispering? . . . A voice,
just his voice, but with deep warmth for the one who adored
him, who held him up as a superior being. "Leland . . ." he
repeated before going on with his thoughts that were being
born there alongside of her like a small new plant and as they
were being born were being trampled on, "Leland, we've lost
the world; we Americans have lost the world."

She muffled the phrase with a long kiss on his mouth, until
she made his head sink into the pillow; after she kissed him
he took his arm out from under the sheet and ran his fingers
through her golden-green hair. It was not the pain of having
lost the world; that can be regained. It was the sorrow of their
being lost, of turning their backs on God. Who can be saved
with his eyes open? The only ones who can be saved are those
who close their eyes and let go. He drew her toward him,
pressing her against his chest, with his eyes closed; and she,
as she felt her husband's sudden and sweet caress, also covered her complete nakedness of a wife with the darkness of her
eyelids.

Very early in the morning the curious neighbors returned.
They had started as his neighbors and had ended up as his
partners, and they came to ask Mead what he had been able
to do for the small owners of plots planted with bananas.
Mead, swallowing a silky banana, answered them:

"Before I say anything I want you to make me a promise:
that you will obey me blindly, because we're in a fight against
the Green Pope . . ." he finished the banana and broke another one off the bunch, and while he was eating it, he was
looking at them with his green eyes, the way he used to look
after pausing in one of his laughs.

The copper-colored faces showed themselves agreeable to

obeying him blindly. Some guttural sounds confirmed what the faces were saying. Yes, we will obey you blindly.

"The Green Pope, for your information, is a man who sits in an office and has millions of dollars at his command. He lifts a finger and a ship starts or stops. He says a word and a republic is bought. He sneezes and a president, whether general or lawyer, falls . . . He rubs his behind on his chair and a revolution breaks out. This is the man we have to fight against. We may not see our victory, because our lives may not be long enough for us to finish off the Green Pope; but the ones who come after us in the trenches, yes, if they move like us, like the strong wind that leaves nothing standing when it passes, and what it does leave, it leaves all dried out."

"But we don't have the means . . ." Juan Sóstenes insisted, moving his head from side to side, always mistrustful and pessimistic, "and right now we want to go back to our village; we don't come from around here, and even though there may not be much to eat back there, there isn't so much fighting."

"The first thing is to use our heads, the second thing is to use our heads, and the third thing is to use our heads. The weak point, the only weak point we have, and that's how they've beaten us and got whatever they want, as Juan Sóstenes has mentioned, is the fact that we lack the means of survival; and in every war survival is the first thing."

"We've got debts . . . that's what we've got! . . ." Bastiancito said.

"That's the business, that's what I've been getting at, now we can make our plans together. This isn't a fight with machetes; and it isn't a battle that can be won with speeches, trying to convince them; no, it's an economic battle."

"They won't buy any more fruit . . ." Lino Lucero complained in a bitter and remorseful voice.

"I know. The Green Pope told me. But the fact that they

won't buy it from us doesn't mean that it's not worth something somewhere else; we'll sell it in order to survive; bring me a figure of what each one of you thinks he'll have available within a week, and I'll go and put it up for sale in the markets of the towns around here, and I'll go to the capital if I have to. I'm just waiting for a truck that I bought and which ought to be here at any moment."

"The whole business would be different that way, even though it wouldn't be much different . . ." ventured Juancho, the other Lucero.

"We'll sell the fruit to keep on paying off the debts that Bastiancito mentioned and we'll live frugally, the way peasants live in other places, the way you used to live before you came here . . ." he took out his pipe, and while he was filling it with tobacco, he added sententiously, "the worst part is that with the good price they gave us for the first bunches, we got into the habit of losing respect for money, and we thought they would keep on paying us the same way; we squandered it all on so many useless things that lie around there, useless . . ."

Macario Ayuc Gaitán found that this gringo was on the right track. Macario did not have many debts so to speak; and, by Jesus, the last resort would be to defend the land with machetes, because it was all they could take away from them! He said in a strong voice:

"Yes, you fellows, we've got to give it a try . . . Between going back there to the village with our tails between our legs like yellow dogs and standing up to the trouble the way Señor Mead proposes there's no choice; it all depends on the truck's getting here soon, because if it doesn't, we're all going to die here of one kind of fever or another, although the worst kind would be a fever of desperation that the truck isn't coming."

"The truck came on the same ship as I did, and it's just waiting for a freight train to bring it here."

"Oh, well, if that's how it is, it puts a different light on things . . ." Bastiancito regained his spirit, and everyone in the group seemed to awaken out of the anguished drowsiness into which they had fallen, roasting in the heat. "If that's how it is, the whole thing's different; let's go get the fruit ready and see how it works out; we're going to be all right; the toughest thing is always the one that never gets done . . ." he got up to leave, holding out his hand to Mead, as the others also picked up their hats off the floor.

"Just a minute," Mead said, "we've seen the easy side of the solution that I'm proposing to you; the hard part is still to come." The animated faces became bathed in a slight suspicion that all of that had been pie in the sky. "The Green Pope can do everything he does because he can count on our human weaknesses; if not, look at what would happen in his territory: the ones who ought to be our allies, natives of this country, are our worst enemies, because of stupidity, ignorance, selfishness, evil, anything you want to call it; they've taught some of them to spend such fabulous amounts of money that they've come to believe that money isn't worth anything and so, even though they earn a great deal, they will never get their freedom, because they've been enslaved like that, getting fat salaries to squander; they make it easy for others to lay their hands on things and they blackmail them because of their robberies; they've made others accomplices in the evil of their banditry . . ."

The Luceros, Lino and Juan, who as children had heard Lester Mead's laughter with fright when he was Cosi, and people would even frighten them by telling them that "the old man who laughs" was coming, had no doubts that this other one, without being Cosi, was still just as crazy as before.

"Why say any more," Mead asked. "We already know that for a few quinine pills José Luis Marzul steals tender young girls; that the managers pass their testicles around among illustrious visiting ladies; that in those private games of roulette and poker gold banknotes flow along with rum and whiskey and soda . . ."

Bastiancito yawned. A lot of talk and nothing on their plates. The others were moving restlessly. He should tell them about the rough part without any sermon.

"Besides going off to sell our fruit with the truck, we should set up an Indian type of economy; I'm not from here, but I know what the Indian can do with his frugality, his simplicity, his constant use of common sense, his way of earning and not spending everything he earns. Centuries have gone by, and the people who are not Indians, the ones descended from the Spaniards, even though it was a long time back, run two or three degrees of proudness fever every day. Even worse here in the tropics when they see how others spend everything they earn and more. Let's go back then, my friends, to an economy based on money tied up in a handkerchief. When the Indian has to spend money, he takes out his handkerchief and he has to untie it with his fingernails and teeth, and that's why he doesn't spend it as easily as we do, the ones who 'get around,' as the saying goes, emptying our pockets and spending by the handful."

In the end they all found it reasonable that what little they would earn with the sale of the fruit in nearby towns and in the capital should be tied up and not turned loose.

"An association with only debts for possessions is certainly crazy," said old Adelaido Lucero, whom they had taken out into the morning sun, immobilized by rheumatism, his hair combed down with violet-smelling hair oil, and wearing in his belt the pistol that Lester Mead had brought him as a gift.

Doña Roselia, holding one of her grandchildren, agreed with her husband at first; but she quickly shook her head from side to side and stated:

"What about the truck? . . . That truck he drives off full of fruit every day . . ."

"That's just a front. You'll soon see how one fine day they'll get tired of seeing what little they're earning, and that'll be the end of the Association and the end of everything, and there'll be even more debts and they'll take the truck away from them . . ."

"I don't know whether I agree with you or not; but you ought to keep in mind that when a person gets old he falls face down all of a sudden and can't see anything else except the hole he's going to drop into stiff as a board at any time. The boys are doing all right."

"They're screwed up all right, you mean, it's written all over them; they haven't been able to get any new clothes, can't even change their sheets . . ."

"It's because they made an agreement; the Association won't let them spend anything."

"But, Roselia, that's just one great big piece of foolishness, what with the commissary right over there with all kinds of good things for sale cheap; what I used to buy for you was perfume, remember, Roselia? They're going to be left with nothing but the shirts on their backs . . . I worked like a dog, but by God I got some fun out of it."

"You spent what we could have saved up by now, and wasn't it me who suggested and insisted that you buy your sons some land? Otherwise they'd still be spending their young lives on the plantations."

"I always thought that a person should stay behind the plow and that everybody should take care of his own chamber pot . . ."

"That's why these boys are going to be able to stand up against the Company, Adelaido; it won't be right away, but it'll happen someday if they manage to hang on and keep on making themselves strong . . . In order to bring these evil people down, what they have to do is be like toads for a thousand years . . . But a thousand years later, that toad's going to shake himself, the way Sarajobalda explains it when she works her witchcraft, and then the mountain will come tumbling down."

"And what good will it do me, me, Adelaido Lucero Peña, if all of this you've been talking about takes place when I'm even more earth than the earth itself?"

Doña Roselia scratched her head with all of the nails of her left hand; in her right arm she was holding her grandson, who had just laid his small head on her old woman's shoulder.

"That's why I think, and you don't have to believe me, Adelaido, but listen to me just the same, that this is like some new religion. I only listen to them, but they talk so seriously about turning all of this upside down that even I come to believe it, and since they're going to do it all by holding on to what they earn, they're going to do all right . . ."

"With all their debts?"

"With all their debts . . ."

"With this new religion now of working and saving, which is really a case of not letting yourself be screwed by the rich people, it's too bad it caught me old and rheumatic, Roselia, because otherwise they'd really see what a strong wind was!"

"We're like old dogs, Adelaido, we bark in the hall without lifting anything except our heads, and all that's left for us is to do our duty and give a little bark now and again."

"What do you mean by that?"

"I mean that I've been chasing away the people who come to the door with their goods: combs, mirrors, soap, handkerchiefs . . ."

"If Comrade Mead—I've heard that's what they call him now—knew that, he'd hang you; he used to live off that when he was Cosi and he used to laugh that Ya-ha, ha, ha, ha, ha! of his."

"Now he says that the one who laughs last, laughs best . . ."

"Well, they know they can count on me, even if I'm old. I'm an old soldier and I can empty this pistol into any one of them."

The flies would not leave him alone and it was a concentrated attack; from the grandson's little face to the face of the old man, the flies came and went. Flocks of parrots stretched out a curtain of green smoke and passed on shouting behind the house. They all lived with their ears glued to the air. They liked to hear the humming of the truck so much.

9

The truck did not hum that day. The truck did not leave. Leland had her husband's breakfast ready very early, but Lester opened his eyes when the sun was already hot. Competition had appeared.

The Fuetés, grandsons of a French gentleman who had arrived forty years before in the days of the cutting of fine woods, were going about in a yellow truck selling fruit at a lower price. In the afternoon, Lester and Juancho Lucero left in search of new markets. Night caught up with them on the road. It was a long trip, but they managed to get a better price. They stopped the vehicle in the middle of the plateau. From a large thermos bottle, Mead poured out an endless flow of rice and milk. In the extreme cold of the highlands, that mixture of half soup and half sweet meal was tasty and comforting. Its warmth as it was sipped and the flavor of cinnamon pleased Lester as if he had never tasted anything better in the world.

They bedded down beside the truck. How long did Mead keep his eyes on the sky above before he closed them? He could not tell. The wristwatch next to his ear reminded him that he was a creature of measured time. The softness of the silence that spread out among the sleeping trees, among the lying animals, was broken by the passing of the truck. Before dawn, the headlights of the heavy vehicle swept the dusty road along rocky stretches and dirt-covered sections where the very fine earth became a white cloud in the air. The lights of the capital were still shining in the soft clearness that began to be tinted with pink in the east. They went downhill with the motor turned off to save gasoline, with the brakes on full so as not to plunge over a cliff. Here and there a walking shadow. The lights of the truck bathed the backs and outlines of the people walking ahead; then, as it drew close to pass them, it seemed to cut off their feet and leave them lying in the still, thick darkness.

They grabbed at the fruit. Yes, literally grabbed. Only buzzards on garbage wagons showed such voracity and such haste as they grabbed leavings. In the blink of an eye there was nothing left of their cargo and there were fights over the large bunches of bananas among men and women who then went to look for some bearers to carry off the burdens.

While they were selling the bananas, Mead placed a large sign next to the truck announcing that they would carry cargo to places along their route and to the end of their run. It was not hard for him to get cargo. A Lebanese hired him to carry some merchandise. His blond hair, his light eyes, his bearing, and his status of gringo guaranteed the cargo better than the best recommendation. They're people who never steal anything, the Lebanese was explaining, because from early childhood they're taught to earn their own living. The people from here, from this country, are nothing but thieves, nothing but thieves.

Later on, the Lebanese's contraband, merchandise that had crossed the border without paying duty, was on its way down to the coast under the protection of the figure of Lester Mead, whom the authorities would never dare ask for papers. When the documents were signed and everything was in order, Mead, who did not know that it was contraband, got back into the driver's seat, released the brake, started the motor, and back home.

For the nearby markets, which the Fuetés only half-covered, because they missed a lot of trips, Mead and his people substituted the market in the capital twice a week.

But one day when they got to the market and stationed themselves in the spot where they were well known to a great number of dealers, no one came over. A shudder ran through Lester's body. It was impossible that the market in the capital, with the little they brought twice a week, should be so dead.

A vegetable woman, the color of raw potatoes, came over to look at the cargo that was still covered with yellow banana leaves; the bunches had not been moved because no buyer had appeared.

The woman looked, sniffed, poked . . .

"You're not going to sell anything, not today, Mister . . ." she told him; "how were you going to sell anything because yesterday and the day before they were giving fruit away free at the railroad station . . ."

Mead started up the truck in the midst of skinny dogs, the smell of spicy food, Indians smelling of cane liquor, and here and there an early-rising vending woman with new shoes. The streets, the traffic, the city. Into a gate that was open so that trucks with construction material, ambulances, and other vehicles could enter; he kept going along until he saw a Sister of Charity in the corridor taking notes in a book. He greeted her and told her that this fruit was sent as a donation from the firm of Mead-Lucero-Cojubul-Ayuc-Gaitán and Company.

"How wonderful!" the sister said, "for them to send us these bunches of bananas, because all we've been getting from there are the incurably ill! Sick people who have left their lungs back there. Our wards are so full that there's no room for more patients, and many, but oh so many, have to sleep on the floor."

While Mead and Juancho Lucero were unloading the fruit, two ambulances came in. The Sister of Charity, with sparkling eyes, thankful to the Lord God who had given her proof for what she had said, came over to Lester and said to him in a low voice:

"Here comes the other fruit that they send us free from those large plantations where all that money flows, but the only thing that reaches us is misery."

Mead stood watching a procession of living corpses. Human bones that were coughing and spitting blood. Eyes bulging out of faces soaked in bitter quinine perspiration. Teeth attempting a tragic laugh between the dry edges of their lips. The stench of weeping and of diarrhea. The sick people bundled up their clothing to carry, those who could walk, the others, on brown canvas stretchers, were carried inside from the ambulances by barefoot attendants in white gowns.

Mead gave a pat on the back to his helper on those trips, still Juancho Lucero. The sister had disappeared inside as if she had flown off with the wings of her hat.

The truck stopped at a shop that sold automobile parts.

"It can't be, because I paid fifteen pesos less for this one; you're charging me a lot . . ."

The tire salesman squatted down to look at the number on the tire; then he stood up to consult the price on a greasy and oil-stained chart, and after rapping his pencil against his teeth, he did some figuring.

"Since it's you, Mr. Mead, I'm going to let you have it for

less; but please don't tell anybody, because we're selling them for more."

Juancho Lucero signaled to Mead with his eyes, drew him aside, and said:

"What you're doing is foolish; back there the company has a whole pile of good tires and they throw them away almost new. We ought to buy some of those."

"They won't sell them," Mead answered.

"But why won't they sell them, they're still good, they've still got some mileage left on them . . ."

"They won't sell them, they'll throw them away to rot, even though we and the whole country need used tires."

"If we offer them a good price . . . there are hundreds of tires they throw away to rot in the dumps . . ."

"They feel it's better for them to rot than for us to use them." The truck was rolling toward the outskirts of the capital with the spare tire that Mead had bought at the price of gold. "What we will buy from them are some of the horses they have left over . . ." Mead seemed to be talking to himself ". . . but we'll have to find someone who isn't one of us to make the offer . . . We'll talk to . . . I'm thinking . . . someone . . . someone they won't suspect . . ."

The truck did not hum toward the capital again, nor did Mead take it out much except for a few errands nearby and to go to the beach one Sunday when everybody went for an outing.

The mouth of the river stopped them; as the river continued on into the sea, the road stopped. The water of the broad river was taking on a tint of soft, greenish fear as it came face to face with the wrathful and salty loneliness of the great ocean. Ceiba trees higher than towers, smooth, with no branches until the crown, a crown shaped like a basket to carry immensities. Long vines hanging from the branches, climbers, parasites, tufts. The vegetation crouched beneath, defending itself against the dampness and the shade, and, like endless arms, the sandbars were shining like shattered mirrors, reddish beaches sprinkled with garnet dust.

The children in the group, of all ages, little men and women, were picking up stones and shells on the beach, while the older people, lying down, scratched in the sand. A solemn bird with a bill larger than its body passed over, flapping its wings above the bathers who were naked, like animals or copper gods.

Other people had arrived from the plantations; company workers for the most part, with bodies shaped like swaying hammocks, arms and hips, as they walked, the same as if they were hanging between heaven and earth. Most of their lives had been spent in hammocks. They slept in hammocks, napped, received visitors, got drunk, took refuge in the breeze from fevers, sought the fever of love, which on the coast is the heat of riding animals. The concave back, the buttocks, the hind part of their legs down to the heels, everything in them matched the ungainly and lazy shape of a hammock.

They became desperate as they faced the sea. Their quadrilateral lives were broken against the infinite curve of the horizon. They felt uncomfortable outside the quadrilateral of their daily lives, living in houses which were long dovecotes raised on stilts. Up above they slept, their rooms and their extended comforts. Below, basins to wash the sweat from their clothes, because what most passed through those washbasins was the sweat of a man, of a working beast. Below too, the kitchens, and the hammocks where they spent most of their lives. And the houses matched the shape of the farms where they worked, quadrilaterals which stretched out one after the other. Their horizon was formed by those green parallelograms covered with banana trees in geometric rows set at equal distances, and the houses in the so-called yards were wooden oblongs, dovecotes that were longer than they were wide. Out-

side and inside their houses they lived within the same
geometric figure, harmless at first, but hostile and disturbing
afterward. The sea, therefore, made them desperate. Their
eyes followed a line that was different from that of the quadrilaterals in which they spent their monotonous lives, a
geometric monotony that was nullifying them, always between
boards, sometimes between the boards of a coffin, a quadrilateral that was also longer than it was wide, and boards too with
the bills they owed the storekeeper, with nothing ever left
over from what they earned with their work.

Bastiancito Cojubul did not go on the outing. He was suffering from a slight attack of asthma. He had gone to see the
doctor at the hospital, and the latter advised him against going
near the ocean. Among the other patients, more women than
men, who were waiting in the clinic, he heard a conversation
that amused everyone, but Bastiancito, even though he had to
pretend to laugh, trembled under his clothes as if he had been
shaken by a malarial chill. The same chill that fear brings on.

"Hrumph, hrumph, they, they almost got the truck that belongs to those people down there with a railroad car," a man
adorned with a huge goiter was saying; "hrumph, almost . . .
they were keeping watch waiting to let the car go and catch
them on the tracks and they almost did it . . . well . . .
hrumph, there wouldn't have been anything left of the truck
and less of the people in it, blood and gore . . . But the big
dopes, when they pushed the car free, the truck had already
gone over the crossing . . . If it had stopped for a second
when it was on the rails, it would have been smashed . . . It
almost, ha, ha, ha . . . hrumph, was . . ."

"But they're not selling fruit around here anymore," one of
the other people in the clinic said. "The Fuetés have cut into
their business because they sold their fruit cheaper, and they
were hit in the capital too when the trains brought in leftovers
to give away free at the central station."

"Hrumph, hrumph," the man answered with a sharp voice, as if he were grinding glass in his goiter and spitting it out, as if he were spitting it out through his bulging eyes. "Hrumph, hrumph, something's keeping them alive. That gringo who heads them up must have made a deal with the devil."

"I wouldn't be surprised," said a nearsighted man with a wormy tumor on his forehead. "Lucero's a good friend of Sarajobalda."

That same afternoon Bastiancito told Lester Mead all about the railroad car that had been pushed down to run into the truck which had passed through, unaware of the danger it was in. The news did not dampen any of the merriment of the outing. They were only sad that Bastiancito had not come.

Lester, jovial as always, took Leland's small accordion and began to sing sentimental songs in English. Leland applauded him, happy to hear him singing, happy to see him happy, and all the others, taken by the feeling of the music, for they could not understand the words, showed their pleasure by applauding.

Lino Lucero picked up a guitar and sang:

> *Oh, innocent morning star,*
> *how you fell into the sea,*
> *and the daring boat sailed far*
> *with you, far away to the lee!*
> *People say you are weeping,*
> *when it rains on the open sea,*
> *and my sailor's heart is underway,*
> *and you will be shipwrecked with me.*

Watermelon time was jolly. Leland ate her slice as if she were playing a tune on a seashell with a green shell and a red inside. Her hair peeped out from her bathing cap and curled silkily over her forehead, became entangled with her nose, got caught on the watermelon until she had to spit out the sweetness and the bothersome hair. The green glow of the

sea had wrapped them in an atmosphere of a liquid banana
grove which added the velvety gold of the sun's dusty light
to the deep-water green; and they drew nearer and nearer to
the breaking of the blue waves to wash in that splendor of a
marine banana grove and feel themselves soaked in the indigo
water, intensely alive because it was water.

Leland came out of the foam with her eyes closed, putting
her hand on her waist to steady herself or pulling on the edge
of her suit, which was riding up and pinching her beautiful
white legs. Lester was playing shark, surprising her as she
swam. His teeth closed on Leland's thigh and made her shake
her leg with an electric nervousness, shout, and come out almost in terror. Lester Mead appeared behind, laughing and
shouting at her:

"I know a woman who was the victim of a laughing shark!"

Bastiancito saw them when they came back. He was visiting
at old Lucero's. Don Adelaido made his way slowly to the
end of the hallway, leaning on his cane, to greet the picnickers.

"Well, if that's the way things are, you're not going to get
very far," the old rheumatic said, "because they're out to kill
you; that business of trying to send that storm-road car down
on top of you is going from brown to black; the only thing is
that this man, gringo or not, is pretty sharp."

"They're going to finish them off, you'll see . . . even though
he says that in the long run they can lick the Green Pope."

"Ah, m'boy, there's no end to this Pope, any more than there
is to the other one in Rome, because when one dies another
takes his place . . ."

"Then . . ."

"That's what I say, Bastiancito, then . . . That's why I
think of this man and everything he's worth; he won't see the
end of this, but he's sacrificing himself so that others who
won't be us will see it."

The old man sighed. The clear night, slightly cool, let one

breathe at Semírames. Except that Bastiancito was worried that he would have another attack.

"Whiskey's good for what ails you."

"That's what they say, Don Adelaido, but I don't like that drink. It tastes like medicine, it's like drinking carbolic acid."

"You ought to go to bed; you have to go to bed early, that way you'll fall asleep right away and even if a coughing spell wakes you up at dawn and won't let you sleep anymore, you've already had a night's sleep."

"Good night, please say good night to Miss Roselia for me, tomorrow's another day."

The old man raised his head. The seven shining objects, the triangle . . . The whole sky was a dust storm of lights and it could easily have been true that luminous chariots were racing up there on an immense circular track.

10

Unforgettable nights. They filled several pages in Leland's diary. Which of them all did she prefer? If they told her to erase one of them from her memory, as if she had not lived it, which one of all those nights would she have left blank?

She could not tell, really, because they were all so deeply clear and at the same time dark: clear for a zone of her consciousness and dark for her love, because she had touched blindly what is visible only in the latitudes of the heart.

The friends from before did not visit very often now. Still, they would appear when least expected, to introduce them to the O'Briens, Miss Morgan, and Smollet the engineer.

The conversation was very interesting from the very first moment. They all seemed to be animated with the spirit of college students, turbulent, romantic, slightly frivolous.

Carl Rose, wearing a carnation in the lapel of his light suit, went into the middle of the living room and tried to drink his glass of whiskey and soda by biting on the edge of the glass to lift it and let the drink pour into his mouth without using his hands and without spilling a single drop of the precious liquid, more precious than the blood of Our Lord Jes—

"Don't be blasphemous," Miss Morgan protested, altering her ruddy look of a person who is always in a good humor.

Tom agreed that it was difficult; but it was more difficult to light a cigarette by placing the box of matches on the tip of your foot, the match in your mouth, and the cigarette in your pocket in an unopened pack.

They all laughed, going over to the group formed by Smollet the engineer, the O'Briens, Walker, and Lester Mead. Walker was overdoing himself with his attentions toward the O'Briens.

"Good poker players . . ." he said into Carl Rose's ear, patting him on the back, "new legs make you forget the old ones."

Walker adjusted the blond lock on his forehead, shook his glass of whiskey and soda with ice so that the ice would settle to the bottom: it was shining on the surface of the amber liquid like a piece from a polar mirror; and he said:

"I demand respect for Mrs. O'Brien; society is based on the respect for married women, even though that respect doesn't mean condemning them to be married forever . . ."

"You devil . . ." Carl Rose said as he clicked glasses with Ernie Walker, who had his glass and his cigar in the same hand, and an ash fell to the floor as the glasses touched.

But those short dialogues, amidst laughter, a friendly clicking of glasses and cigarettes being passed around did not deter engineer Smollet as he spoke about the Anderson case.

"He's the man who made all of this possible . . . there wouldn't have been any plantations without him. I don't know how much of it's a myth, but when you visit places like this you really have to think of him as a supernatural being."

"Anderson and the flight of the green butterflies," Mr. O'Brien said. "My wife is thinking of using that as the title of a *Lied* she's been composing, she's heard so much about Anderson as a legendary figure."

"Why 'green butterflies'?" Miss Morgan asked, as her round face appeared from behind the cigarette smoke.

"It's easy to see," Leland put in, "that you're a newcomer; after you've lived here for a time, when your world becomes geometrically square and in that quadrilateral the light of your days and the shadows of your nights become a single green haze, then you'll see how green butterflies flew out of Anderson's pockets to form this world of an underwater sky."

"Leland has rounded out the picture," Carl Rose said, "because I know that Anderson would take handfuls of earth from these places and put them into his pocket to have analyzed later, which was the basis of his findings that it was land well suited for the planting and cultivation of bananas."

"How beautiful! How beautiful!" Mrs. O'Brien exclaimed, casting her peach eyes on Leland, "the handfuls of land went into Anderson's pockets as if they were the cocoons of those caterpillars that hang down from the mangroves around here, and they came out one fine day changed into green butterflies, those slender banana leaves that filter the light below which is like the constant flight of green butterflies."

"But besides that, and I think it's the most important part," Walker added, "Anderson did a study of the climate which did not appear on the topographical maps of the region; and what most convinced them to accept his plans was that as far as winds were concerned, he was able to prove that on this coast we don't have that 'strong wind.' As a matter of fact, there's never been a case of it."

"A powerful enemy!" engineer Smollet stated; "anyone who hasn't seen what happens when it comes can't imagine what the 'strong wind' is like. It's something fearful. I can only tell you that I've done a lot of sailing and I've been through heavy storms at sea, a hurricane in Cuba, but none of those storms made me feel the terror I felt when the 'strong wind' hit the Atlantic coast three years ago. A person feels strangled, asphyxiated, turned to dust. It's a hurricane wind that doesn't only shake and knock down everything on the surface, but it tears up trees and buildings by the roots."

Lester Mead, who had remained silent, raised his voice:

"Those who maintain that wealth is produced by business enterprises in which there isn't the smallest bit of a dream, a fantasy, or a fable, are not aware that there are exploitations that are like great dreams and that this has been one of them. Anderson dreamed up these banana plantations and their owners think they're dreaming now when they read the figures of their profits . . ."

"That's why Anderson seems like the devil to me," Miss Morgan said.

Lester Mead looked at her. She had anticipated him. He too thought that Anderson was the tropical incarnation of the Tempter. A devil. Miss Morgan had said so.

"Oh!" Mrs. O'Brien accepted a place on the piano bench next to Leland while the men and Miss Morgan remained standing, "if he's a devil, my *Lied* ought to be something else, don't you think?" she said to her husband, Mr. O'Brien, who cleared his throat slightly as he answered her:

"If you follow that level, you'll end up composing something that could be called 'Anderson, or the Green Temptation.' "

Lester jumped up:

"The Green Tempter, that's what I've always called Anderson—right, Leland?—in contrast to the Tempter of hell in the Bible, who must have been red."

"Yes, because you say that he climbed up to the summit of the mountain of hope that exists for many, for thousands of men, and which is green in color, and he called to them and said: 'Do you want to own the world?' "

"That's very beautiful," Mrs. O'Brien said, almost into Leland's ear, as Smollet the engineer applauded with his boxer's hands, adding aloud:

"Do you want wealth?"

"Let's have Lester tell us all about it," Walker proposed, "as soon as we fill our glasses and Miss Morgan finds a chair."

"I wouldn't know how to tell it in front of so many people with their whiskey glasses empty, maybe when . . . No, not for me, Leland, I'll pass because I've had quite a bit to drink already," Lester said.

"Me either . . ." Miss Morgan covered her glass with her hand, "I'm halfway there . . ."

"But a drop won't make the river overflow . . ."

"Thank you, you're so kind, a person can't resist . . ."

Ernie Walker went over to sit near Mrs. O'Brien. He was the kind of man who is satisfied with having the woman he desires close by, being within the orbit of her breathing, drawing in from the air all those infinitely small particles of saliva which, it was proven scientifically, emanate from the mouth when one speaks and from the air when one breathes. And he noticed her perfume, an exotic scent whose essence, in the tropics, broke up until it became violent and intoxicating.

"At that time," Lester Mead began his explanation, "the men of a strong race, the sons of Puritans, climbed the mountain; each carried before his eyes a vision of the city of good; long paths of stars, reflections of light on the water stretched out before their eyes; the bad weather did not bite their root-hard skins: they were too hard to be weak and too innocently good to be bad. They all slept under the stars. A great darkness with a mineral glow and shining lights down below where the city began. The green devil approached those men; hidden in his darkness he carried the color of the realest of hopes, of money in its most tempting manifestation: gold-coin-paper-money green. 'Do you want wealth?' he asked them without showing his face clearly, hypnotizing them with his bovine eyes. They answered that all wealth cost a great deal of work and that they were happy with what they had and because they did not have to work anymore. 'Work?' the Tempter laughed in their faces. 'A great deal of work?' a drivel of mangled snakes came from his mouth. 'This fabulous wealth will not cost you any work: open your eyes, look there below, find between the seas those blue and mountainous lands and I will give you the seeds that will change into plants that are the color of green money, plants whose fruit will make it seem that their foliage, their leaves, all of their leaves cut into a thousand pieces can be exchanged in banks for gold coins and gold bricks . . .'

"And that race of strong men," Lester continued, "the sons of Puritans, accepted the offer. The millions collected from the banana groves made them masters of the world, lords of creation. They needed a chief, and at a stockholders' meeting where they sat on gold bricks, they elected the Green Pope. Nothing more fantastic than that demoniacal growth of riches based on the color of the hope of man given to a race that had been called to the highest destiny, which made them leave the straight and narrow path; and that was Anderson, the Tempter, the one who offered them those lands and on that land wealth which they did not have to work for, because other men came to work it, for there were legions of sweaty men, greasy men, men soaked with fever, men blinded by physical misery, men whose destiny was that: working for the Tempter's strong race . . ."

A long silence reigned after Lester Mead's words as he brought the last sip of whiskey to his lips, more water than whiskey, for as he had been speaking, the ice had melted in his glass.

Miss Morgan said timidly:

"It's curious, but I'd thought about that strong race too, that this wealth of the Green Tempter has changed into . . . into what we are . . . nothing but exploiters . . ."

"No, please, no conclusions!" Tom shouted as he leaned on Walker, who could be heard repeating:

"No conclusions! Don't draw any conclusions! What's been said should stay just the way it was said, nothing else!"

"Then why have we been saying it?" Miss Morgan asked with a certain courteous annoyance.

"So that Mrs. O'Brien," Walker savored the letters of the beautiful Mrs. O'Brien's last name as he held them on his lips, "will know how to proceed as she composes her *Lied*, whether she does it about the fable of the man and the flight of the green butterflies, or about Anderson the Tempter, the creator of green wealth and of the Green Pope . . ."

Only Leland's eyes had guessed the storm that had passed through her husband's heart.

"The conclusions are obvious, we don't have to extract them or state them. Why should we, since they're obvious? Because of a few handfuls of money, because of all these plantations we have, because of the wealth that adds up to millions and millions of dollars even when it's broken up into annual dividends, we've lost the world, not the domination of the world, we still have that, but the possession of the world, which is something different; we're masters of all of these lands now, we're masters of these green temptations; but we mustn't forget that the time of the devil is limited and that the hour of God, which is the hour of man, is at hand . . ."

"The 'strong wind'!" engineer Smollet said, making use of desperate measures; he was a practical man and that peroration was like a Sunday sermon to him.

"The engineer has said it; but not that 'strong wind' he spoke about, something fearful, like an incomparable force of nature . . . The hour of man will be the 'strong wind' that will raise its voice of complaint from beneath the entrails of the world, and it will make its demands and sweep us all away . . ."

Tom Baker took a broom he found behind the door and began to brush his friends, telling them:

"Out, out, out! I am the broom, I am the strong wind . . ."

They all jumped away to escape the sweeping on their feet or moved forward so as not to receive it so strongly on their backs or legs.

"Have Tom dance with the broom!" someone shouted.

And Mrs. O'Brien began to play a happy tune, which they all took advantage of by jumping up and pairing off, until a moment in which the rhythm of the piano became faster, when everyone abandoned his companion to change partners, while the one with the broom dropped it on the floor and looked for someone to take. In the change of partners, the one who was left alone picked up the broom and danced with it until the music speeded up and the change of partners took place again.

Walker, while they were changing partners, picked Mrs. O'Brien up from the piano and asked Leland to go on playing. Leland picked up the rhythm and kept the music going. Mr. O'Brien was having such a good time with Miss Morgan that he was unaware of the switches, even more so when it was his turn to relinquish his young partner. There was a time when Mr. O'Brien had his wife as a partner. He immediately leaned over and picked up the broom. Walker sensed the perfect husband in that discreet man, and with a loving but disguised tug, he drew that sweet friend with the peach-colored eyes into the liveliness of the dance. If only he were able to kiss her right there as he held her. A moment later he was dancing with the broom. It was a stupid switch, but it was obligatory. A broom, a dirty broom instead of his beloved fruit who came from "the garden of another."

"These friends here are like the devil himself, not the green devil," the engineer said to Lester Mead, "but actually, what they think is a reason for dancing will bring on a *danse macabre* if they don't correct their procedures. The strong wind, as you said, will be the revenge of these hard-working, humble, long-suffering, exploited people; I intend to say just that, spelling it all out, when I turn in my report."

"There was no broom, there was no piano, but the couples were still swapped . . ." Walker was saying as he shaved the following day to Tury Duzin, who was listening from the small anteroom, "the Morgan girl with O'Brien."

"That aged young man gives me the impression that he's impotent," Tury Duzin exclaimed.

"You're jealous . . ."

"Miss Morgan isn't my type . . ."

"And me, of course, with pretty Mrs. O'Brien . . ."

"I like her better."

"Me too."

"What other couples were there?"

"Tom Baker and the engineer, both drunk . . ."

"But they understood each other too . . ."

"I don't know whether they understood each other in the meaning you give to the word, the lion thinks that everybody else thinks the way he does, Tury Duzin; what's certain is that Tom wanted to kiss the engineer, because he was saying that he was his father, and the engineer was embracing Tom because he said that he was his brother. If you'd been there who would you have danced with after dancing with the broom?"

"With Leland."

"You really would have lost . . ."

"Completely. Like all of them, she's a disgustingly normal woman; and with that husband, crazier than a loon, a worthy citizen of his Phalanstery."

"He was preaching last night. He said that an unknown strong wind, more devastating than the one known by that name, will blow across the plantations and sweep us all away when the green devil is overthrown by God in the hour of man."

"He's a most unbearable bore, I'm glad he lives outside of our geometry, because I don't know whether you've heard him talk about the parallelo-geometric mentality that he assigns to us. We're condemned to parallel lines according to him. The parallel lines that form the rhombuses of our horizon on the plantations and which are repeated in the workers' quarters, maintain in all of us creatures with reason who live here a state of an unattained thing, something unattainable, because the parallel lines not only never come together, but they also go along equidistant, and that equidistance makes us all live apart from ourselves in two equal persons, alike, parallel . . . According to Lester, from the point where the ends of the cultivated parallelograms on the plantation stop, the human eye takes off in visual or imaginative flight with the help of the mechanics of the deeper being to extend such lines, and it never gets to bring them together, because they go on like that, equally parallel, to infinity; that is, there's something in us, those of us who live here, that is never realized; never at the horizon; and when a person in desperation takes refuge in his house after a day's work, he finds his quarters conceived geometrically too, equidistant parallel lines that are only erased when his eyes are closed in sleep . . ."

"You sound like a disciple of the new doctrine too," Walker said as he shaved, bathed, and put on a light blue suit. He shook hands with Tury Duzin and received a cigarette from her along with the greeting.

"According to him," Tury Duzin added, "it's a diabolical formula invented by the Green Pope so that the people who work with us will never feel hemmed in, so that they'll live in a stable situation, because the axis of their vital mechanics, at work and at home, which establishes them, makes them feel secure, will always remain where the parallels of the rhombuses meet, that is, nowhere."

"It's all very much like dancing with the broom, waiting to change partners!"

"Ah, if he's thinking about sex . . . He's crazier than I am . . ."

"He must have wanted to convince you that you're not very adorable because of your parallelism . . ."

"No, Mead is respectful, don't think that . . . He respects my way of being masculine without growing a beard or wearing men's clothes, and without men's silly attitudes."

"I'm going to see if I can cure my pains with a horse's neck. Do you want a drink?"

"It's a little early for me; it's only eight o'clock in the morning; but with this damned heat, just to get my lips close to some ice, fix me one."

In tall glasses, long, like horses' necks, the surfaces of which were decorated with picaresque motifs, Walker's trembling hand served two enormous drinks of whiskey, then he put in some water, ice, and a few drops of lemon juice.

"Take a look at this glass, there's a beautiful dark girl with chubby legs and proud breasts."

After savoring the figure of a beautiful Latin American Venus, Tury Duzin began to savor the whiskey. After the first sip she offered her friend a cigarette from her jeweled case, which on a gold background had the figure of a woman who seemed to open her legs when the case was opened.

"You ought to put some tobacco from a light cigarette there so that it would look like hair . . ."

"I smoke them dark . . ."

"Ha, ha . . . ha, ha . . ." Ernie Walker laughed and the ice hit the sides of his glass as he did.

He drained it almost as if in haste.

After the drink that went from the horse's neck to his neck, Walker put on a somber defensive smile as he went over to Tury Duzin to tell her in confidence that he was in real trouble.

"The wife of the senior foreman, the one he married for the third time, a young girl, came over to my house the other day and . . ."

"A pause . . ."

"Her husband shuts himself in to gamble starting on Saturday and he doesn't come out until Monday, and when there's a weekend holiday he disappears for three days."

"Introduce me to her . . ."

"That was my idea, to throw the husband off the track, he's become an Othello, because the poor fellow wouldn't be jealous of you, he'd think his wife was protected with another woman."

"No, my dear; several times now the managers have used me as their protection. But it's a role that smacks of a go-between; my sexual morals are strange, but they're honest: the role of a go-between is repugnant to me; in every go-between there's a prostitute *manquée,* one who was halfway there."

"But that isn't the real trouble; what has me worried is that I've been accused of getting the daughter of one of the people down below pregnant, and it's not mine, it belongs to Carl Rose."

"Oh, no; look for somebody else to get rid of your guilt on, not that decadent Don Juan!"

"Well, we could put the blame on Tom . . ."

"You can put the blame on anyone you want to, but I don't have to get involved in your affairs."

"Tom Baker or somebody else . . . I'm going to see the man in charge of the warehouse, that fellow from Tabasco. He takes care of lots of jobs that don't belong to him for money, because since he's in charge of merchandise, he can appease the parents with goods from the commissary. He gets paid in the price of gold, but the fact is that the parents of the future mother are happy with some rice, sugar, canned goods, rum, and perfume."

"He must have a whole army of little blond children all over the place . . ."

"Everybody is thinking up ways to make money and that someday they'll disappear from here . . ."

"And those children will be left behind . . ."

"There won't be many of them left . . . they'll be eaten up by the climate . . . devoured by their miserable diets . . . torn to pieces by bacteria . . . the invisible little fangs of measles, mumps, scrofula, scarlet fever, croup, whooping cough, not to mention those lovely worms . . ."

"The green hell . . . Men and women come here and you can't tell whether it's because of the big doses of cane liquor, the climate, the parallelism, why, nobody knows, but they live like animals in heat; and that was what I was going to explain to you about Lester Mead's sexual theory."

"I need some reinforcements; do you want another?"

"No, I don't like to drink in the morning; I'm a night drinker, and besides, I don't like that whiskey; it's got too sweet a taste. Let me explain Lester Mead's sexual theory to you. It's very strange. According to him, life in parallel, quadrilateral horizons produces that urge in the libido to exchange women, the one men get here, and the ease with which the women themselves change over and give themselves up, no matter what race, social class, or future, because men and women feel caged in, and it's the desperation of a caged animal that makes them try to escape through their senses into the sexual game. If imaginary bars were placed on these plantations with equal horizons, two long sides and two short sides, we'd have the real picture of what we are, animals in cages, one cage after another, cages and cages all the way down to the sea."

"Cages, wild animals, and their trainers . . ."

"You're right, because Lester gives us the role of trainers, and the whip we use to make the poor animals obey is the work contract, and the lead slugs on the end of the whip are the dismissal clause."

"Ha, ha, of course! It's horrible to have to admit that he's right!" Walker emptied his glass while Tury Duzin lit another cigarette; then, wiping his mouth with a paper napkin, he added: "Which one of us really doesn't feel caged in? Me, you, our friends . . . It's a kind of asphyxiation in cages where there's a sky, but it's behind bars and bars that can't be broken because they're not there . . . those damned parallel lines . . . It's horrible! It's horrible! It isn't the tropics, the jungle, the swamps, the mosquitoes, the black and yellow fevers that kill; what makes us die, what makes us sick is the desperation of a life of wild animals pacing back and forth in their cages! Worse than hell, because in hell a person will burn, the same as he burns here, but it's the punishment of the unobtainable, perhaps, of the unreachable, of the thing found where the unending ends!"

Walker's bloodshot eyes wandered slowly about the small room they were in. His mother's picture in an embossed silver frame was shining in the background over half a dozen books.

"Those people were happy," he said slowly, "because . . ." he put his glass of whiskey down on the table and trembled slightly, shrugging his shoulders, while Tury completed his thought.

"You don't have to give it much thought to finish what you were saying if you follow Lester Mead's theory. They wouldn't let themselves be tempted by the devil, they rejected the world of riches, the fabulous profits, the economic domination that was offered to them from the summit of the mountain of hope. Those people had enough virtue and strength to reject it.

Those of our generation listened to the Tempter's voice and we accepted the pact, we fell into the cage . . ."

"Wealth piles up here in a fantastic way. The figures are astronomical. If a child began to count what has been earned from bananas, not counting peso by peso, but counting by thousands and thousands of gold pesos, he'd be an old man before he got to the final figure."

"You're exaggerating!"

"And the power, the power, Tury Duzin . . . I think that power is the diabolical part, and wealth gives a power that . . . Paris is well worth a mass."

Tury Duzin got up to leave, having found out what had happened at the Meads' party. Walker put on a Panama hat to go along with her. He was leaving too.

"Since I'm already late for the office," he said when he closed the door, "I'm going to look into that business of the girl who's looking for a father."

"She has one already, the warehouse man . . ."

"It's not that easy, the guy asks questions, he has scruples . . ."

"The way we all did once; but the Tempter appears, and who can resist him."

11

Papa-Wetnurse, that was the nickname of the man in charge of the warehouse, a dark Tabascan, not shiny dark, but ashen dark, with scaly skin and a huge family of blond children, was going about his business when Ernie Walker appeared with his lock of hair over his forehead, his Panama hat in his hand, stopped at the door, and with a strong English accent, a little drunk already, said:

> *Higgledy, piggledy,*
> *which of the two?*
> *Piggledy, poggledy,*
> *the daddy is you . . .*

The warehouse man, who did not find the jingle funny, was counting the ribs of one of the many people put in chains by his system of installment selling. The skeleton of the man opposite him was visible through his coarse cotton clothes, pants and shirt, a kerchief tied around his neck.

"So there you are; pay me what you're behind or bring me back the goods."

"You hadn't ought to treat me thataway, because we're like kin, since that girl of mine got mixed up with you; and what did we git, fer me, just the things fer me, nothing but a hoe, everything else was clothes that she thought you were giving her for free."

"Well, that was a big fat mistake; in these little installment sales I make I don't make no distinctions; and they all bring me what they're able to pay. When they got their mouths open and are yawning 'cause they're hungry, they come running to the warehouse man to butter him up; I'm some kind of flesh-and-blood saint then; when it's a question of paying, they come around with their buts . . . Just the other day one of them came by to holler at me, I forget his name, he said I'm the first one they're going to string up to a pole."

The customer left without saying a word; but Papa-Wetnurse thought that it was convenient to keep on sounding off in front of Walker . . .

"Hang me? Why not the superintendent of merchandise? I'm the one farthest down the ladder in this system of taking away everything the workers earn, why should I be the sucker when it's them; it's you people," he aimed his long gnarled finger at Walker, "it's you people who use those tricks to make a little more money. You people aren't ashamed, even though you manipulate millions, to do something that's nothing but robbery if you look at it right . . . They ain't going to hang me! Let them hang their mothers, the bastards, just the other night they came by here hollering that they were after my hide . . . God damn it . . . it's nice to see you here, Mr. Ernie, because you're on the list of us who's going to decorate the lamp posts like so many bunches of bananas until the buzzards take care of us!"

"Me? Why?"

"For being a whoremaster; you've got more women than a sultan; there are six harem masters who are going to go off to a better life; the sons of the good screw, starting with you. There's half-breed Cifuentes, Don Medardo, Mr. Abernathy, the twins, and that other fellow they call Minor, he's got the biggest urge of all of you."

The Tabascan was laughing in his face, rather at the blond lock on his forehead, smelling his breath, enjoying the delicious aroma of whiskey.

"Ho, ho, the Rippys are on the list too, and Señor Andrade or Andrades, I don't know which it is, and the great Don Juancho Monge . . . No matter how often they go to the capital on Holy Week to carry images in the procession, wearing their paper cones so God will forgive them for all their dirty tricks, virgins and married women, they may be forgiven there; but the thing's hot here; and the old warehouse man is a thermometer . . . sons of breeches . . . they all try to get out of paying . . . you saw the one who was here just now . . . he used to be one of the most regular . . . his payment every week . . . and that business of fertilizing accounts stinks to me, but it must smell worse to the one who has to do the fertilizing . . . Now they don't pay anymore, not even if you scare or pressure them with one reason or another . . ."

Outside of the shade of the warehouse, protective, like a tunnel of cool tar, the sun was burning now with its white fire of noon. A foreman came in with his hat in his hand, almost dragging it, his spurs could be heard for a long time in the silence of the warehouse, where the rats were going back and forth like pendulums with eyes.

"Fuck it, I couldn't make a deal with nobody; they're all on the warpath, even the Indians, and they've always been so peaceful."

The Tabascan and Ernie Walker were silent while the foreman continued speaking:

"But they don't do anything, people drowned in cane liquor don't move, all of them sad, the same dead flesh, like fetuses in a bottle of alcohol! Huh . . . drunkards aren't men, they're great big fetuses pickled in alcohol, and you, Mister, in whiskey."

Ernie Walker looked at him with annoyance; the Tabascan came over to see what it was all about.

"It's about Sarajobalda being beaten up. Huh . . . and they're not working . . . They've started already . . ."

The Tabascan, big and dark and fierce as he was, pouted like a child when he heard the foreman say that Sarajobalda had been beaten up.

"I'm for closing up the warehouse and hiding; it's good this is such a big place, because in order to find me they'll have to move a thousand of the crates in here."

Sarajobalda was, in fact, in the hospital, wrinkled like an old rag, with her head grayer, as if the great fright they had given her when they went into her house had turned her hair.

"I left Sarajobalda at the hospital," the foreman said, "poor woman, she was cut up like a piece of meat."

At first Sarajobalda ignored their threats, but when she was in the middle of the scuffle, when she saw her potions on the floor, the little frogs starting to crystallize like emeralds with feet, her unguents evaporated, her prayers scattered, her special decks of cards to tell fortunes with on the floor, a pair of bottles with mixtures that she had not buried . . .

The worst is that it began to get bloody, because with the shove they gave her when they went into the kitchen that was her laboratory, they caught her from behind and she fell to the floor. Only one of the lot of them, a one-eyed man, took pity on her and took her to the hospital. But since she was dropping annatto seeds on the way with every step she took, he decided to carry her. He threw her over his shoulder, risking the possibility that she would stain him with blood and they would put the blame on him. But the one-eyed man said, if you're going to do somebody a favor, you do it right or you don't do it at all, and with Sarajobalda on his shoulder like that, he reached the hospital.

A doctor with large, velvety eyes, moon-faced, with short arms, came to take care of the case. When he saw Sarajobalda he said:

"You old witch, you finally got what was coming to you . . ." Sarajobalda, her face bloodless now, death on her features, barely saw him in her agony. ". . . and the way she got it . . . some Negro must have given it to her . . . these old women take advantage of every chance they have to get back to their streetwalking . . . war is war, she must have said . . ."

Some young ladies with their hands in begonia-colored pink gloves took out instruments and more instruments from some glass cases.

The one-eyed man who had brought her sneaked out. He was not her husband, so why should he stay there; but one thing, yes, not without first having looked at Sarajobalda all over to see what she was like.

"You poor devil," the doctor was explaining, "you weren't capable of any other work except selling potions that turned people's heads. Now that I've got you, why don't I do the same thing? Why don't I call in the person who raped you and tell him here's your rotten hairy thing and let him be disillusioned once and for all?"

Sarajobalda, with her heart beating inside, could feel him shaving her down there with one of those things men use.

"And this should be seen," the doctor went on, "even if people say no, for the change in feelings that got hold of old John Pyle's wife and other dirty work . . ."

The doctor fell silent and went into action with some things that were like small spoons, while Sarajobalda bit her purple lips in pain, twisting, trembling from her waist to her head and from her waist to her feet; during all of this, one of the attendants had put in an apparatus down there that felt like a set of false teeth so that the doctor could scrape.

And the doctor was still speaking with a loud, jovial voice when, after the scraping, his gloves off now, the water spurted out of the faucets to wash away from the palms of his hands and from in between his fingers the soapsuds white as his teeth, which, as he took the towel to dry himself, he showed, laughing and repeating:

"War is war, right, you devilish old woman?"

It was hot, the fans were buzzing incessantly. In the operating room the acrid odor of permanganate, with which they had washed her before covering her with cotton gauze, was spreading out.

The foreman, when he left the warehouse, took it upon himself to spread the news everywhere about the attack on Sarajobalda. The most alarmed were Don Andradito and Juancho Monge. In spite of their gaudy pistols, their rifles, and their good marksmanship, in spite of their prayers, which they were pouring out now in front of the pictures of the saints framed in glass, which had previously hung forgotten in their houses, it was as if it were their very breathing, their breath, and neither of them felt safe. The workers on the farms where they served as foremen, overseers, or straw bosses saw them as they always had seen them; but the bosses felt that they were looking at them in a different way, they could not explain why, but it was as if they were feeling them over to find out where the mortal blow would be given when the time for settling accounts arrived.

Their wives could count on their being home all the time. It was dangerous to go out. From work back home to do some reading in magazines and old books, to look after their children, to replace the candles that burned in front of the saints and Jesuses night and day. A silent mass, a sea of shapes with hats, gigantic hands with dark, knotty fingers with granite nails, long metal blades that cut the air that the overseers, foremen, and straw bosses were breathing.

They unbuttoned their shirts in order to breathe. They had to open their arms wide, like doors, to get out of themselves, out of the frightened selves that were inside of them. A swimming race in the darkness of the night pearled with dew that was not dew but sweat, the sweat of Christ, distributed on a thousand peasant brows bent over the land until they could bear no more.

The overseers, foremen, and straw bosses slept with their ears everywhere. At the slightest sound they would leap from their beds, as naked as they went to bed, naked and roasted beside their naked wives, their naked children, and go out to search in the deep green-black darkness of the land to see whether some shape was moving, some shadow. Sometimes they would shoot point-blank at their own fear in the night. A howling dog, an evil gust of wind that had sneaked up and slammed a door, the flapping of the sleeping birds in the chicken houses.

"Machine guns have come! . . . Boys," that was the great news, "machine guns have come . . . and soldiers . . . they're camped there behind the station!"

The overseers, foremen, and straw bosses went out very early in the morning to see for themselves. Groups of workers were also walking around. The bosses no longer stayed home after work that day. They forgot about their reading, their children . . . What a bore! . . . And they also forgot about praying. The machine guns were the best prayer against all the threats that had been made against them by the fathers, brothers, relatives, or merely friends of the abused girls.

The Tabascan, just as if he were dragging chains, dragged his metal cot around the warehouse night after night in order to sleep in a different spot every night.

"Those machine guns," the warehouse man was saying, "I've seen them in my country . . . Now they're coming to protect them; but the soldiers are men of the people, they're Indians just like the workers, and I wouldn't trust them . . . Someday those machine guns are going to come, ha—they'll remember me, Papa-Wetnurse—to mow us down."

A string of prisoners was brought in, Bastiancito Cojubul and Juancho Lucero among them, all strong men, the kind that does not retreat before danger, the kind that says come here to death.

There was weeping on the faces of the women who reached the station among the soldiers, clinging to their men, when they piled them all into a crowded cattle car. Bastiancito looked out unemotionally, while Lucero put out his calloused and tanned hand and waved good-bye to his people.

On the following day, Lester Mead, under his broad-brimmed hat, his pipe in his mouth, his suitcase in his hand, left for the capital.

The train was way behind schedule. For two long hours and forty minutes he sat waiting on a bench at the station next to Leland, looking out at the same countryside. They did not speak. Leland felt so good sitting silently next to him. The street dogs passed in front of them, sniffing, looking at them, as bothersome as flies, sad four-footed skeletons. An occasional passenger, the kind who does not know which window to go to, would ask them if they knew when the train was due. They answered him and told him. The same countryside of light and heat. The same silence. The same flies. Through the groves that looked like squat clouds of green smoke, palms and coco-nut palms, the locomotive appeared, waddling like a duck. Whistles, bells. The good-bye.

Lester Mead went to see his lawyer, a former judge whose

conduct called for the disinterment of such buried words as integrity, intensity, industry, incorruptibility, and for all those *ins* a two-story INRI over his head.

The lawyer, wearing a suit that was now frayed at the elbows, a shirt that had been hospitalized several times, a bow tie that had been dissected like a butterfly a thousand times, hanging on by the button at the back of his collar, and shoes too large for his feet, explained to his client that as soon as he had received his telegram, he had gone to the military tribunal to find out what the charges were and there were none.

"None, and still they're holding them as prisoners!"

"Let me finish, Mr. Mead. The only thing they have are some documents, lots of documents; but nothing that justifies holding the prisoners."

"My men are prisoners, that's all I know; that means, my dear counselor, that there must be something."

"Naturally; but in my opinion, it's a matter of illegal procedure no matter how you look at it, unconstitutional, of course; an illegality aimed at avoiding a recurrence of these things." The lawyer took out a hand-rolled cigarette, homemade, lit it, and after the first puff, added, with the typical voice of a man who is ashamed to be poor, his honesty had led him to that point: "It seems to me that if the courts function in complete isolation from legal norms, if we follow the course of legality, all we will do will be to increase twofold the amount of official paper and still not obtain the release of the prisoners."

"Whatever you say, counselor."

"We have to find a subterfuge, a sub . . . ter . . . fuge . . ."

Lester Mead looked up the name of the man who was attorney for Tropical Banana, Inc., and went to see him before noon.

The office of the company attorney exhaled the comfort of

a transatlantic liner, the kind that makes the movements of bosses and employees in American offices so pleasant. The lawyer, dressed in an impeccable suit that had been tailored in New York, had Mead come in as soon as he saw him enter, despite the fact that there were several clients in the waiting room.

"Foreign clients come first," he told him, leaning his head over as he closed the door to his private office.

Mead sat down in a leather easy chair, and when the lawyer sat down behind his desk he said to him:

"I'm the neighbor of two farmers who were arrested yester-day, and I've come as a neighbor to see what I can do for them. I suppose that you're making the accusation in this case."

"I thank you for your visit, but I must inform you that we haven't accused anybody. The most we can do when things are going badly is to suggest to the press that they publish information for the benefit of the public, who, in our opinion are the best judges in these cases. You've already seen how many columns have been filled with news, commentary, and pictures of what we can't call an uprising, just a small distur-bance, but which the government, eager to maintain order, and in light of the alarming news in the press, has determined to cut short by sending troops to the place where it happened and arresting the ringleaders."

Mead got up, shook hands with the company attorney, who had a diamond stickpin in his English silk tie, and he left to pay a call at one of the newspapers with a large circulation to obtain a clarification of the facts even if he had to pay for it.

At the newspaper he walked among tall rolls of paper that were being unloaded from a truck. When a roll fell to the ground, everything shook, then they rolled them along slowly with levers past a good number of bystanders. He got to the editorial offices, glass and wood enclosures where the sound of the linotype machines could be heard like rain when a person is sleeping.

A pockmarked newspaperman with intelligent eyes, thick lips, and some missing teeth took care of him. Mead outlined his plan. The reporter took some notes for the subsequent clarification of the facts, but he stopped suddenly and said that he could take care of the matter better with the editor.

He then disappeared and returned a moment later to tell Mead to accompany him to the editor's office. When he entered, the American's green eyes met those of a very tall man, bulging at the waist, short-necked, graying and balding, and with brownish skin, the color of a flesh-eating parasite.

A typewriter could be heard in the background, closer to the somnambulist environment produced by the interminable rain of the linotypes. The editor, after greeting Mead, sat down to sign a letter with his gold pen, then he pressed an electric button with the tip of his finger that lay between the ivory of the button and the ivory of his nail, beautifully polished by the manicurist. He turned at once to attend to the visitor, whom he asked with Franciscan softness to explain the case.

After listening to Mead for five minutes, he replied to him without changing the tone of his soft and convincing voice, saying that one of the norms of his newspaper was not to publish retractions of news items except in cases where the law required it or when it was a case of facts that everybody knew about.

"Perhaps it could be done on the commercial side," Mead argued, reaching for the wallet he carried in his breast pocket.

"That's not the point. Money is of the least concern in this case."

"My money, you mean . . ."

"I'd better fill you in on how things stand. On the commercial side it would be going against the best interests of one of our best advertisers, Tropical Banana, Inc. Still, I can advise you to try other newspapers; there must be one of them willing to publish your clarification."

But there was not. With less unction, the editors of the other newspapers told him the same thing.

That night, at the American Club, Lester Mead ran into the editor of the first newspaper he had visited, who was playing billiards, a high priest of the three-cushion game, and a man of great generosity.

"Did you get what you were looking for?" he asked Lester Mead affably.

"No, I couldn't get anyone to publish the truth about what happened to the men who were arrested; but the worst part is that I was at the military tribunal where the trials are being held and the newspapers belonging to you people are a part of the case for the complainants. The version published in the papers, according to what the company attorney told me, is just what Tropical Banana said. The Company, which is an interested party in the matter, supplied the details and those details were put through the linotype machines and the presses and have appeared as the proof of facts that are completely false."

"I'm going to have a cognac . . ." the newspaperman said, still holding his cue, which he was waving like the bow of a violin. "Oh, bartender, let me have a cognac with a glass of ginger ale and ice on the side. What can I offer you?"

"A crème de menthe."

"How would you like it, Mr. Mead?"

"With chopped ice."

"Ah, yes, a Huguenot!" the bartender specified.

"You probably think that what we're doing is bad," the editor of the paper admitted. "When a person is an idealist . . ."

"I'm a practical man," Lester cut in, "and I don't think that what you or your colleagues are doing is bad. What seems bad to me is that your paper, and I can generalize, all the newspapers in the country, call themselves organs of public opinion, when the frank thing would be to call them what they are: organs for the interests of Tropical Banana, Inc."

"Bravo, bravo! Except that in that case we'd lose our customers, because if it were exposed to the public eye, we'd lose our usefulness."

"That's the worst part of it: using freedom to do away with freedom; that's what—some more than others"—Lester Mead sipped his crème de menthe on ice, green as his eyes—"they always do in these countries. They get freedom, and when they put it to use it's to do away with freedom!"

"Then you would advise some kind of control . . ."

"I don't know what to tell you; I'm an Anglo-Saxon, and freedom of the press makes me prefer to tolerate the building up of false public opinion the way you do in your newspapers that are not free but think they are and call themselves free rather than to accept the smallest attempt at censorship or control."

The newspaperman half-folded his eyes into the small pockets of his eyelids as he took the last sip of his cognac. As he raised his arm, his jacket opened, and sticking out of his belt in front, Lester saw a dark weapon.

Bastiancito Cojubul and Juan Lucero were charged with rebellion, disrespect for the authorities, and vagrancy, all of which the military prosecutor summed up in one word: dangerousness. Their heads were shaved and they were dressed in the classic zebra outfit.

"We do not have at our disposal," the prosecutor said to Mead, "the laboratories they have in the U. S. States [that was what he called the United States], where they can measure the degree of dangerousness of these types. Penal science in the U. S. States has made great progress, and it's the law, the whole law, and nothing but the law."

A clerk dressed in purplish-blue stopped at the door, and when he saw his superior with a visitor, he was about to turn away, but the prosecutor called him back:

"Don Casimiro, go see if you've got on your desk the trial material of those people involved in the uprising on the coast. These are things, my friend," addressing Lester, "that don't happen in the U. S. States. It makes me upset to send them off to split rocks, but if they're not punished the way the press has demanded, everybody would kick over the traces; if it hurts them to be poor, let them rise up in their hearts, but they shouldn't revolt, because that's why we have the law."

"The case has sixteen parts," explained the secretary, the same Don Casimiro who a moment before was about to come in and who was now coming toward the prosecutor's desk with a bundle of official papers.

"Are you a lawyer in the States?"

"No . . ." Lester Mead answered.

"Then you must be an official of Tropical Banana . . ."

"Not that either . . ."

"But on the side of the complainant of course."

"No, I've come now and I came before because two of the people you've accused here, Cojubul and Lucero, are partners of mine."

The military prosecutor did not doubt for a moment that this foreigner and partner of those dangerous types was, purely and simply, an anarchist, the kind who threw dynamite bombs at kings, spat into the chalice, and . . .

He cut off his thoughts. He settled himself comfortably on his broad buttocks of a man who has spent his life sitting down, until he was in just the right position to face the alleged anarchist.

There is a policeman dormant in every lawyer, but in this one there was a whole regiment.

"I should like to see your papers before I show you the documents."

He found them in order.

"Well," he went on to say after leafing through the passport and other documents, such as military discharge, tickets, "this type of crime does not call for bail; but since it is a question of owners of cultivated land, the matter is different, we can find a solution. Give me a petition to that effect. My secretary here can draw it up."

"A tamal nicely wrapped in green leaves . . ." Don Casimiro murmured in a jocular voice, but the allusion was direct.

"I've got plenty of green leaves . . ." Mead answered, as he caught it on the fly, and he added in a joking tone, "just as long as they build a good fire under the tamal so that it will cook fast."

"When do you plan to leave?"

"I'd like to leave tomorrow; but I can wait until everything has been arranged."

"A couple of days, all right? But you have to find some banana leaves, because they give the tamales such a good flavor."

"That's the way I see it; those company tamales are so delicious . . ."

"Sweet tamales, don't you think?"

Lester took from his wallet a bundle of green banknotes that were like leaves for the tamal, green leaves, banana leaves, and since Bastiancito Cojubul and Juan Lucero were owners of cultivated plots that were in production, and since their presence was needed to save the crops, and a few sinces more, Lester Mead returned in the company of his partners.

They left on a night train, the three of them riding the seats of a second-class coach, and they arrived the following morning. Veils of clouds, a fine blue-green in color, mauve, pink, pale yellow, hung over the narrow coastal sky at that great hour of dawn, when the heat is only annoying, before it makes its presence felt.

The stench of death obliged them to move the heavy cases in the warehouse after several days of commenting on the disappearance of Papa-Wetnurse the Tabascan. He'd run away. A Mexican to the end. He'd run away with the warehouse funds. That was why he had been collecting and collecting during the last few days. They could no longer tolerate his refrain. He was as hungry as a weaned calf for what they owed him. A person who could not pay ten, paid eight, and if not, he would pay five, and if not, three for what he owed at the warehouse, and he was even satisfied with two pesos. A kind of final plucking to reduce the debts, a lot of money flowed in, and to build up the funds. That was the pretext. What was certain was that he had set himself up and disappeared. And all of his children, a swarm of blond heads, here, there, everywhere, came out like peeping chicks. The superintendent of sales, a gringo with a cork leg, took charge of the keys and began an examination of the books and an inventory of the merchandise.

But he could only go in for a moment, because he came out of the warehouse as if his cork leg were falling apart as it echoed on the boards, sounding like a noisemaker, and when he was outside his stomach was still upset; he was on the verge of vomiting, a strong and pestilent smell of death filled his flat nostrils. He called for some workers to make a search and in one of the corners, on the creaky iron cot, under a pile of coffee bags and crates of powdered milk, lay the Tabascan with his chest pressing against his back. In his fear of being killed by the workers, night after night he would drag his cot from one place to another with the noise of chains, hiding in the darkness itself, and on one of those many occasions, the darkness of death had caught up with him, the final shade had fallen down on him, had crushed him in his bed. Women of all ages attended the burial, his artificial concubines, whom he did not even know well, for he had earned them a good deal of money through the children whose paternity he had assumed. An old clay jar with a layer of ashes on top and underneath a coat of charcoal to simulate a brazier concealed his treasure. The women passed by, one by one, with their blond children and received from the cork-legged gringo what was their proportionate share of Papa-Wetnurse's treasure.

12

"It's funny, but I don't get moved very much, sometimes not at all, by personal problems. It takes collective ones. When I hear that animals are starting to die because there's no water, I feel thirstier, but at the same time all I can drink is one glass of water. That remorse of having too much when someone else has nothing!"

"There really are people who can be moved by the collective struggle . . . maybe it's because they've already been through the little personal one and they know that every personal struggle is something reduced, circumscribed; while the other one, the bigger one, the one that doesn't come from frustrated convenience or wounded self-esteem, is the direct, blind, and broad reality of the great majority." They were riding in the sulky; Leland had on a green band that held her hair back like a crown and let the breeze play with her silky locks of greenish-gold, and he, a little tired from the business of the day, unshaven, was chewing tobacco.

"The Indians didn't live in these hot climates and that's why they were able to invent good, generous, and human gods, so much like the divinities of the isles of Greece. Everything seems to be on fire in this hot dampness, there's no room for any benevolent divinities. A great hidden and flameless fire . . ."

"I feel a nostalgia for those good gods too sometimes, Leland, and I'd like to get out of this tropical hell."

"We will leave, Lester, and then the salty taste of sweat that burns our faces as if we were weeping through every one of our pores will seem so far away. Yes, without noticing it, we weep when we sweat . . ."

The bridges extending out over the small rivers that flowed between flowering canyon walls brought them back to the reality of the two wheels of the buggy as it disappeared like a racing car through the banana groves, the geometric plantings that they soon left behind as they went ahead into the forest that was noisy with insects and the sound of the watch-ticking of the hot and stifling air.

They went a long way. Perhaps Leland did not notice the road. The sulky went down through a pass of sand and old bamboo into a small valley, until there was a flat stretch where a small lake bathed in moonlight shone in the center. Something at last, Leland said to herself, that reminds one that there is such a thing as cold, the poles, dampness, a winter's night beside the fireplace, a street carpeted with snow, skaters, and birds that peep and hop about.

The sulky went along the side of the shining flat spot, deep, dark silver, to a house with only the roof and four supports left. There they stopped. Lester used his small flashlight to light up the sound that under the round face of the light turned into a black reptile with red speckles.

Leland clutched her husband with both hands, jumping back, looking for protection.

"A varmint . . ." Lester said as he picked his wife up; Leland was shaking as if stricken by a deadly fever, and he put her on the seat of the sulky.

"Take the reins," he said to her after he had seated her and given her a few love pats so that the fright would pass, "take the reins and I'll lead the horse, we're going along this way so you can see what I wanted to show you."

Between the moon and the reflection of the moon dropping like sweat on the water, Leland could see a shadow that was repeated many times in the same shape. They were the shadows of horses. On hearing the sound of the sulky, one of the animals shook itself and whinnied. The whole air seemed to quiver with the sharp and prolonged whinny.

"A yearning mare will whinny when she smells a stallion."

"There seem to be a lot of them . . ."

"How many do you think there are all together?"

"There must be a hundred . . ."

"Fifty-seven, and all fifty-seven are pregnant." The sulky drew close to the mares and stopped. Mead went up to one of them, patted her on her pregnant belly, sonorous, like a strong chest, and he added, laughing in the light of the moon, "they have their strongboxes in banks and they keep their riches there, I have the bellies of these charming ladies, and we bought them as castoffs, no need to tell you that when they gave a price they didn't take into consideration the fact that they were pregnant."

The night of the horses, that was what Leland called it, making no distinction between stallion and mare. Then they went along through some long and reedy stretches of road opened up through the underbrush.

"This land belongs to the Fuetés," Lester explained, "the ones who were selling fruit cheaper than us when I started with the truck; and now they want to sell it and I intend to buy it, except that I'm waiting for the noose to get a little tighter. People like them who have inherited what they have don't take long in getting rid of it by living high and squandering. All of this was planted with coffee trees and they cut them down as if they were weeds in order to plant bananas."

"Fools!"

"Not entirely, you shouldn't say that, because bananas in those days were getting prices that they'll never get again. The worst part is that they thought that a fatted calf would live forever, and when the price of bananas went down, they were left without anything, because they'd spent everything on trips and fine clothes, instead of saving it or putting it into other crops. Now people say that all they have is snail stew for breakfast, lunch, and dinner . . . easy, boy!" He was leading the jet-black horse that was pulling the buggy. "But one thing certain, they were ready to go out and sell bananas cheaper than us in a truck the company gave them. When a rich man becomes poor, it's easy to make him take part in any kind of dirty deal."

In the vegetable mass of the green sky, which was the color of a geranium leaf in the part toward the sea, the stars, their glow made faint by the splendor of the moon, were shining like hazy little spots. The crash of the waves began to be heard clearly. The great round waves were barely visible as they came out of the surface like frothy carriage wheels and broke on the rocks.

And the days went by . . .

Leland's eyes fell closed on her that Sunday. It made her so tired and sleepy to watch the waters of the huge river flowing with the repose of a sheet that covers an enormous birth-giving woman after a painful delivery, a surface of muddy talcum into which her husband's fishhook disappeared like a question mark, while he patiently waited with his pipe in his mouth, changed into a statue, waiting for one of his favorite fish to bite: a redmouth, a sambuco, a juilín . . . Piles of stones among which the water sobbed, small clumps of brush that went halfway into the river, groups of flowers with their reflection standing out on the crystal surface, pink herons, others sugar-white, ducks, alligators with hypnotic, glassy looks, long-legged birds that fished in flight, others with spoon-shaped bills, and the motionless heat that was sweating its intense burning over the land.

Carl Rose's dogs, three big young hounds, announced his arrival. Leland turned her face to see their friend approaching step by step, having a hard time walking through the stones and brambles after he had left his car, a late-model coupé, on the road, if that high point could be called a road.

The Meads and their strange whims, more and more impossible with their eccentricities. Spending Sunday fishing instead of organizing a poker game or an evening of music. And besides, it wasn't any time to go wandering through the brush. The workers were showing their teeth in that icy laugh of theirs with which they used to take anything, even blows, but which now was a disguised urge to take a bite and carry off the chunk.

"What a wild notion, coming here, Leland! A sensible woman letting her husband expose himself and expose her to the workers' revenge . . ." He went over to Lester and shouted in his ear, "Did you hear me, did you hear? Aren't you afraid?"

Mead, without moving, answered like an automaton.

"No, because I've got my warships patrolling the seas!"

"You nut!" Carl Rose exclaimed, patting him on the shoulder, ". . . my warships patrolling the seas!"

The dogs, thinking that when Rose patted him he was indicating some prey for them, jumped on Mead, boisterously playful and panting, with their mouths open, their tongues hanging out, and their eyes happy at being free, because they spent most of their time chained up in their kennels.

"I run more risk with the company's dirty American dogs than with the workers!"

And saying that to annoy Carl Rose, he fell to the ground and played with the hounds as Leland took his fishing pole and adopted the same serious and rigid posture as her husband. In addition, he had dropped his pipe while he was playing with the dogs, and she picked it up and put it in her mouth and struck a caricature.

"Bravo! . . . Bravo, the perfect fisher girl!" Rose shouted, applauding Leland. Then he said, "Aren't you afraid, Queen-fisher, that the river will carry you off?"

"I'm not afraid," Leland answered, imitating her husband's voice, "because my diplomats are watching out for me!"

"Ordinary bodyguards," Lester Mead managed to say, crawling among the dogs with whom he was playing, huddled over, his hair mussed.

"I think this whole thing is going to end up badly. I intend to ask for my leave and not come back."

Mead, standing up now after having worn himself out without tiring the dogs, brushed himself off, smoothed his hair, and . . .

"Oh, no," Leland shouted to him, still holding the pole, "we've done enough fishing for this morning!"

Carl Rose helped her so that she would not get hooked and they went back, one after the other, accompanied by the dogs.

The car, with its cut-out open, roared through the tangled tropical jungle that was full of birds and flowers, determined not to let itself be ruled by man.

Why had Carl Rose dared to come and look for us at the riverbank if things were so bad, Mead wondered; and he was not long in finding out.

Over the roar of the motor came the voice of his friend who was driving:

"The logical person to intervene in the conflict with the private banana growers is you, since you head up the Cojubul-Lucero-Ayuc Gaitán group . . ." He fell silent, it was not clear whether to turn a corner or to wound Lester with his mocking smile.

"Well, just so you know, the firm of Cojubul-Lucero-Mead-Ayuc Gaitán is not selling a single bunch this time, and it's bought the land belonging to the Fuetés. We have other plans. Now that Tropbanana has obligations to fulfil, let it fulfil them, and leave me out of it."

"Let the corpse come to life or bury it!" Leland said, more emotional than her husband.

"They're rejecting a lot of fruit, and that isn't right; the same ones who see that nothing is rejected when the company needs it have decided now to reject everything systematically, without any appeal, without any recourse . . . Get away, you dirty things, the inspectors say now with the power of a God, to the rejected bunches. It isn't right! The people are weeping blood!"

The farmers with lands planted with bananas who had gathered together in town adopted the war cry of: "Tropbanana shall bow its head!"

Telephone and telegraph networks linked officers near and far. Undersea cables carried the news, but its vibration did not leave any trace on the metal protected by a waterproof coating from the attack of the corrosive seawater but not from the corrosion of false information.

Tropbanana shall bow its head, a war cry of commerce, legal in any marketplace. But the telephone, telegraph, and cable messages made patrol ships change course and aroused the zeal of diplomatic watchdogs.

Carl Rose stopped his car at a prudent distance. The atmosphere, almost unbreathable, was like soup with a scum of heat on top. The speakers finished their orations, voiceless with thirst, bathed in sweat, as if instead of speaking they had been boxing. Tropbanana shall bow its head!

The speakers were shouting themselves hoarse. There was more and more fruit being rejected. They were rejecting it for no reason: the bananas are too thin, they're broken, they're old, they're bruised, and they could not explain why a year ago almost to the day, the same thing had happened. It was a coincidence that the fruit today was identical with the fruit of a year ago. Large groups of banana growers repeated: Tropbanana shall bow its head.

Carl Rose headed his car toward a cold beer stand. They drank from the bottle, among flies that were buzzing around and customers with their shirts unbuttoned, some wearing only shorts and with their shirts hanging out or with the shirtails tied together in front. One of these touched his foaming glass to that of one of his companions.

"Well, there's got to be a reason . . ." and after drinking down half a glassful without wiping the foam from his mouth, ". . . the worst of it is that you can't say that Tropbanana is all bad, you've got to remember all the good things they do without anybody's forcing them to."

"Yes, but remember that they do it because it's good for them to keep the mule blindfolded. It's not out of goodness. It's all calculated. Haven't you ever noticed that whenever they do some shitty little thing they buy whole pages in the newspapers and there's no end to their patting themselves on the back."

"A little bit is a little bit. You don't have to expect everything."

"You're a fine one. It means that just because I do you a favor I can forget about what we've agreed to do in a contract. But the gringos are losing their support, and when they haven't got anyplace left to hang on to, there won't be many machetes left for them, because they're going to turn into tongues and come out with the truth."

Leland was no longer standing. The heat was too much. The houses, even with their thatched roofs, were burning inside and out everywhere in town. They decided to go back while the speakers were still shouting in the distance: Trop-banana shall bow its head. And that Sunday, starting with the fateful omen that not one single fish had tried the bait on his hook, had not seemed promising to Lester Mead. Not only had he not caught any fish, but Carl Rose had come along, and they were beginning to suspect him of being a spy from the office.

When he saw the Luceros, Bastiancito, and the three Ayuc Gaitáns at the house, Mead went ahead of Leland and Rose, who were talking about different makes of cars, and said to his partners in a low voice, enough for them to hear him, however:

"Say that you came to congratulate me on my birthday."

Carl Rose also took part in the pleasant cordiality with which they all gave Mead their best wishes. Cold beer and some whiskey and soda on ice were served. When Carl Rose left, the friends dropped their party faces. A message from the Chindent, which was buying all their fruit, had warned them to stop cutting because the railroad would refuse to carry it.

"I'll take care of that," Mead said, between the suffocation of the heat and the displeasure which made his mouth bitter, completing that Sunday for him, as if a glass of bile had been poured between his teeth along with that bitter message.

Early in the morning, Mead was sitting on the bench at the depot, waiting for the stationmaster. His pipe in his mouth, his hat on his head; hats became wet around the crown with the heat and they would become soft and slide down on top of bent ears.

"I'm not coming to see whether or not it can be done; it's a special service I'll pay for in hard cash, without any discount, and I can even pay double, because I want to get some balsa wood out; but I want to sign a guarantee that there'll be freight cars available when I need them."

"The price would be . . . Well, the price has probably gone up a lot . . ."

"I'm not asking what the price will be; you name it and I'll pay it."

"I'll still have to inquire . . ."

Mead nodded at the telephone next to the stationmaster and said to him a little threateningly:

"Go ahead and inquire, I'll wait."

"I have to warn you that there may not be anyone at the central station, it's still early for them up there."

"I'll wait in any case."

Mead went out onto the station platform. A woman passed by selling coffee and milk. She was carrying it in a tin can and Mead asked for a glass. It was more water than milk. But it was delicious. Others bought straight coffee and corn bread from the woman.

"It's worse than ever," the woman said to a lady who stopped to chat; "really, because that's the way it always happens; it'd be better . . . No they haven't let them go, they're still in jail in the capital . . . that's the way things go, but now you can't find enough of anything to eat. They say more soldiers are on their way and they're going to arrest more people. It must be God's will, people around here fighting all the time as if they'd been bitten by some evil animal."

The stationmaster told Mead that he had taken care of it and Mead gave him a check at once. But unfortunately, the stationmaster had forgotten to ask for how long Mead could count on transportation for his balsa wood; and while he was finding out by telephone, *runk, runk, runk* went the machine as the stationmaster cranked it, *runk, runk, runk,* Mead went back out to his bench on the station platform.

An Indian-Negro half-breed wearing a yellow shirt with blue stripes sat down near him. Greater than his bulk was the strong odor that surrounded him as he imposed his presence with his sweat glands.

"Times like these, Mister, it's better to get out; they're coming to cut throats, hammocks moving all night long, ricky, ricky, ricky, all night long, and people talking and talking; money don't get nowhere; kids hungry; women hungry; people hungry no good . . ."

"But soldiers, machine guns, bayonets are on the way . . ." Mead said to draw some words from the half-breed, who showed him friendly eyes.

"Yes, they's on the way . . ."

He did not say anything else. A yes that was the strongest evidence of the inability of men who had no arms and had to accept the imposition of working conditions that were unfair, not to say unjust.

"The contract will be for a year . . ." the stationmaster shouted to Mead through a window of his office, "as long as there's rolling stock available . . ."

"I can't accept that condition," Mead went over to say, "unless there's a clause . . ."

"Mr. Mead," the stationmaster interrupted him with a friendly and confidential voice, "the railroad won't approve any contracts with clauses that put them under an obligation. If the laws of the country don't apply to the railroad, contracts will be worth even less. Let's sign it the way it is and you go ahead and load your fruit . . . when they find out the trick, they'll say there isn't any rolling stock and we can take it from there."

And the days went by.

Juan Sóstenes Ayuc Gaitán parked the truck by one of the inns near the Colón theater . . . The gringo Mead was going to meet him there. He buttoned up his pants, because when he drove he always kept them unbuttoned, and he got out to take a walk and stretch his legs. Not very far away, about a block, he came to a church. From what he could tell, there were prayers for a feast day. He went in and when he saw all the people kneeling down, he doubled his knees on the icy floor too. He remembered to cross himself and the "Our Father"; but it had been so long since he had said the prayer and that "Our Father" part attracted his attention . . .

It had a meaning that earlier, when his daddy was alive, he had not given any importance to. Now that he no longer had anybody, how pleasant it was to say from time to time a few words that began with that "Our Father."

"Our Father who art in heaven . . ."

It's not childishness, he thought. He's up there. The daddy who art in heaven must be the daddy of all of them, when a person's father is dead, the ones who want to make themselves the only judge become the only warning voice, and that is a person's daddy. And this one who is in heaven can be addressed in the familiar form, without the formal address a person has to use with daddies on earth. It was nice for a man to be able to say: "Our Father who art in heaven . . ."

A great hoarse burst of music deafened him. His whole body was not in the middle of the church now, among the kneeling people, but in the midst of the music, in that great sound, that deep rumble that would grow soft for moments, then stronger. The music was like cloudbursts on the coast. It began suddenly with heavy blows, then it would let up for a while and remain as if sleeping, falling for a long time, until it grew stronger and stronger, just as if it were not a downpour of water but the lashing of whips. He was going out the front now and "he was still a-hearing." He wondered what it was being played on. A great marimba of flutes.

The organization had recently acquired the land of the Fuetés and with the land the yellow truck that Juan Sóstenes was driving now, and as he went down the steps of the church to the street he saw from a distance Mr. Mead's red truck by the door of the inn, parked behind his yellow truck.

He had arrived. He hastened his step. Mead had brought the other partners with him and they slept there that night.

Bastiancito Cojubul protested, because their situation was not so bad that they had to spend the night in the capital lying on cots in a cheap inn. But Lester Mead was unyielding in the matter of spending.

"A cot's just as good as a bed when a person's at war. Whoever among us forgets that he's in the front line against the Green Pope is a bad soldier. The Indians sleep on the ground, they don't spend what they earn in the commissaries, and they're the only ones who go home rich from that banana hell. We'll go home too! We'll go home with our railroad cars full of our fruit, singing!"

"On that day," Macario Ayuc Gaitán, Bushy, said, "it wouldn't be such a bad idea to lay a few of those people, you know who, on the trucks so that the train will run over them."

The next day they went to the customhouse. The two trucks and all the men.

"Socorrito Cruz . . ." the customhouse official who took care of one of the warehouses shouted.

"Here," said a feminine voice behind Lester and his men, and a chubby and rather short woman passed through them.

"Here, Socorrito Cruz and ze Niño de Goya . . ."

Behind her there appeared a Spaniard with a dull face under a Cordovan hat.

The customhouse employee asked:

"Are you the people with the banana meal mill?"

"Ze what . . . ?" asked the Niño de Goya.

"Whoever had the bright idea to import that piece of junk can go to hell!" Socorrito said. "We've come, you should know, for my wardrobe and the clothes that belong to this one here!"

"I didn't know that a machine like that existed!"

"The only thing that exists for me is the Virgin of Pilar!"

"And she grinds stars . . . Whenever she feels like it, she sets her eyes to grinding and the light falls down turned into gold . . ."

"That's back in Spain! Here in America they grind even what shouldn't be ground; because take away wheat, Niño de Goya, and nothin's worth grinding; mills is noble when it's wheat they grind, when you've got a miller girl like in the zarzuelas; and the rest of it is a lot of crap!"

"How many items are there?" the customhouse man asked the Spaniards.

"Only thirty-six bundles," the Niño de Goya answered. "Our modest belongings came in that . . ."

At the other door they took care of the people with the mill to grind banana meal. Lester and his men were dragging the heavy crates, the large boxes with the machinery, and, heaviest of all, the millstones. They were loading it all into the two trucks with straining wrists and with the help of levers and rollers.

Socorrito Cruz lifted her skirt to fix her garter. Lester Mead saw her flesh the color of guitar strings and there was no more peace for him, except that his desire was coupled with a certain annoyance at what she had said about the mill. Grinding her in revenge would be something. He made the pretext of a telephone call he had to make to New York as soon as he heard that the actors' baggage was being sent to the Hotel Paris, and he watched the trucks go off in convoy, one behind the other, loaded with the mill for making banana meal.

Socorrito Cruz lived alone in a room that opened both on

the inside and onto the street, the room next door was occupied by the Niño de Goya. Mead took another empty room not far from them.

The first day he observed the movements of the two dancers. Socorrito Cruz was aware of the looks she was receiving from the tall, blond gentleman, who soon was nodding at her. Well, if this isn't funny, she said to herself, men in Spain don't greet bulls or women, they make a pass at them, first with the cape, then with the banderillas, then with death.

And it was with death that Mead entered the room. She heard the heavy footsteps. The Niño de Goya made practically no noise at all when he walked. Socorrito slowly turned her head to give the impression that she was sure of herself and that she was a lady who did not let herself be surprised by an abusive stranger. And one who did not change her voice to put him out, because that would start a row, and a row would make people think that she was a loose woman.

"Did you get the wrong room?"

"No . . ."

Mead crushed her with that firm no, and with his menacing steps toward her.

"What do you want?" Socorrito asked, rather startled, going toward an old silk screen.

"I want what I see in front of me!"

"What you see in front of you you can want all you like, I don't say that it isn't desirable; but it has an owner, an owner."

Mead had taken her by the arms and she, like a lace doll, when she felt the large warm hands of that man, let him do it. A woman who had been courted by many men, she was disarmed by her surprise at the crushing procedures of that giant who was acting like a schoolboy. All of Mead's fingers were sunk into Socorrito's arms and his blood was throbbing. The desire for the woman, but also the urge to mill her.

"No . . ." she said, trying to repel him; but her negative was like a spur for the big man, soul of a mill, son of an evil bitch.

"Yes . . ." Mead answered, sinking ten yeses in the form of fingernails into the dark flesh that already belonged to him by the rights of the male, by being the stronger, the master of what he dominated.

"Now that you've come in here thinking that I was the thing you were looking for," Socorrito tried to disarm him, "I'll do it, but only if you've got enough money to pay me what I'm worth."

"Whatever you ask . . ." Mead hastened to answer with his mouth full of saliva, trembling, his green eyes firmly fastened on Socorrito Cruz's black coals.

"A thousand dollars . . ." she said with a nervous laugh.

Mead lowered his green eyes to look at her, not at a distant Dulcinea del Toboso, but at a poor creature who belonged to him. He let go of her arm, took out his checkbook, and wrote a check. Socorrito took the piece of paper in her hand, which felt asleep, rigid. Mead had written two thousand dollars.

"You made a mistake," she said, trying to swallow her saliva, her dark eyes on the eyes of Mead, "it says two thousand dollars."

Lester thanked her for noticing, tore up the check, and after writing and signing another one, he gave it to her. He had put down five thousand dollars. He would have paid more to grind her, to turn her into flour from a different sack, to pass her through his mill teeth like greenish banana pulp, through his muscles, through his urges of a man, through his fingers, through his knees, through his loins, under his stomach, under his chest, under his weight, under everything he could be for her, nothing, no one, a man who paid five thousand dollars.

And there was nothing. He strode out of the room. His spirit of revenge had overcome his mad desire for that woman.

Humiliation for humiliation, despising her at the moment she gave herself to him for money was worth what she had done to him at the customhouse when she had chanted "Whoever had the bright idea to import that piece of junk can go to hell!" . . .

"Hey! . . ." she went out without shoes, she had already taken them off, running after him, "here's your money . . ." and since she could not catch him, she shouted: "Well, I'm going to tear this piece of paper up, because ain't nobody makes a fool out of me . . ."

The Niño de Goya came running and tried to stop Socorrito from tearing up the check, but he could not, it was already in pieces.

"Zis may be money for him, but for me it's just confetti . . ."

13

Doña Roselia de Lucero's eyes were liquefied from so much weeping; she had been weeping night and day ever since Adelaido, hindered the way he was by his rheumatism, had suddenly recovered his motion and stood up in front of his son, Lino Lucero, to throw him out of the house after an argument during which, only because she intervened and knelt several times, the angry father had not turned the edge of the machete on him as he caught him with the flat.

Doña Roselia called on the Holy Trinity, Saint Caralampio, Saint Judas Thaddeus in the midst of the whirlwind that was rising up between father and son, and only when Lino disappeared, pale and trembling, among the hedges and the banana trees could she release the sobs that she had been swallowing so as not to infuriate her husband more, as he sat shattered now in his chair, bitter, sweating from every pore.

Doña Roselia thought to give him some water and she huddled next to him. Semírames was like a strange house without the children, because everything had happened at once: Juancho had been taken off under arrest as a rebel, even though this had not upset the old man. If it had been for theft, we would have had to bury ourselves. But for demanding justice, let him go to jail, there's a man for you. And that was what had happened. The grandparents were silent. They, the old folks, were silent. But the third generation is the one destined to speak for them all, for the living and for the buried.

Sarajobalda, whom Doña Roselia went to see in great haste, remained more silent than the earth they were standing on when her old friend told her when she entered that . . . she did not dare say it . . . that . . . she twisted the kerchief soaked with sweat and tears . . . that . . . she passed the kerchief over her forehead and her eyes . . . that . . .

Sarajobalda knew and helped her:

"That . . . he's mixed up with a woman from the sea . . ."

"Oh, what's to become of m'boy! And he has such a good wife, such a patient girl, and since there's no man who doesn't lose his head sometimes, I've always prayed to God that he wouldn't up and leave the mother of his children, because the poor little things. No one's ever seen that fish-woman."

"No one, old friend . . ."

"And he must see her just the way she is; remember that when he was little he used to walk in his sleep. With God's help you got him to stop that getting up when he was asleep with his eyes open, but still asleep . . . We were so afraid . . . Even though what we did was bad, leaving water under his bed so that when his feet hit the cold it would wake him up. I think the sleepwalking has been cured, but m'boy there, Sarajobalda, he's still asleep."

"And what do you hear from Juancho?"

"Mr. Mead went to the capital to see if he could get him out, because they took Bastiancito away too. Everything's getting so ugly, Sarajobalda, and being old when things like this catch up with you. But what hurts most is this thing with Lino. Them that are in jail have got a way out. But Lino. If you could talk about his case with the Shaman."

"Rito Perraj hasn't been seen around; but in Lino's case, he's my godson . . ."

"Yes, he's your godson, you did us that favor . . ."

"Lino's case is something like heresy . . ."

"What's that?"

"Heresy?"

Sarajobalda was silent and could not explain.

"Well, let's sit down, old friend, it doesn't matter what it is . . ."

"Yes, old friend, let's sit down, I've been so worried that I've kept you standing."

"So many things are bothering me; and what you were saying, because in the old days they used to burn heretics."

"The good part of it is that if that's the case he might be cured with a good rubdown with holy oil. Let it pass, Good Lord, that ugly possession of his!"

"And right soon, old friend, the poor boy is down to skin and bones."

"I'm going to keep on trying to find Rito Perraj. I was reading the seven grains of thick-shelled rice, I crushed them against the nine stones and I slept with the seven of them in my nose until they were moist in the morning and I sneezed them out before the rooster crowed into a fire made of blue spruce cones."

"Blue spruce, old friend?"

"Yes, that pine tree that grows up on the highest peaks and looks like a crawling snake. There were still a few small coals."

"But Rito Perraj."

"Yes, Rito Perraj can give some good advice. He's wise because he has the four sides of his body turned toward the four parts of the sky; his strong eyes can take a handful of what can't be seen; his mouth, his teeth, clean as words, like white clothes on the line; his fingers, long as cañadistula pods, and fingernails the color of burnt horn."

Lino Lucero was listening to all the noises of the woods. The deep throats of the gorges where the water meditates as it passes through, the heavy sand of the shadows, shadows that can be touched and are hard and cutting in each one of the minute black grains. Finally, after much listening and watching, without seeing anything in the darkness, he stayed there with the hollow of his hand stuck against the sweet and salty mouth, which felt like a small wound opened in the green flesh of the trunk of a water-banana tree.

Since threats were no longer worth anything, he would drown her, in spite of all her moaning of an animal made of banana flesh, of moss and shadow soaked in sweat and water.

She sank her teeth into him with all her force, as far as she could close her doglike jaws on the injured flesh; but when she tightened her sharp water-dog fangs and felt the hot liquid of Lino Lucero's blood on her gums of bluish flesh, she loosened her bite slowly and remained lying on the ground where the banana grove met the sea.

Lino Lucero lost no time. His nostrils were about to leave him without breath, not even keeping his mouth open was sufficient, bathed in sweat, his body quivering all over. He lost no time, he leaned over her, knees on the ground, with the hesitation of one who is about to kill. Now his hands were climbing up under something like garments of algae, along a single leg, she did not have two legs. And suddenly he was all swollen, with the hesitation of one who is about to break out of his skin, of one who cannot reach where he wants to go and leave behind what he is carrying and what is most his, that which it is painful to abandon, and a person will not abandon it, but he finally does abandon it and he expands and is enchained.

She leaped up and disappeared.

"Lino! You poor bastard! . . ." Macario Ayuc Gaitán woke him up with the tip of his foot; it was after four in the morning. "Look where you came to fall asleep . . . your wife's been out looking for you . . . you were tight . . . hugging the trunk of a banana tree . . . you're worse off if you thought it was a woman . . . because that's what happened to me . . ."

Lino Lucero, in the hot fogginess of dawn, was squatting, huddled like a worm next to Macario Ayuc Gaitán, Bushy; he was the only one who could understand him. And he explained.

"Because it happened to me, didn't I tell you about it; except that I kept my five senses and my thoughts; an ugly heat got into my soul and I went out for a walk; I came along this way; a half-moon and heat; heat from the ground, heat from the air, heat from everything that gives off heat; no time passed and lots of time passed; I was wandering when I saw two green arms come out from one of the banana trees, fleshy, cool, with hands of dead women who died virgins and who you see later on in dreams with you . . . I got mad as the devil and I ran at it with my machete and cut it."

"That was dumb!" Lino said and hunched over as if it were his flesh which was receiving the slicing blows.

"Yes, Lino; that was dumb; the trunk split and it came toward me; but it wasn't a plant, it was a woman with only one leg, I could hear through my ears while the leaves were talking to me, a cool and juicy splotch of green stem and moon covered my face . . . I'm the only one who knows how nice it is . . . I rolled on the ground with that female . . . Too bad, it's too bad now that when I come out I never run into her again . . ."

They were silent. The hot, salty, lustful sea, and the heavy heat that squeezed one just before the sun came out.

"And to see her . . . Just because I figured that the same

thing had happened to you, to you, that's why I told you about what happened to me. Next to you there is the trunk of the banana tree you were embracing."

"I don't know or will I ever know, Macario, what brought me here. What time did I leave home? . . . What I do know is that the woman I was holding last night doesn't come from banana trees but from the sea; I saw her jump into the foam on the shore and disappear, over there, look, where it's half-dark . . . I was afraid to follow her . . ."

"Thank God, man, if you had they would have found you all drowned there, or you'd have turned right into a shark, an alligator, or a fish. Have you thought about what Rito Perraj says, Lino?"

Lino was trembling, in a fever.

"If up here on land," Bushy Macario continued explaining, "there's everything we can see, out there under the water, right there, three hundred feet away from us, there are monsters with the heads of people and the eyes of a hawk, they stick to the rocks like glass trees, but there's a drivel of dreams that moves through their branches the same as their bodies . . . there are crabs so fierce that when a cow falls into the sea alive they eat it up in seconds, not a bone, not a single hair, not even a little piece of hide is left, they eat everything, and thousands of little gold-colored fish come and in a few minutes they clean away the spots of blood . . . and there are sea stars that walk and talk . . ."

"Leave me alone, here I am shaking with fright and you tell me all that stuff!"

"Now what you ought to do to make the possession go away is to feel like a calf had licked you all over and lay a silver coin on your forehead at noon, when there's the most sun; the coolness of the metal will get into your heart and take away the tired feeling that the woman left there."

"Lino Lucero, you cannot take me to your house because in your house they do not eat what I eat!"

"And what do you eat, tell me."

"Hair from fish from the bottom of the sea . . ."

Lino fell on top of her, avid to kiss her, but she averted her mouth and only showed her white teeth, which gleamed in the starry and warm night. Her eyes of a sea goat, her half-sunken forehead, her black, straight braids, sweaty with saltwater and the sweat of a burning woman.

"Lino Lucero, you cannot take me to your house because in your house they do not sleep the way I sleep."

"And how do you sleep?"

"In deep sheets of water and on a mattress of foam."

He reached her mouth with his mouth. Something like a moan could be heard as under the weight of his lips she twisted her neck and rested her head on banana-grove earth, damp and spongy, and on the sand which had embers of sun in its grainy and slightly metallic coldness.

"Lino Lucero, you cannot take me to your house because in your house they do not drink what I drink . . . water from the bottom of the sea."

Like the body of a woman sleek with soap, she slid out of Lino's embrace and began to run, taking the shape of a water-spout; she swirled her tail, swift as the breeze, as he chased her and could not catch her. Finally he caught her. She let herself be caught. He caught her, he clutched her against his chest, he joined her to his flesh, he kissed her hard. She laughed, smothered, innocent, with her eyes glowing from the heat.

Bushy had not neglected Lino and he went off to look for him, while some companions who had gone fishing helped the experts throw the nets, not into the sea, but into the mouth of the immense river, into the parts where the water rushed through narrow channels of unsettled mud, sandbars, what were almost trees; frogs, rocks, and a world in disintegration.

Lino Lucero, brought by Macario Ayuc Gaitán, joined the group of fishermen and the voices of those shouting from the banks:

"I'm going to catch me a good peche! . . ."

"Me a guapete! . . ."

"I'll be satisfied with a redmouth! . . ."

Bushy handed Lino the guitar.

"A guitar," he said in his ear, "has the shape of that woman, except that it has its tail on top."

And Lino Lucero, before he played, tuned it, caressed it; ran the tips of his fingers over the trembling of the strings, which made him tremble too.

> *There was once a poor dove of clay,*
> *who fell apart in the dark! . . .*
> *Where, oh where did you go, O Dove,*
> *that I never saw you again? . . .*
> *A downpour of tears*
> *that clung to the willows;*
> *I've wept for you over and over so much,*
> *that here turned into a willow am I . . .*

The fishermen, on shore now, waited in the light of the bonfires they had made to frighten away the wildcats, who could be heard roaming in the underbrush when the roar of the sea would diminish; and the members of the fishing party began to play cards and started drinking rum from the bottle.

Lino Lucero went away again after he had sung, like a sleepwalker in the drowsiness of the midnight heat, cushioned on a deep dream; his body the color of lemon mud was covered with thick drops of sweat-spittle.

His hand pulled her by the hair and he drew her again toward where he had lain down on the beach, watching the waves break, furious, roaring. It was a banana trunk and the flesh of a woman and he fell across her and kissed her endlessly, no words now, no ears, no eyes, just sex and soul now.

Nothing could be heard, the sea could be heard, but except for the sea, nothing but his panting, which had turned him into a beast and had turned her into a human being made of living waters, bejeweled with stars and deep as the silence that accompanied the entry of the river.

"Get the hell out of here!" Lino Lucero protested.

"No, old man, I won't let you alone, you might get drownded," the hairy Ayuc Gaitán told him, returning from where the bonfires of the camp were twinkling. "A drink'll do you good, maybe it'll go away . . ."

"Let me have it . . ."

And Lino tipped up the bottle until Macario took it away from him; almost half a bottle of rum had gone down his gullet without his drawing a breath.

It was getting time to haul in the nets, and then the argument began. There were those who wanted to throw some barbasco into the water so that the poison of the plant would kill more fish and they could go home with a good catch.

Lino Lucero went berserk. No man had ever acted like that when he heard that they were going to throw barbasco into the water. He was more than berserk. Some frightened person shouted at him:

"Hey, you, you'd think there was a member of your family in the water!"

Lucero jumped up and waved the machete he carried in his belt, someone else disarmed him with a blow on the hand; several people jumped to pick up the machete.

"No, this is too much," someone exclaimed, "this kid has four drinks and now he wants to slice everybody up! . . . A fuck-up, a real fuck-up; if a person doesn't know how to drink he should lay off . . . drinking is for men . . . you shouldn't never drink, Lino! . . ."

But Lino the madman, when the attack had passed, was limp as a rag. When they took away his machete, he humbled himself, knelt down, begged them by all they loved most dear not to throw any barbasco into the water.

Macario, watching the whole uproar, cleared things up.

"What's going on, fellows, is that our friend here, and I know what I'm saying and why I'm saying it, is in love with a fish-woman . . ."

They all fell silent, with that somber silence of the questions and answers that were going on in their heads. The one that Lino had been about to decapitate went over and embraced him.

"I'm sorry, Lucero, but I didn't know that you were that drunk and believed in those things!"

"Well, we won't throw in any barbasco. Who wants to play a game of videma? Call in the boats . . ."

Lino did not want to play, but he played and he began to win, win, win. There was no card he called for that did not fit his hand at once. He would sing it out and there it would fall.

One of his companions patted him on the back and said:

"Let me touch you, maybe the clam-woman will bring me some luck and something will come my way."

"Save some to make it come my way too!"

"Give him the guitar," another one suggested, "it's better to have him sing than to pluck us bare. With all that luck, Lino, that fish-woman must have given you luck at cards!"

The fish that came out in the nets looked drunk as they began to strangle on dry land. Their round, glassy eyes. The light of the blue-gold dawn began to show between the infinite green of the sea and the green shadows of the banana groves.

Lino sang in his alcoholic voice:

Little fish-woman of the seas,
come see what's happened to me
from all the trouble you made;
but I'm worse off still inside!
Good-bye Guatemala, I say,
as off to marry I go,
in Puerto de Amapola,
to the Mermaid from the sea!

Bushy Macario, as soon as Lester Mead came back from the capital with Bastiancito and Juancho, the prisoners, visited him with a great air of mystery to tell him with every scaly detail about the love between Lino and the woman of the sea. Doña Roselia went to the Meads' later, not only to thank him for the favor of having got Juancho released, but to tell him what had happened to Lino, who, God's will be done, Lord . . .

Lester moved his large green eyes in those white corneas of his without giving an opinion, without reacting, which was very strange in him. He gave no opinion and he did not carry the matter further. Not even shaking him up, giving him some advice, doing something so that Lino would come out of his wanderings. Nothing. He had assigned the Lino affair to a dead world.

"What did they expect him to say . . . quiet the way he was," they said, "because he's a son of the sea woman himself and he came out of the sea laughing here on the coast!"

"You're right, because his green eyes are like a mermaid's and his white skin is like that of a fish."

"He's a real son of a fish, he is, and that's why he doesn't say anything!"

Leland told him that she had chatted with Lino's wife. She was weeping like an ocean, but she was adjusted to it all.

"It's better if she adjusts to it all . . ." Lester answered.

"Oh she isn't pleased to have a fish as a rival . . ."

"As far as she's concerned it would have been the same if he'd been cheating with a Spanish dancer . . ." Mead said as if he were letting out the tail end of something that he could no longer keep secret.

"In any case, you're the one to speak to him, man to man; he can't go on like that . . . Talk to him, tell him to change his ways . . . he's being so stupid."

Mead did not answer. Socorrito Cruz was the name of his mermaid with guitar-string flesh, with fingers that smelled of sandalwood and stopped him from speaking.

"Speak up," his wife proposed after a long pause; "take Lino's part, tell them to leave him alone, to let him be, he's got to get over this bad spell. It seems that old Lucero threw him out of the house and tried to cut him up with his machete . . . The old fool! . . . Most fathers, when they scold their children, turn into regular savages; but nobody can understand except those of us who haven't had any children."

Days later, after dinner, the theme came up again with Leland's question as to whether mermaids really existed.

"It wouldn't surprise me at all," Mrs. O'Brien offered, suffocating in the heat which was like a very hot spice with the meal and made her perspire.

"Any woman who doesn't belong to a man is his beautiful mermaid!" Mr. O'Brien declared, making an effort to do away, once and for all, with the sweat that was abundantly bathing his face as he used his handkerchief like a sponge to pat his cheeks, his nose, his chin, his brow, behind his ears, even behind his neck.

"That's it . . . that's it! . . ." Lester said.

"That's a bore!" Mrs. O'Brien added.

"But getting back to the subject," Leland continued, "do you or don't you believe in mermaids?"

"When I was young and in college, I had to memorize something about mermaids. I know it by heart."

"Recite it for us!" Mead exclaimed.

"No, for heaven's sake," Mrs. O'Brien said quickly, "I practically know it by heart too; he recites it to me every time we're alone, waiting for a train, a streetcar, when he shaves, when he's tired of reading."

"But we haven't heard it and we want to. You're being selfish . . ."

"I had heard tell of mermaids . . ."

"There goes the lesson! I'm going to take a little walk while my dear husband . . ." Mrs. O'Brien exclaimed, getting up from the table with a demitasse of coffee, and she disappeared into the hot shadows, hot and dark, as if they were coffee too.

"I had heard tell of mermaids, but I had not believed that they existed. The heat on that tropical night at sea in the Caribbean was very strong. Nothing disturbed me when I first went to sleep. The ship was sailing with a favorable wind and on a friendly sea, rocking back and forth like a child's cradle. The stars were following it from afar. There were so many that the studded sky was like a golden breeze. Above that deep shadow, like a fish made of crumbling diamonds, there appeared and disappeared a light that left the vision of a sparkle in the atmosphere. I leaped up. Could it be a mermaid? . . . But I had jumped in my sleep, because years later I had come to realize that I had been in danger of falling into the sea. I could not see anything else. Had it been a mermaid? I have my reasons for believing that it was. Ever since that night I can feel my body wrapped in an opal, cold, and warming light, a feeling that menthol was being rubbed all over my body, and I can feel that I am comforted and I can feel, how can I describe it, more seaworthy . . . Those who do not know what has happened to me should not scoff. Nor do I ask their pity. Let them listen and rub my limbs with their common hands to see if the spell shall leave me and begin in them so that they will share a little of the light of that mermaid. But, I ask myself and I ask you, do you think that I really saw her? Although I cannot remember her body, her face, or the color of her eyes, I can say yes. We wake from many dreams startled by a knowledge that we cannot explain, the way in which we came by it, that of a person whose physical being, like that of a phantom, is completely beyond us. And then, the perfume of that night, the tepid air, the waltzing sea, the shadow of hammocks that had been woven with eyelashes . . . everything comes together so that I can feel in me, whether sexual and only sexual, the memory of that fugitive submarine light that for one minute, on my body, held me on the brink of the abyss, which the immensity consumed."

Leland made a motion to applaud, but Lester Mead interrupted to say:

"Wait, he hasn't finished. Go on, it's interesting, and you've got a good memory."

"The ants eat mermaids that get lost in the tropics, along the green paths of the coast that are covered with underbrush and banana trees, travelers say, and sometimes one of these mermaids, washed up by the waves of the sea, will be carrying millions of ants, who, after they have bitten into the flesh of the mermaid's corpse, will return to shore, leaving luminous wakes in the agitated waters . . ."

Tired of walking on the ties, one after the other, one after the other, as the railroad tracks made sharp turns like the tail of a mermaid, Lino Lucero would sit down and talk to the track crews or simply nod his head. He would drop down onto his legs as if he had been broken off at the waist, his hat thrown back, and as he scratched on the ground as if it were part of him and were eating him, he could be heard speaking. He would like to work as a track man, but during the night. It was rough working in the sun. The track men, Negroes, opened their eyes and their white teeth and laughed at the sleep-

walker's notions. The sun was not so bad for working. It would
sting, but it was nice working in the light of the sun. The smoke
from the gravel train made Lino sneeze. It was not mucus but
soot that came out of his nostrils. From smelling so much black
smoke as the train crapped into the air, and even if he was not
a track hand, he was like them. Those men who carried earth
and locomotive smoke inside themselves, oil and clouds of
sand that gave them the scaly and exhausted voices of old men.

They were a bunch of skins, shiny from sweat and sun,
muscles that moved with the slightest motion, as if underneath their skin there was some anatomical puppet swimming
about. Some of them were smoking cigars or cigarettes, others
tipped up bottles of cane liquor in great swigs. Lino Lucero
was among them, among the crowd of track workers in whose
hands the huge hammers were toys, the ties toothpicks, and
the rails guava jelly.

They hovered around the sleepwalker and they asked him
to sing the "Who-Who" song. After he strummed his guitar,
Lucero nodded at them and they all began: who-who, who-
who, who-who, who-who . . .

Lino signaled them to lower their voices, without stopping
their who-who, who-who, who-who . . .

> *Who lives, who dies, who*
> *sings beside the donkey*
> *loud . . . The trackman! . . .*

The voice of the chorus: who-who, who-who . . .

> *Two rails, two rails, two*
> *rails on my guitar . . .*

The chorus: who-who, who-who, who-who . . .

> *Who sings, who eats, who*
> *sleeps along the fire*
> *line . . . The trackman! . . .*

The chorus: who-who, who-who, who-who . . .

> *Six days, six days, six*
> *days a week . . .*

Who-who, who-who, who-who . . .

> *Who knows, who knows, who*
> *knows, trackman, who knows*
> *whether you're alive or dead . . .*

Who-who, who-who, who-who . . .

> *One year, two years, ten*
> *years, life is done . . .*

Who-who, who-who, who-who . . .

The story that they sang was endless and sometimes it would grow vulgar. Others would join in merrily:

> *Who sucks, who fucks, who*
> *shits along the line*
> *of the train . . . The trackman! . . .*
> *Who pays, who pays, whose*
> *shit makes us stick to the line*
> *of the train . . . The gringo! . . .*

And like that until the sun went down, smoking, drinking, and the who-who, who-who, who-who . . . The motionless heat of the beginning of night made them drowsy. The locusts, the frogs, and the drowsiness of sleep seemed to follow the who-who. Lino went off silently, wildly, in search he could have said of that divine enchantress who was made of green flesh light, the vegetable green of the sea, and when she came out onto land she would change into a banana tree. But he could not find her anymore. His legs were swaying like hammocks, he was so drunk. Bushy Gaitán looked after him. He kept telling him the same thing: You've got your kids, you've got your wife, you've got your goods and you haven't got what you ought to have! . . . Lino would only shake his head from side to side, his eyes staring and his lower lip fallen.

At other times Lino would spend the night drunk among the clearing crews, singing to them:

> *Usebia, when I die,*
> *eating a banana,*
> *don't bury me in town,*
> *eating a banana,*
> *bury me in a pasture,*
> *eating a banana,*
> *where the cattle*
> *can tread on what's*
> *left of me . . .*
> *the tip, the tip,*
> *the tip of the banana! . . .*
> *Make me a tombstone*
> *of a red banana,*
> *with a sign that says:*
> *Here I buried a poor devil,*
> *banana and all,*
> *banana and all,*
> *banana and all . . .*

"For the love of God, man," Juancho Lucero, his brother, would scold him. "There's no hope at all for you. You'd be better off dead. You're the death of us all. Ma's blind from crying so much. If you'd only go talk to your godmother, Sarajobalda, maybe she could cure you. You're getting worse every day. A cane-liquor mermaid's what you've got! A cane-liquor mermaid in the shape of a bottle!"

The difficulty of consulting Rito Perraj, the Shaman, to whom he had been sent by his godmother, was to guess which one a person was consulting, whether Rito Am Perraj, Rito Was Perraj, or Rito Will Be Perraj. To get on his good side it was quite essential to say to him without hesitation and with no mistake: Rito Am Perraj if he was Rito Am, the father, Rito Was Perraj if he was the grandfather, and Rito Will Be Perraj if he was the grandson.

And he never intended to consult him; but nevers do have a way of arriving. He had had an attack of malaria. A snake malaria that had kept him frozen, his hands congealed, his hair like that of a dead man, his teeth with the taste of bull bile, a stiffness in his joints. If it were not for the illness, he would not have given in. Bones and eyes set in the slightly freckled face of a stained cloth that had been left out in bad weather, from sleeping in the dampness by the banana tree, which for him was the warmth of the body of the woman who was his confused love. Sometimes he would show Bushy or his brother Juancho what was inside the banana trunk, and in those vegetable tubes the small interstices were like those of the tail of his mermaid. They were like small honeycombs that wept acid water. What also made him ride off to where the Shaman was was the pity he felt for himself when he felt his muscles and admitted to himself that the only work he was capable of doing now was that of a sprayer on the plantations, like the kind of man who comes from the city with his face full of family trouble. Not for me, he told himself; if you're going to end up as a sprayer, you'd be better off begging outside a church! Working, yes, but as a clearer or a track man! Of course, but at . . . at . . . no need even to think about that: Carla, as an Italian said was the name of his mermaid, always kept him swimming in sperm! Lino Lucero kicked his legs and almost wept; Lino Lucero, now only good for spraying. He would rather have not had the occasional litanies of pity from the Negroes on the gravel train. He went to look for the Shaman, like a banana leaf being carried off by thousands of army ants; blue acid on his long, tangled hair, because now he was passing by the sprayers. Carla is-a no *donna*, is-a no mermaid!, the blue-eyed Italian would tell him, a man who had accepted being sold into slavery to Tropbanana in exchange for the few *fiaschi* of Chianti wine he would pick up at the commissary every day. My-a Carla, she's-a no *donna*, no mermaid, she's-a grape from-a Italy, from-a my-a Italy!

The Shaman shut one eye when Lino Lucero appeared at the door with his sleepwalker's face. The great night was beginning, great, and a great moon was rising on the horizon yonder. One of those hot moons, coastal moons which when they first rise spread out the slight tremor of a cold bath. And he had that great luck, just like the night, of being correct and calling him:

"Rito Was Perraj . . ."

The hand the grandfather was holding on the other door to shut it stopped moving. He leaned his white head out. In the shadow Rito Am and Rito Will Be had faded away, and Lino added intuitively:

"Good evening also to Rito Am and Rito Will Be Perraj . . ."

Three sets of teeth made of yellow corn glowed in the semidarkness; but from one set of teeth there came a soft word of welcome, one that came over the ages in the voice of the grandfather, who greeted him and bade him enter.

The hard touch of an old man's hands, bones already surrounded by the emptiness of death, led him into the anguished pitch-wick light that was burning in the small kitchen that was off the room where they were, where the Shaman had him lie down on a long mat.

He was not there, Lino Lucero, even though his known terms of existence had come into his thought, calling himself by his name: Lino Lucero de León, son of Adelaido Lucero and Roselia de León de Lucero, brother of Juancho Lucero and brother of the Newt, an intimate friend of Bushy Gaitán, a member of the cooperative . . .

Nothing concrete. The restfulness of the Shaman's breathing turned him into an abstract mass, as before baptism, as silently the flesh of his mother and father, silently in an unobtainable desire of the two, together, as they loved together in that time when time did not exist for him.

When had time begun to exist for him?

On April sixth . . . in nineteen . . . nineteen . . . back to the forgotten day of his birth.

The Shaman dissolved him, picked him up with the tips of his fingers, as the trembling of his breathing blended with the small moans of a little old man and took him to the cave of bats, of bats made desperate by lice and the heat, unable to fly because they were asleep. Those wind bats who keep the wind rolled up in cobwebs in the web of their wings, and which they release once every hundred years, if the Shaman does not let it be released before. The hungry lice grew fat-bellied with blood as he passed through there, buzzing like a malaria mosquito, and from their eyes there emerged circles of sliced onion, circles and circles and circles, as if a stone had been thrown into each eye. His forehead was like a toasted leather headband. The hand of the Medicine Man drew the sticky sweat off his hair so that it would not fall into his senses, which he had daubed with a compost made of mint leaves.

He only knew that he had been asleep when he awoke in his house, not the house of his wife, but the house of his parents, and he heard, like an outpouring of clean water, the voice of his mother who was telling his wife about the purge the Shaman had told them to give him when he woke up.

With the simple miracle of the medlar seed he grew fat and regained his strength in two or three weeks. The seed was opened, the dream of the black shell that covers the pit was broken, and when the pit was ground, only a touch of it was needed to fight off weakness, and a touch more and a man would stay virile.

Old Lucero repeated from his rheumatic immobility:

"It was good I threw my son out, because that was why he wanted to come back; now he's even more my son . . ."

"Hush, Adelaido, stop saying unpleasant things . . ."

Lester Mead's steps surprised them. It had been a long time since he had put in an appearance. Doña Roselia went out to receive him. He came in and he embraced the old man and Lino. Then they sat down in a circle around the rheumatic's chair, facing the panorama that dominated the terrace of the house at Semírames. Lino, according to what Mead said, should go live in the capital.

"But how will he be able to live there, where everything costs so much . . ." Doña Roselia managed to say after a moment of silence.

"He'll have some funds for that."

"And what will he work at?" Lucero ventured, thoughtfully, because what Lester Mead said was almost always law. He didn't give us any help in that mermaid business, and now he comes here wanting to send him away.

"He'll work at whatever he wants to. But he mustn't leave his guitar behind, and up there he'll have to learn to read music."

Old Lucero, who was getting ready to say that he would not let him go, felt relieved. A father's vanity is the strongest of vanities. Doña Roselia was silent, deep, she almost had to close her eyes so as not to see the idea: the mermaid was hidden in Lino's guitar, and this fine gentleman wants him to go on with his guitar.

"The first thing would be for Doña Leland to teach him something about music here," Doña Roselia said in a slow voice. "Adelaido is sick, and a person dies more quickly when there are no sons around. Because without sons, the thing that is most a part of a person, a person begins to feel as if he had no place in life, and then he's ready to call on death. Sons are a person's warmth, Mr. Mead . . ."

"Yes, Leland can start teaching him the notes; but the best thing is for him to leave."

14

Adelaido Lucero, you're going to die! You're already on your way! You don't have any more accounts pending! Every son with his own sons! Roselia is old, what can you do about it, old! The old man was toasted by his coastal rheumatism, hot rheumatism, his skin was like a saddlebag!

He would weep like a child when they left him alone. He scratched and he scratched and he scratched. He scratched his head for a long time. Finally he looked to see if they were home. He would straighten up his neck at times with a great deal of effort. Who was there? Roselia. Well, Roselia, then . . . He would have prefered it to have been one of his sons. There was always one close by in case something happened. The most loving was the smallest, Rosalío Cándido, the one they still called the Newt. But that night in some buildings bedecked with paper streamers and pretty leaves, under bulbs that gave off a strong white light, they were celebrating the opening of the banana meal factory.

The hands of Lester Mead and the hands of Leland, and the hands of all of them dug in and out of the receptacles that began to fill up with the precious powder as the pulleys turned and vibrated and the belts, like endless snakes, brought the magic of movement to the machines, all run by a one-and-a-half horsepower engine.

"I'm going to die, Roselia, Adelaido Lucero is going to die without knowing the truth! Everything you tell me about the organization the boys have with crazy Cosi [for old Lucero that Lester Mead business was a trick] shows that there's more than meets the eye. I'm not convinced, I know the whole works, how they say they've been able to do everything they've done with only small payments. Even setting up that mill. There's more than meets the eye."

"What about the balsa wood and the pregnant mares?"

"No, Roselia, that man must have a pact with the devil. Do you remember when we first met him? He was selling . . . what was he selling? . . . nothing . . . it was mostly his loud laugh that punctured people's ears from far away . . . Ya-ha, ha, ha . . . And he would fall asleep, ha, ha . . . wherever night found him, and he would eat, no; it probably would have made me laugh too, he wouldn't eat."

A marimba brought from town was playing at the mill. And now some couples were dancing on an earthen pavement with pine needles scattered over it. Mead took Leland in his arms. A waltz. She was breathing in the happiness of being loved by that man. Her happiness was greater than that of any other woman who felt herself loved, because for her it was feeling herself being loved by an exceptional being. She clung to him, she wanted him to carry her next to his heart. And Lester pressed her softly, as one would a sweetheart with whom he dances for the first time. He loved her because she had noticed him when he was simply Cosi, that picturesque vendor of "everything a seamstress needs," who used to announce his wares with a long, strident, terribly tragic laugh; he could not resist the temptation to kiss her, and he laid his lips on his wife's hair, on her ear, then he rested his mouth on the fragrant, silky, warm hair, golden with the glow of a banana leaf. Underneath was the bone of that small adored head. She felt so beautiful underneath that kiss that she would have liked for everybody to see her like that, dressed in one of her husband's kisses.

"They don't spend anything, Adelaido, they don't spend anything, I tell you! Anybody can keep afloat that way. They keep everything they earn, and out of that, out of their nest egg, they take what they need the most."

"You tell me all that. The mill only cost two pesos; the mares they got for eggshells; the Fueté land and the Jarrín land; and always shipping on the railroad, which won't carry anything for anybody . . . that all costs, costs, Roselia, and only if they've sold their souls to the devil, and the devil gives and gives until his day comes around . . ."

"Well, yes, you have got something there . . ." Doña Roselia murmured; "but the ones who should talk, who should talk the least are us; just look how much he loves the boys and how much he's done for them, and how he worried, remember, and brought Juancho back to his wife and family."

"That's what I'm getting at! Before I give up my soul to God . . ."

"You're not dying, so stop making up stories . . ."

"Let me talk, woman. Before my end I want my sons to confess to me under the sign of the cross that they haven't yet and never will make a pact with the devil."

"You tell them that . . ."

"Could we do it today, Roselia?"

"They're celebrating today and we're not going to bother

them and make them swear to things that make them sad. Think about your grandchildren, the delight they are, and stop talking about Satan."

"And what if it was stolen, what they spend, and one fine day my boys will be sent off to jail as thieves."

"It'll be proven that they're innocent."

"It'll be proven . . . But while they're proving it, as accomplices . . ."

"You start me thinking, and I don't want to think; if that's the way it is, they might just as well have a pact with the devil."

"Woman!"

"Neither of the two, then; but it's your fault for making me think; there's nothing worse than a tongue, and old people's tongues are either poison or sweetness!"

"The one who could get rid of our doubts is Mr. Rose; I know him and sometimes he comes by here, except that I'm so hunched over that I look like a wilted floripondio, and so as not to bother me, I imagine, he doesn't wave; I'd have to raise my hand and it's so hard for me."

"You can ask him . . . When Lino had his trouble he came by to see us, he was interested."

"I'll ask him . . . We parents have got to look out for our children, even if they're already such big galoots. Not prisoners and not thieves and not with their souls sold to the devil . . . Let them work clean the way their father did, but free men on their own land, selling their own fruit!"

"But they've got all that, we can't complain."

"They've got it, but . . . Don't make me say any more, Roselia, don't make me talk; they've got it, but who knows which one's worse . . ."

That night the countryside was full of luminous dots of green color, as if the banana grove had let loose eyes in the form of fireflies in the midst of the heat of the sky. From Semírames the two old people could see the bright lights of the party house behind a green curtain of trees that climbed halfway up the hill then turned to stand between the gulley where the mill was and Semírames, visible above.

"Listen," old Roselia said after a long pause, "it sounds like somebody coming."

"At this time of night it could only be the doc—if it's him, I'm going to ask him, Roselia, I can't die with this doubt on my mind."

The joviality of the medical man made the Luceros feel happy. While the old man pouted, the doctor felt him, making a spider of his hand, on his front ribs, around his heart. With his fingers opened in the form of a compass, he traced a half circle. He traced the other half almost at once, and he put his ear over a silk handkerchief he held there.

But the doctor seemed to be listening more outside of Lucero than inside, because he raised his head and asked:

"Is there a marimba close by?"

"They're opening the banana meal mill," Doña Roselia said as her husband buttoned up his shirt, or, rather, brought the edges of his shirt together, because with his crooked fingers, how was he going to put one of those shell buttons through a buttonhole.

"Look, doc, I'm what you always said I was: a screwed-up old man; but so damned screwed-up that I was thinking that with this opening of the mill that maybe there's more than meets the eye . . ."

"Your sons ought to know . . ."

"They don't know anything; I'm the one who wants to make them open their eyes; it's very funny, everything that happens with Mr. Mead . . ."

Doña Roselia cleared her throat, feigning a cough to indicate to old Lucero that he was spitting at the sky.

"Well . . . what I know," the doctor answered, "is that Tropical Banana, Inc., had three of the best detectives from the States down here and nothing was proved about the mystery of Lester Mead. Is he an adventurer? Is he a technician working with the cooperative? Is he a visionary? What we do know, Don Adelaido, is that he's won everybody's sympathy and respect."

"He's been so helpful!" Doña Roselia exclaimed.

"As far as I'm concerned, he's got a pact with the devil."

"The only thing that's known is that he was always traveling around banana plantations here and in other countries."

"Sit down, doctor . . ."

"No, ma'am, I have to go . . . The other day I was talking to him and he gave me the key to his economic system. The San Jacinto Indians go down to the other coast, work on the banana plantations, and they all go home rich; on the other hand, those who aren't Indians come with their heads full of heroic dreams and they don't even ever get home . . . and if they do, they're social outcasts . . . The economy of the San Jacinto Indians, think about that and not about the devil!"

The doctor, when he said that, motioned to Doña Roselia to follow him for a way. The old woman went with him and came back with heavy feet, like sacks of sand on the floor. Lucero had closed his eyes, the mask of an old man bedewed with sweat. But he was still breathing, he was breathing softly. She put her hand on his head with an old woman's tenderness. There beside him she no longer felt anything. It was the night, the shadow, and the land of death, where her old man was going to go when the penny whistle in his heart gave out. She closed her eyelids to break off the tears that were like fat grains of corn under a millstone. It was sad to see a life breaking apart, to feel already around the poor, worn-out old man all the futility of the world, all the futility of things. She squatted down beside him. She opened her lips to say, at the same time as she sought his hand, she had to carry it to the end, to say oh Lord, Lord!

"The economy of the San Jacinto Indians! . . ." old Lucero whispered, word by word.

The last attack was a long one. They carried him down to see the mill one day. He had never seen banana meal. Everything for export. He held the white flour of gold in his hands. He tasted it. He asked them to put a little on his lips, and more than tasting, he kissed it. Banana meal. Flour from the God of the tropics. Flour for the host of a new religion. That of man. Then they showed him the small boxes in different sizes according to weight, for export, and the labels.

15

Bastiancito Cojubul's wife stayed to take care of the Meads'
house. They would be away for a few weeks. Now they could
take advantage by searching even under the stones. It's too
bad that I can't get around, that I can't move . . . Old
Adelaido Lucero, in spite of the matter of the "economy of the
San Jacinto Indians," did not stop his doubts from revolving
in his head. And with them, one day when they went into his
room at Semírames they found him turned into a scarab covered with flies, dead at last. The wake. The nine days. Doña
Roselia could not bear the color black. Mourning roasts on the
coast and, as she said, what better mourning than old age.
Old age is mourning for life. A person grows old for everything
that has died. April and May were great bonfires. Although it
usually began to rain earlier along the coast, that year not a
drop had fallen. Finally the rains came. But rains that seemed
to be carried by birds on wing. A downpour and then the sun,
drying everything out, turning the ground into an unfired brick.

Not those rains in which one could sit and watch it rain, sleep while it was raining, wake up while it was raining, and go to bed again while it was still raining.

To get away a little from Adelaido Lucero's body, which had remained in the coldness and the emptiness of the house, Doña Roselia would go down to the Meads' place. A curious building, made out of logs, and which they called a "bungalow" in their language, surrounded by gardens that for Doña Roselia were nothing of the sort, but rather some well-kept plots of green grass. Bastiancito's wife was very nice to her. She served her chocolate as soon as she arrived with her sad face of a widow and mother, wearing her everyday clothes. That foreign chocolate that tasted so delicious. The native chocolate was very badly made, mostly sugar and very little chocolate. One of her sons said that before Lester Mead had left, he had bought some land where he planned to make an intensive cultivation of cacao trees. The cacao business was more golden than coffee and bananas. I never imagined my sons would be so rich, old Roselia reflected, sipping the cup of hot chocolate, there on the coast at two in the afternoon. She had asked God to make her sons hard-working, but not rich. Riches bring many misfortunes, many disappointments. If we could only have seen! Rich people's hearts grow hard. And what greater misfortune than to have a hard heart. But since luck is luck, they were born to have, just as there are others who spend their lives always cursing their bad luck . . .

Leland Foster, since she came to the Tropical Banana, Inc., plantations with her first husband on a vacation trip, could not remember ever having left there. She had not gone to the capital, much less to the United States. Once, a long time ago, she had packed her bags, but then Lester came back and she never moved again. The train bothered her nerves. Mead arranged to go by car. On the way he would leave it in a garage to be tuned up and painted, and it would be like new when they returned.

The surprise that their friends were going to have when they found out, after they were already away from the plantation, that they were taking a trip. For her especially, because Mead was a gadabout. And the first time that she would travel for so many hours in an airplane. She only had time to buy a halfway presentable dress, a hat, a purse, shoes, and to take a short spin around the city, where the clear air gave her the impression that she was in another world, on the top floor of the atmosphere.

But after a few hours of flying she was in another world again. The smelly iron atmosphere of New York. How many years had it been since she was last in New York? She shook her head in front of the mirror in her regal room. The home of some of Mead's friends in the most beautiful part of the suburbs of New York. When Leland came into the dining room, Mead was waiting for her, reading the newspapers and some messages. She went into the library and took *The Taming of the Shrew* from among the works of Shakespeare. The greenish-gold of her hair, her eyes like almonds made of toasted bread crust, her white beauty, everything laughed in her when she said to Mead on returning to the dining room:

"I'd better reread Shakespeare; I don't want the girls to get ahead of me . . ."

"I'm the one people have got ahead of. My lawyers called just now."

"Have you inherited a fortune, I hope?"

"Well, you'd better take the other car . . ."

"What other car, my lord Duke?"

"The one that these people left for you . . ."

"What people? I haven't seen anyone. Since I've been here all I've seen have been pictures."

"The owners, those friends of mine who take care of their affairs from some place in Europe."

The lawyers were waiting for Lester Mead. Twin brothers, the two lawyers. When they were together it was not easy to say who was who, and when they were apart it was impossible to identify them. Mead felt a great joy, therefore, when on greeting them he managed to say Alfred to the one named Alfred, and Robert to the one called Robert. They were the famous attorneys Alfred and Robert Doswell.

After the greetings, Mead sat in a chair across from the desk, which was a very large desk, especially made for two people, two people who were one, so alike physically and so identified in their business, their tastes, in everything.

"Our stockholders," Robert Doswell said, "are anxious to know about your experiences. Could we call a meeting for this very afternoon?"

While Alfred was talking, no, it was Robert who was talking; while Robert was talking, Alfred took out a pad and got ready to take some notes.

"It seems all right to me to have a meeting this afternoon," Mead answered. "Just tell me the time."

"We have it all set," Alfred Doswell said as he wrote: "at four o'clock."

"Fine . . ."

"Uh, just a moment, Mr. Stoner . . ." it made Mead a little surprised to hear himself called by his real name, "we're going to call Washington, because the stockholders in our group want someone from the State Department present during your report."

"In the meantime I'll call my wife; perhaps she hasn't left the house yet and I can tell her to stay there."

"At four this afternoon, Mr. Stoner . . ." one of the lawyers said; but this time Lester had no way of telling which one it was, Alfred or Robert.

The report was slightly tinged with humor, although of a very bitter kind. Wearing a suit the color of old copper, Lester Stoner began to speak at one minute after four. The stockholders were sitting in low chairs. An official of the State Department had arrived from Washington. A gruff man with white hair and a walrus moustache.

"Now you know," Stoner concluded, "the methods used by Tropical Banana, Inc., to which I have the honor to belong, if it can be called an honor to be dirty dealers, slave traders, and slave owners, are methods due to the policy adopted. It is up to you to set it on the right road. Things can't go on like this in the American tropics, unless we want to lose our prestige and our investments forever. Practice shows that if we go there with hands clean of bribery and if we cooperate in the welfare of those people, without the sacrifice of a single cent of our current profits and perhaps even increasing them, they will look on us as friends and not as enemies. We are not honest and we have no respect for the laws of the countries where we operate. They're not against us because we're Amer icans, but because we're bad Americans. It's sinister to crush every day the hopes of men who have planted their fields and want to live in peace. Those men make war on us because we went to them on a war footing. We haven't learned how to deal with them on a level of legality and decency, which honest industry and business imply. We think that everything is legitimate because we have the power of the dollar. But I believe, maintain, and defend the idea that if the world situation goes contrary to us someday, the hatred of those people will follow us, multiplied by the number of bunches of bananas that our inspectors reject each day."

Lester Stoner drank some water and continued his report.

"Those people are beginning to become tired of us and we of them. The threat that if we are hindered we will abandon the plantations and take our investments elsewhere does not frighten them anymore. Things are going so badly for them with us there, that without us they couldn't be any worse off. And geography is against us. Where could we take our agricultural enterprises and stay in our own backyard? Nowhere. The press that defends us is discredited and our lawyers are more policemen in our service than attorneys who serve the law. We enslave some of the people with our credit system, we corrupt others with our largesse; we ruin the local economy with our monopolistic greed, and we pretend to cover it all with the benefits of the civilization we brought with our teams who remove from man the dignity of dying from malaria, for example, to find the slow death of whiskey and soda for some, rum and cane liquor for others; and we remove from ourselves the dignity of defending like men the things we can defend with a quick phone call to our diplomatic representative."

Stoner drank the rest of his glass of water; his lips felt feverish, and he went on with his report.

"The complete figures, aside from my human convictions, that prove that we will get good profits without any need to exploit the workers, to ruin the private planters, or to kill off competition are with my attorneys and available for inspection by the stockholders."

He raised his voice to say:

"The crux of the matter is to replace those who are running the company today with a policy that sacrifices everything in the name of profit, with directors who will use our immense financial power to afford us a stable investment, which is slipping from our hands day by day. I ask for a policy aiming at safeguarding the future without reducing the profits. You have never thought about this change in policy. The other stockholders either, because you are not in a position to know what is going on down there. Let us do some recruiting, then, and soon, among those who are unaware of the truth of the

matter, some new followers, and when we have a majority
. . ."

The long silent car went along one of the highways leading
out of the center of New York to the country. Leland, beside
her husband, who was driving the car fast, put her body
against the door and turned her head to take a good look at
him, and after the challenging look she said to him:

"I think that I ought to talk to you in all loyalty, that you
should know what I'm thinking . . . yes . . . it's best that
you know . . . the pedestal where I put you has crumbled,
the pedestal . . . you're such a great hypocrite that I don't
know whether I can bear you another day, another minute
. . . on the plantation you would sleep on the ground with
the boys sometimes . . . there you didn't spend anything that
wasn't necessary . . . wasn't necessary? . . . even when it
was . . . nothing that was a luxury . . . you were angry with
Macario over that nothing of silk that he bought for his wife
in the commissary . . . all in order to appear in the eyes of
those poor ignorant people as something you're not . . . you
faker . . ."

The glow of the city spread out over the country like the
tail of a great comet. Leland was wounded by her husband's
silence, as in spite of the offensive words he did not move a
single muscle on his face, or his green eyes in their white
corneas that he kept glued to the gray strip of highway, and
she remained silent, stifling her tears.

After a long while, Lester, without moving his head, said:

"Would it be possible to know your preference between the
puritan of the plantations and worldly man of New York?"

"Cynic!"

Lester was silent again and she could not hold herself back
anymore. Teardrops were bouncing down her cheeks, thick
and abundant. She was weeping without movement, as if she

were part of the clockwork of that long and silent automobile. Only by the small lace handkerchief that she had taken out to blow her nose could one tell that she was crying.

"Certain expenditures, even though they seem to be luxuries are not that at all when it is necessary to obtain a loan like the one I've asked the banks for. A long-term loan which will allow us to develop industries based on bananas and other crops native to the country."

Leland raised her head. Her eyes, wet with tears, had two small points of light in their depths, and she said, almost in a whisper:

"I'm sorry, Lester, I'm a poor fool, and the city has upset me, I'm upset at not finding the New York that . . . what New York means to a person . . . what a person thinks New York is, what one has dreamed New York is . . . finding a city that seems to have been created to exploit all human effort to the bitter end . . . to devour us all . . . an ugly, senseless giant . . ." and moving close to him: "Darling, you're divine! You play so well your roles of a man-about-town and a hermit, a Wall Street banker and a tropical planter, so much that a person can't tell which role you're better at; at all of them, I think, because you're authentic in all of them; that's why I was suffering so much a few moments ago . . . sweet . . . because I thought you were going to destroy the beautiful picture I have of a man who has the capacity to do anything he wants to do in an authentic way . . ."

"Let's get out of here; I've got the urge to leave too; I'm a prisoner who's counting the days until he can escape. When I think that there are oceans, mountains, volcanoes, lakes, great rivers with the smell of liquid fruit, and that here, on the other hand, there are millions of people closed in from the day they're born until the day they die in houses and offices, putrid, gray . . ."

The twin lawyers again showed Mead, Stoner to them, their double face, a single person in front of two mirrors, Alfred and Robert, Robert and Alfred, when he went to say goodbye to them and sign some important papers. With just his signature they had advanced a loan of half a million dollars. Then his will. The sole and full heiress his wife, Leland Foster Stoner, and in the event of her decease, the Mead-Cojubul-Lucero-Ayuc Gaitán organization.

When Leland entered the lawyers' office they all stood up.

"I'm all loaded down . . . Just before a trip a person has all the things she forgot to do, little things to buy at the last minute . . ." and after her excuses, turning to her husband: "Are we late?"

The lawyers Doswell bowed to her and kissed her hand, then they shook Lester Mead's hand, Lester Stoner to them, and a moment later the door of the office closed behind the couple, noiselessly, automatically, the way it had opened.

"I don't know how you manage to tell your lawyers apart. Which is which?"

"That's why I only see them when they're together; when I call them on the phone to set an appointment, I always say that I have to consult with them both, and so far I hold the record among their clients for being able to call them by name as soon as I go into the office."

"It's hard to believe that morning will come, that I'll be leaving tomorrow. I'd only live here if I were a millionaire . . ."

"But you are now . . ."

"Then I'll stay . . ."

"You're the heiress to one of the most powerful stockholders of Tropical Banana, Inc., and your income per month is no less than . . . put down whatever figure you want, a hundred thousand dollars and up . . ."

"I will, I will be a millionaire because Mead-Cojubul-Lucero-Ayuc Gaitán is going to absorb Tropbanana, and then I hope that our stocks will be the most powerful."

"All we have to do before we leave is for you to put the Shakespeare book back. There's still time . . ." and Lester's laugh was heard repeating: "There's still time," as the car went up through the shady garden of the house.

Leland was surprised at the profusion of lights that could be seen in the living rooms, stairs, hallways, balconies, and other corners of what at that moment looked like a palace.

"Your friends have come back. It's a pleasant surprise. I wouldn't have wanted to leave without meeting them. We should have come earlier, as soon as we left the lawyers, that way we would have had more time to be with them."

Leland was saying all those words helter-skelter as they were getting out of the car.

A group of ladies in evening gowns and gentlemen in tuxedos came over to welcome them. The strange thing was that they did not call him Mead but Stoner. Leland thought they were making some mistake, and she hastened to ask her husband to tell them that they were not Mr. and Mrs. Stoner, but Mr. and Mrs. Mead.

But her confusion was even greater when she found the twin lawyers among the guests. The party bothered her because of the annoying mistake that the people honoring her were making, and she even began to have bad thoughts about her husband. Perhaps he was passing himself off as someone else. Wives have a great propensity toward having bad thoughts about their husbands. Then, when she learned the truth, Leland was depressed. How suddenly she had become what her husband had told her a few hours back as an apparent joke, a millionaire. But with the first glass of champagne the cloud dissipated in laughter. She was laughing with

Alfred and Robert Doswell about the trouble she would have
in recognizing them now that they were going to be friends;
she laughed with the very grave members of Tropical Banana,
Inc., who were backing Stoner in his plan to change the financial policy of the Company; she laughed with the ladies who
congratulated her and found her charming; and she brought a
smile to the face of the very important person from the State
Department when she told him that her husband had passed
as Cosi. "Everything a seamstress needs," and Leland laughed
with the "ya-ha, ha, ha, ha, ha," which rang in her ears like
the stream of water in a hot shower.

Lester took her out onto the terrace. Had she got drunk
on one glass of champagne? . . . Was she drunk with pleasure?

She did not answer her husband, she put her arms around
his neck and kissed him and said:

"I'm drunk from you . . ."

A chamber orchestra was playing Leland's favorite musi-
cal pieces. Later on, when they went back out onto the terrace
after dancing, Leland was no longer laughing.

"I'm crying . . ." she murmured, and her face was bathed
in tears.

They stayed alone. The guests disappeared the way out-
siders disappear, good friends as they may be, when those moments arrive when it is not good for anyone to be present
except the couple that is in paradise. Those guests who measured their shares in the Company in gold had disappeared.
That little old man with the joking eyes under white eyebrows,
sideburns, and goatee, with his chubby little hands always on
his stomach, the main proponent of a plan to change the financial policy of Tropical Banana, Inc., not as his moderate colleagues wanted to do, but at the very heart of it by socializing
the enterprise.

The music could be heard in the silence not because it was playing but because the sound of it was remembered. Leland slipped out of Stoner's hands and fled through the garden.

"Where are you going?" Lester caught up and asked her.

"To where Mead, the poor man, is waiting for me!"

"Not in the garden, he's waiting for you in Shakespeare!" Leland felt frustrated in her acting role.

"Christopher Sly," she turned and said to him, "enough of dreams, Christopher Sly," and she ran her hands over his face, over his eyes, caressed him, "or let us dream it is forsooth the truth!"

The guests had not left. She was standing by the old man with sideburns and goatee as another stockholder, a Jew with a pointed head, explained how Stoner had got into that banana plantation adventure because he had become bored with the life of a millionaire.

Little by little, Leland was getting her senses back. She had laughed, she had cried, she had run out into the garden. The guests surrounded her, the twin lawyers, and on her finger she was wearing a ring which, not content with looking at it, she had to feel. It was not an emerald. It was a piece from one of Lester Mead's eyes. He was still Lester Mead for her.

The guests began leaving again, or were they only leaving for the first time. Calmer now, she was giving them her hand to kiss. Now they were leaving, going out . . .

"Yes, sweet, Lester Stoner will stay in New York, in this house, and Lester Mead will go back to the plantation with you. Do you want me to tell you something?"

"Anything you want, love . . ."

"Lester Mead is the one I prefer; Lester Stoner is the heartless millionaire; the millionaire who did not give himself the luxury of ceasing to be a swine; the millionaire of the Waldorf-Astoria, yachts, racehorses, hired women . . . The millionaire of baccarat and roulette, the sweat of underpaid people gambled away at blackjack . . . The millionaire of political arrangements to keep governments at his service in countries where he operates with the voracity of an octopus . . . I prefer Lester Mead, the millionaire who organizes planter cooperatives, who installed a small banana flour mill, and who, as if God had kissed him on the brow, millionaire and all, found love."

"Yes, sweetheart. Lester Stoner will stay in New York, in this house, and back will go my madman who laughed on the plantations, my millionaire who is going back now like a simple worker . . ."

"I got so annoyed when I realized my usefulness and hadn't yet found any way to use it, because nothing caused me the slightest emotion anymore, that I made an arrangement with my lawyers and some stockholders to undertake at my expense this investigation of the conditions in which our company operates in the tropics; and the worst part . . . not the worst part . . . the best part, is that I wouldn't be able to live here anymore; the case of the captor's capture . . ."

"And rapture . . ."

"Let's go to bed, because we have to leave early tomorrow . . ."

"But first back to its shelf with *The Taming of the Shrew* so that everything will be in its proper place."

16

A naked sun, so terrible that spiders came out from among the stones, not by ones but by hundreds, not by hundreds but by thousands in an endless outpouring, coming out so as not to burn up inside. Everything in a daily and nightly oven and not a drop of water. The people would stop to look at the sky, their skin dry, their breath dry, sweating, suffocating. The blue tint of the sky. The animals defeated by the heat, and thirsty, would double over like limp rags. The trees were part of the immense bonfire, like flames that did not burn, and the banana trees were sucking up all the dampness of the earth for their thirst. The Shaman took out the jars of whitewash he had prepared and he set out for the graveyard. He alone in the great flat space that extended to where the horizon curved. Step by step, he alone with the jars of whitewash. The ground creaked in the graveyard. It was necessary to take advantage of noon on the ninth of March. He could be seen entering the cemetery. He alone. So much alone that the half-buried dead

could grasp him with their hands of cold fire, for the ground
was like an oven and the dead had the temperature of living
people. A cemetery of hot bones, of green and reddish flies
with the buzz of fans flying over a vegetation the color of
old hair.

He alone. So much alone that the dead could have spoken
to him. Short in stature, wrapped in clothing the color of the
bark of a tree, rags that had been soaked by the rain, clouds
of dust stuck to the threads so that they were like cardboard
and had a wrinkled vegetable quality. His jacket, without
shoulder pads, buttoned up to the neck. A dark, carbonized
tinge on both sides of his cheeks, like a beard. He could be
seen making a great effort to open his eyes that were en-
tombed in wrinkles, his lids nothing but wrinkles, his forehead wrinkles, his ears wrinkles, his hands wrinkles with
fingers, his feet toes with wrinkles.

"Sugusán sugusán, sugusán . . ."

That was what the Shaman was saying as he went into the
graveyard. The jars with whitewash splashed on the road, it
sprinkled his feet. Thick, fat, white drops.

He passed among the first graves with his slow step.
Sugusán, sugusán, sugusán . . . He left other graves behind,
the ones behind the first. *Sugusán, sugusán, sugusán* . . . And
he left even farther behind the graves that were behind the
ones he had just passed. *Sugusán, sugusán, sugusán.*

His mask of wrinkles began to change from sadness into joy.
He raised his head, covered by a hat that was shaped like a
toadstool, shade for a frog, to be able to see something, since
he could no longer open his eyelids very wide in order to see
well, he raised his head, stretching it out, and he scurried
toward a rock pile, where he left the jars of whitewash on the
ground, and he huddled for a long time too . . . who knows
what for.

Some sign . . .

Sugusán, sugusán, sugusán . . .

The Shaman's eyes closed on him, the lids fell, but he was not asleep. A sudden shaking made him arise electrified. From one of the recently covered graves where the earth was still fresh, and the wooden cross still new and the inscription clear, he took out a dead man. With a great swipe of his knife he separated the head and threw it into one of the jars of whitewash. Then he went back the way he had come. He alone, *sugusán, sugusán, sugusán,* he alone with two jars of whitewash, one to cover his tracks, and the other with the head of Hermenegilo Puac.

When he got to his house, the Shaman Rito Perraj took the head of the dead man out of the jar. Fetid, heavy, white with cold lime, the firm and grainy teeth between the purplish lips. And he threw it back into the jar. He would go to the sea along with that moon which does not drink water, leaving the head of Puac in his house, pointing toward where the sun rises, on a pillow of hawk feathers.

He did not take off his hat, he took off the roof of his house, which was like a straw hat above his toadstool hat. He walked away two steps by two steps, three steps by three steps, five steps by five steps, ten steps by ten steps to the sea. The beams of the hut, its ribs, its arms, its shinbones . . . The foundation stones of the hut at his feet. And then it came, it let itself come in from the sea against all things, turning them into pieces.

The wind picked up a hut . . . the people said and they all hid, because the wind was blowing strong, stronger and stronger, the wind became a hurricane, devastation . . .

Hermenegilo Puac died because when he had no one to fight with, his heart became paralyzed. That was why he died! And he did not have anyone to fight with because when he resolved to kill the manager people told him: You kill this manager and they'll send another manager, you kill that other manager and they'll send still another manager! . . .

He buried his nails into the flesh of his workingman's hands, not knowing what to do. They had to write to Chicago. The great people up there were the ones who had the last word. Hermenegilo Puac did not know where Chicago was, but he would have gone there on foot, finding out where it was, to save himself from ruin, from which he did not save himself in the end. And who are those people, he asked. Everybody, it seems, knew who they were, but nothing concrete. Chicago. The people up there. The bosses.

The day when he was left with his fruit, with his bunches of bananas larger than a normal-sized man, unpurchased by them, he wept and said:

"Gringo sons-of-bitches, if they've got something that can't be seen and crushes us and which a person can't fight against, not even by killing, we too, ha!, I'll cut my balls off if there isn't some kind of revenge!"

And he went to see the Shaman Rito Perraj, so that the Shaman could oppose that indeterminate will with an invincible force that would ruin them, and the Shaman asked for his life, and he, Hermenegilo Puac, gave it to him, and the Shaman asked for his head, and he, Hermenegilo Puac, gave him everything, as long as there would be vengeance.

A force that leaves nothing standing. Hermenegilo Puac asked for that. A wind that would blow from underneath, uprooting the banana trees of Tropbanana, uprooting them forever. The wind that sinks its teeth into the earth, dirty, atmospheric, salty, and unburies everything, even the dead. Hermenegilo Puac asked for that with the presenting of his death of the heart and the giving of his head to Rito Am Perraj. Will everything change shape? It will. The railroad tracks will wiggle like snakes. Nothing will stay put. The poor vegetable resistance to the unleashed elements of the natural will be beaten down by one lone element unleashed within the supernatural and the magical with the destruction of man, the strength of great sea beasts, and the incessant pounding at the roots of the foundations, the paws of the animals, the feet of the horrified inhabitants. Hermenegilo Puac asked for that. And the avalanche of a hurricane like an aerial earthquake, a dry tidal wave, would be, would come, would overcome because of what Hermenegilo Puac had asked Rito Perraj, the one who manipulates the fluid and stony breaths of Huracán and Cabracán with his fingers.

That night. The following day. The second night. The second day. The third night. The third day. The boxcars on the railroad lines began to move against their will, jumping off the rails, while the cattle lowing in the corrals came surging out like so many locomotives, running blindly away and jumping the tracks. Little by little, houses were leaving their foundations, the wind was blowing so strongly. Water pumps passed by light lightless stars, iron towers broken into pieces, telegraph poles pulled up out of their mud, and in the banana groves nothing was standing, everything was beaten down to the ground and had become an unmoving vegetable misery.

The soft metal of the hurricane in the hands of the Shaman Rito Perraj blew wrathfully like dust made out of swords. The first impulse of the banana trees, not to let themselves be uprooted, was just an impulse, because the whole sea, transformed into whirlwinds of air, fell upon them, and then, torn up by the roots, trunks snapped, falling down suddenly, offering no resistance, so that the wind could pass by more rapidly to sweep away everything that it was sweeping away, houses, animals, trains, as if it were sweeping trash.

The presidents of the Company, the vice-presidents, the local agents, the superintendents, the . . . all of them, all of the representatives of the great people up there, those people who had neither face nor body, but did have an implacable will . . . All of them were spinning about like blond rats, dressed in white, with eyeglasses on their poor myopic eyes, in their tumbling houses that were about to be torn up and swept away. They were all trying to find the face of that someone else who was opposed to their designs, who was facing them with superior elements, who was annihilating them in spite of their foresighted system to avoid any possible causes of loss.

The dry wind, hot, almost fire water, not only knocked down everything in its path, but it dried it, left it like stuffing; it emptied out the substance of the banana trees it had knocked down, just as if many, just as if many days had passed and they had lain there in the sun.

Sugusán, sugusán, sugusán . . .

The Shaman went back to the graveyard with Hermenegilo Puac's head and he buried it. The crosses had fallen into pieces when the hurricane passed over the graves. Of the village which fed the cemetery with its dead, there was just the mass, with great destruction, a great sad mass, a pile of collapsed houses, some roofless, others without front walls, as if they had been disemboweled, leaving their viscera of furniture at the mercy of the elements; over the empty alleys where the frames of stores, warehouses, and bars faced each other, flew the bodies of cats, dogs, chickens, and an occasional child.

Sugusán, sugusán, sugusán . . .

Fear took hold of inanimate objects in the midst of the wind that was pushed from behind as it blew, pushing everything, everything, everything, wherever it passed, so that nothing would be left where it passed, and what resisted did so at the cost of great destruction and the suffering of living things, to such a degree that nature itself seemed to have surrendered and was going along with the hurricane, trying to save the

large trees that were standing up elastically with all of their
foliage now pieces of the great wind.

"Leland! . . ."

Lester was repeating the name mechanically, heading toward his house in the midst of the wind.

"Leland! . . ."

"Leland! . . ."

Inside his skin, his nerves and his blood vessels and his
muscles and the bones of his neck were twisting with the urge
to let out his earthy laugh as if to announce "everything a
seamstress needs," and he had to bring up his fist to squelch
that desire to laugh, laugh, laugh.

"Leland! . . ."

"Leland! . . ."

"Leland! . . ."

The hurricane was almost knocking him off his feet as they
weakened on the surface of plants that had been twisted by
the wind, and now not even by clutching the trunks of the
trees could he go forward. He was being dragged, he was face
down, on all fours, or snaking along for whole stretches so that
the hurricane, which left no solid mass in its place, would let
him reach his house.

"Leland! . . ."

"Leland! . . ."

The laugh of other days, the ya-ha, ha, ha, ha, ha, came to
him like a vomiting of laughter and blood, and when he felt
it pouring out of his teeth he swallowed it, he made it return,
soaked with water changed into wind, with sea changed into
wind, with light changed into wind, with trees changed into
wind, with stones changed into a wind that was blowing
crudely with the smell of an ocean beast, wild, prideful, a
mixture of the shriek of the elements and the roar and complaint of an inland creature in the complete affliction of death.

It made the banana plants vanish, it swept them away, it lifted them up to throw them farther, where least expected. Tables, chairs, beds, everything destroyed and scattered hither and yon for miles, over trees, under bridges, in the lashed waters of the rivers which were also infuriated, not because of any increase in their flow but from the snakelike passing and passing of the windstorm.

"Leland! . . ."

"Leland! . . ."

He was about to let out his laugh when he saw his wife as he reached the house, in the midst of the storm, her hair in disarray, her clothes about to be torn off, struggling with the horse and the sulky.

"Leland! . . ."

He fell on her like a part of the windstorm. To touch her. Touch her. See that she was there. See that the wind had not carried her off and broken her to pieces. Broken her to pieces, left her flung down, inert, dead, or unconscious, the way so many already were in different places, indifferent corpses in the path of the hurricane.

"Leland! . . ."

She did not answer him, mute with terror, trembling at the thought that it was the last day of her life, but not thinking it, feeling now that it was like a brutal imposition, like something inevitable, absolutely inevitable, right there, there with her, there with everything that was happening and what would come afterward . . .

The horse, once out of the stone corral behind the house where they had the chicken house, the buggy shed, the stable, did not stop for anything. The sulky was a ball of fire and Lester Stoner (danger hammered his real name into his ears) was back in his good, old student days, when at college, dressed as a Roman, he had driven a chariot in some bastard pageant.

The applause of thousands of spectators was there in the thousands of leaves shaking constantly, branches with a thousand tongues savoring together the bitter bravado of being firm branches and not the ones that were going off loose, flying away like aerial objects. The wheels of the vehicle began to weaken. In a moment they felt that they were traveling on one wheel, because the other one had already flown off. Luckily the thing did not fall down, and they could still go forward, flee, cover ground toward the town, even get to Lucero's house. Her whole being clung to Lester, made into a single person with him, her head sunk into his back, in back of him so as to give him room to work the reins, but at the waist her arms were like a taut rope to hold on better. If they fell, they would fall together. Their ears were full of that world in movement, gust after gust, of those hundreds of thousands of banana trunks flying off as if they were leaves which at any moment would be transformed into the wings of green buzzards to carry them through the dust that prevented them from seeing more than a few yards. The road slipped down a small incline where, as the sulky struck a stone that had rolled into the middle of the road, they remained after a tremendous fall to the ground, leather seats and all, he with the end of the reins and she pressed between Lester's back and the ground, with a horrible scratch on her face from her forehead to her ear, where her skin was torn, although she did not feel pain but fear, a fear not of the immediate resolution of everything, because they had already come to that: there was not much hope of surviving now that great stones had begun to roll, passing over them like silent worlds . . . The horse, down below, had been crushed by an immense tree that one of the big stones had knocked down quickly as it rolled toward the bottom. The poor animal had fallen to its knees helplessly, with all four legs broken, changed into a single stain of blood, horse, and moan.

Lester knew the terrain, but in the midst of the catastrophe and with the anguish of what might happen to Leland, he was disoriented. If he had been alone, he would have known where to drag himself; but with her . . .

He half-arose from the ground where they were lying so as not to be swept away by the wind, lying down and hanging on to the roots, and he could see that they were not far from the place called the Gambusino caves, a mile or so from Lucero's.

"The phenomenon covers a wide area" . . . That was what the Meteorological Institute said. The Shaman knew it, Hermenegilo Puac's whitewashed skull knew it, back in the graveyard, laughing with all of his teeth at the gringos, at their power, at their machines, at the great people from up there, the secret heads who governed them and who, in all truth, were not a single head, or two, or three, but the heads of all the stockholders put together in the great head of the Green Pope. Hermenegilo Puac, with his white skull, was laughing at the twelve million banana trees that the strong wind had knocked down, tearing them out of the damp soil where they had been placed like bowling pins.

In the small depression in the ground there, along which they were crawling, they could go forward without being knocked down, and they went behind each other, leaning, leaning over so as not to expose their heads to the windstorm, which was coming more from the side than from the front, in short, staggering steps, as if they were drunk.

When they reached the Gambusino caves, Leland let herself go, without any sign of life except a moaning breath between her lips. She was as white as hardened wax under her greenish-gold hair in the midst of an atmosphere that was murky like saltwater. Lester had brought one of the cushions from the sulky and on those remains of horsehair and leather he placed his wife's head as he looked for a handkerchief to sop up the

stream of blood that was running down her neck behind her
ear. The shadows of ghost trees, of trees that did not exist, but
which did exist there, began to prowl around and come into
the cave like gigantic animals. Lester knew it. Sarajobalda
had told everybody. When there was a storm, the shadows of
the trees that had been cut down many years ago during the
lumbering come into the Gambusino caves like ghosts, and
the person they discover inside will have everything alive
under his skin taken out and he will be left as a doll of skin
and bones. Lester opened his green eyes as if he saw a wild
beast coming at them, he strangled in his throat the laugh that
was coming from his chest like a gravel train and he shouted:

"Leland! Leland! . . ."

The shadows of the giant trees, ebonies, mahoganies, matilis-
guates, chicozapotes, guayacanes, which no longer existed,
continued crawling fantastically, coming into the cave with
the movement of animals, of the waves of a heavy sea.

"Leland, let's get out of here, the shadows are coming in,"
and he pointed with his stiff finger. "Look how they're crawling, look how they're advancing, look how they're spreading
out, look how they're cornering us, look how they're catching
us, and if they wrap around us they'll empty us inside and tomorrow the only thing they'll find of us here will be two dolls
of hide and bones!"

They ran out of the cave so fast that Leland tore her clothes,
with half of her leg exposed; and they fled on to Lucero's be
tween the tall poles on the top of which the distant splendor
of the day was trembling at ground level; still fleeing, with
their looks now lost in the irremediable, under the immense
stones that the hurricane was moving along like trash.

They managed to arrive, breathless, footless, like robots,
to a sheltered place near the woods by Lucero's house, and
there they stopped. The hot dust that was rising up from
the ground would not let them see well. But what was passing

by near them, frightening them, almost hitting them, could be made out in a kind of lightning flash of awareness. A truck that looked like the roof of a house ran into a pole that was still showing its wires, a pole or a hand that was saying: see how I didn't let go of my telegraph line, herds of cattle, cattle that had become hard leather from so much beating, their legs stiff, dragging their tails, and a great chunk of house with the name of the boys' school, and desks and blackboards, giving the idea that they too had gone out for recess, everything scattered among thousands of banana trunks that did not seem torn up from the earth but rained down from the sky, loose . . .

"Leland, let's not go on, we should wait here until everything is over, because it's all over. I knew it . . ."

The wind was whistling among the trees against which they were leaning, wrapped in the torrent of destruction. An awning and a piece of bench came tumbling down, just like a great broken bird, and the remains of colored chairs passed by in the gusts, as did things from kitchens and bedrooms, becoming motionless when they hit the ground, but only for a moment, for then the strong wind would lift them up and carry them off and toss them where things no longer had any use. It was the awning from Tury Duzin's house. And some human shape passed, it passed like a Judas making the gestures of an animal caught in a trap. They did not know who it was. Very close by they heard the wail of a woman. Then nothing. Everything went back to the noisy silence in which the hurricane was dancing about. Chickens with chicken house and all; dovecotes with many blind eyes of terror; and bureaus with clothes hanging out like entrails, and mirrors where the faces of the catastrophe were smashed; rugs like pieces of paper, spinning at the mercy of the wind . . .

They did not see anything more. Lester repeated, his breathing cut off by doubt and fatigue:

"Leland, let's not go on, we should wait here until everything is over, because it's all over. I knew it . . ."

Horses and horses and horses went by at a gallop, raising
clouds of dust that mingled indecisively in the light of the
saltwater and muddied up the atmosphere. From the dust and
their shape of flowing-free beasts it was known that they were
passing, because the hurricane was whistling to erase even
the echo of their gallop, while a strong wave of the smell of oil
made one suppose that the sheds where the gasoline was stored
were jumping about.

Leland, milk-bland in her whiteness, only moved her features when she made efforts to swallow her dry, sticky saliva,
or when pain mounted up in her, pain, undefined and unde-
finable pain. It was no use. Who would have believed all of
that. Covered with earth from head to toe, she tried to make
her husband feel that they were together, that she was his
definitive companion in the hurricane, but she did it without
reasoning, without speaking, hugging him as he repeated:

"Leland, let's not go on, we should wait here until everything is over, because it's all over. I knew it; I knew that a
great darkness was waiting for us, a great darkness, a time
without time, a hurricane with the skin of a sea frog, terribly
vengeful . . . That's it . . . terribly vengeful . . . a cluster
of all the most elemental forces, because in the end this, all
of this, is wind, just wind, a wind that is passing by, a wind
that is howling, wind that never stops passing by . . ."

His back, the trees, the starless night, without a light, had
fallen like a chunk of darkness.

"Leland, I knew it, I knew that a great darkness was waiting
for us . . ."

They no longer saw each other. They no longer saw each
other. All ears. That was what they were. Just ears. And not
even that, not even ears. What for? . . . To hear the sea
advance over them, because now that they were in the dark,

completely in the dark, they felt themselves on a great tongue that was twisting to speak without saying anything but the same thundering sound, on an immense tongue of torrid sea that had changed into wind, and wherever it passed with its unleashed force it burned, lashed, swept, dried, overturned, dragged, tightened . . .

"Leland, let's not go on, we should wait until it's all over, because it's all over. I knew it . . . I knew that a great darkness was waiting for us."

Everything was blended into a single depth at their feet, a pit of fatigue into which she felt herself slipping, into not being able to stand up anymore, her back against the tree that was like her whole body, paralyzed with terror; she was falling out of her body, she, out of her body; her body was still able to be like that leaning on the immensity of a tree, while she was falling, beaten down, just like any poor animal that was breaking itself apart to flee, harnessed to death which was waiting for it there, right there, there now . . . Yes, she slipped out of her body and fell, changed into fatigue, only fatigue, nothing but fatigue; but when she reached her feet, she brought down the rest, the matter, and now she was a body and she was fatigue, a single motionless thing, resolutely abandoned to whatever God willed . . .

"Leland! . . . Leland! . . . Leland! . . ."

Mead was calling her and shaking her mercilessly, as if the hurricane had got into his body too. His hot hands rubbed her, he wanted to touch her heart underneath her full breasts, and it was painful to feel that he was not caressing her as before, but that he was rubbing her to find what he could not feel underneath her breast, because he would not let his hand rest . . . until at last, yes, now, now, now, now . . .

"Leland! . . ." he leaned over to kiss her, his teeth hit her teeth and he repeated in a low voice, almost in secret, ". . . I knew it, I knew that a great darkness was waiting for us . . ."

He sat by her side. He made a pillow for her with some branches and he took her carefully by the waist to hold her better, because she had fallen, all crumpled up, just like the branch of a tree.

"Leland . . ." with his eyes closed, hugging her, ". . . Leland . . . perhaps tomorrow . . ." He used his hand to push away a black branch that the hurricane had not moved, a branch of mourning leaves that had fallen on her forehead . . . The hand was no longer there . . . his hand . . . It had gone away, it had gone away with the branch . . . as he grasped it . . . as he went away where he was now without his hand . . . without either of his two hands, handless and footless as his feet lay there far away like a pair of tired shoes.

EPILOGUE

"They met each other here and they shall stay here! . . ."

The determination of Doña Roselia, the widow of Lucero, dressed in black, her eyes pouring tears, her nose red from blowing, her lips burned from the elements in which they had lived so many hours of anguish, she would not allow the old bailiff who functioned as mayor or even the justice of the peace to do it any other way.

"They met each other here and they shall stay here! . . ."

The stretchers made of fresh leaves on which they had carried the bodies were in the courtyard, surrounded by dogs who sniffed indifferently, hungry, in search of food, and Doña Roselia, to work, and she put them on a bed she had brought into the main room. For lack of space, the two of them on the same bed. One beside the other, together in death, icy, as if their hands and faces had been exposed to the full moon on a high mountaintop. The boys, her sons, were going about helping people. So many things had been pushed out to sea by the strong wind. So many land creatures were floating among the sharks now, lost in the waters that after the hurricane had passed went back to being an array of emeralds, mermaid tails soaked in foam, the luxury of the sun, a feast of crystal banana trees.

Someone spoke about the houses down below there. What houses? There was nothing left but the sites. The big wind had taken them off. At the spot where the Meads' little house had stood there was only an uninhabited plot, swept away, just as if a furious broom had passed through to sweep away all that decoration.

Luceros, Cojubuls, and Ayuc Gaitáns stood by the corpses, not knowing how to act, in a misty atmosphere, impregnated with dampness and still menacing.

Doña Roselia had the ground opened beside her husband's grave in the cemetery, where in another grave, the white-washed skull of Hermenegilo Puac was laughing with all his teeth showing, surrounded by the three yellow laughs: the laugh of Rito Was Perraj, the laugh of Rito Am Perraj, and the laugh of Rito Will Be Perraj. The justice of the peace came to claim the bodies. There was room for them in the cemetery for foreigners.

The whole Lucero family and the Cojubul and Ayuc Gaitán families, ready for the burial, accompanied the bodies of Lester Mead, they knew him by that name, and Leland Foster. On the same stretcher on which they had brought them to Semírames they carried them to the train, wrapped in two white sheets. From one of the bundles a lock of greenish-golden hair was peeping out. The train went off slowly, rolling along without making much noise through a cemetery of fallen, broken, destroyed banana trees.

THIS BOOK WAS SET IN

CALEDONIA AND BODONI BOLD TYPES

AND PRINTED BY HAMILTON PRINTING COMPANY.

IT WAS BOUND BY MONTAUK BOOK MFG. CO., INC.

DESIGN IS BY LARRY KAMP